A Tale of Wizards,

Dragons and

Fracking

Noel. P. Morgan

ISBN:

DEDICATION

This book is dedicated to everyone who believes in justice, conservation and oh, of course, magic.

CONTENTS

ACKNOWLEDGMENTS

I would like to thank my family for nagging me into writing this book and Jill Evans, Paul Court and Lucy Gowland for their constructive feedback and keen eyes editing and proofreading.
This would not have happened without you.
So, this is all your fault.
Enjoy.

1. WHY DRAGONS DON'T NEED SAT. NAV.

The dragon banked left, for she knew that within a few more miles she would be approaching the giant factory stacks of Port Talbot. Although not averse to a little bit of smoke or steam, some of the chemical cocktails spewing up from the giant chimneys would leave her with a horrendous headache and the sort of sore throat that was reminiscent of the good old days when knights in armour were in plentiful supply. Her mouth watered as she recalled how delicious, if not somewhat difficult to swallow, those metal clad warriors tasted after a gentle roasting. She had always had an odd penchant for tinned food.

Her new course would take her to her destination, the hills and mountains known as Brakin' Wind, but first she would have to fly over the home of her hatching, an odd little village nestled at the foot of Brakin' Wind called Pant y Gussett.

Pant y Gussett, not so much a place that time forgot, as a place time avoided to escape embarrassment.

Many years ago, Pant y Gussett lay undiscovered by man, inhabited only by the abundant wildlife and the magical folk who still live there to this day. Amongst many others there were gnomes, an industrious race with an almost obsessive passion for gardening and fishing, and pixies, no larger than a domestic cat with a talent for mischief and pranks that although they were not necessarily evil, they were definitely considered a pain in the sit-upon. Up on the side of Brakin' Wind were the dwarves who worked the small copper mine. These were a hairy bearded race tempered by toil and labour, making them very muscular, so much so that they might have to stand on a box to look a human straight in the eye, but they were always wider. Various types of elf could be seen throughout the area, they came in all shapes and sizes (mainly tiny, though there are some fossil records to indicate an extinct species that reached a towering two-foot-high), and could be found among the flowers and grasses of the landscape.

Keeping the peace among them all was the immortal good Queen Megan and her loyal fairy clan, including her internationally renowned guard The Resolute Aerial Fairies, or RAF, as they are affectionately known. Queen Megan was far from being the monarch of Pant y Gussett but was so respected by all races that she was the first port of call in the event of a serious dispute.

Great Britain has always had the unfortunate habit of attracting invaders throughout the years. They have been repelled by bow and arrow, musket and cannon and in more recent times giant ships and planes, all suitably decorated in ominous grey.

Back in the day, even before Long John Silver still had two legs and an egg on his shoulder, even before King Harold famously yelled,

"Oi careful with that arrow, you'll have someone's eye out."

There was another threat to this septic Isle, from the Ogres. The Ogres had been cast out from Continental Europe for their anti-social habit of eating people and thought they would try their luck in the UK. Their first mistake was to attack Scotland where the red-haired men in dresses proved to be every bit their equal in both ferociousness and sheer savagery. Licking their many wounds they turned their attention on the English where they encountered an organised and well-disciplined militia who easily sent them packing. Undeterred the King of the Ogres, "Bert the Bludgeoner" rallied his army of red-eyed, stuff of nightmares soldiers and bellowed,

"To Wales my boys, a bunch of choir singing, sheep breeding farmers will be no match for us!"

Now the Welsh are not famed for their ferociousness and savagery nor could we be accused of being disciplined and organised, but we are a proud and courageous nation and also bloody sneaky.

During the first few weeks of the conflict the ogres thought that they were getting the upper hand, after each bloody encounter there appeared to be fewer and fewer Welsh soldiers; but then they started to notice that their ships were developing leaks and some had even gone missing. (They turned up a few weeks later as part of a private fishing fleet based in Milford Haven.)

The camp's stores of fresh water had mysteriously become too salty to drink, with some of the ogres' sentries reporting seeing a load of Welshmen with funny grins on their faces and their flies open fleeing the camp. There was a marked increase in the amount of flea infested rats appearing in the tents while rousing choruses of "Men of Harlech" emanated from the surrounding trees keeping them all awake at night. The final straw came when the ogres awoke one morning to find all the signs throughout the camp depicting important details such as "armoury", "latrine" and "Officers' Quarters" had all been painted over and replaced with the equivalent Welsh translation.

"Sod this!" cried Bert the Bludgeoner" angrily, "back to the boats you lot, let's try that place that Columbus fella's been banging on about"

Defeated and demoralised the ogres left for the new world. History has shown that they didn't fare that much better over there.

With the fighting over, the Welshmen, joined by a few

of the more enlightened ogres tired of mayhem and violence, were now free to find their way back home to their loved ones, but not all of them. Many of the single men and possibly some of the married men, who would rather fight ogres than face their wives, decided to take the long way home and explore the parts of the country they had not seen before and should they encounter an inn or two on their way, then so be it!.

One small group, while following the main track between Swansea and Llanelli, took a detour to find the shortest crossing over the Loughor river. They happened upon a small ferryboat operated by a tall shadowy figure in a black cloak who seemed to be perpetually shrouded in mist, but despite the very reasonable charge of a penny, they decided he gave them the "creeps" so they opted to wander a bit further inland and find a way to cross by foot. Eventually they found a section of the river that was quite narrow and by chance was bridged by a moss laden, fallen tree that they decided to walk across.

Cursing the moss, they all hung onto the tree for support and swam to the other side. Freezing cold and soaking wet the men dragged themselves on to a grassy bank, where to their surprise, there crackled a huge log fire.

"Hello", said a diminutive feller with a bright red pointy hat, as he shoved another log on the fire. "I saw you trying to walk over that tree and I thought you might appreciate this. "Cheers" said the men crowding round the fire.

"Once you're dry, you're welcome to join me at my place for some hot broth and sandwiches."

Blown away by the gnome's hospitality and the beauty and tranquillity of their surroundings, the men unanimously decided that this place, the gnome called Pant y Gussett, was where they wanted to make their new home.

Over time the men met girls from neighbouring towns

and villages and brought them back to settle down and raise families, some sent word home to friends and loved ones to come and join them in this new found paradise. Eventually Pant y Gussett became a well populated village with people and magic folk happily living side by side in a comfortable harmony. Painfully aware that the anonymity currently enjoyed by the village could easily be compromised by this burgeoning population, bringing with it the violence, greed and corruption endured by most major towns run by government and politicians, they consulted an elder, who used to be a solicitor in nearby Swansea to see what protection could be sought. After months of research, going through dusty scrolls, law books and notes scribbled on the back of fag packets, the elder discovered that as Pant y Gussett was hitherto unknown to the government, there were no statutes or laws pertaining to the area and it could legally claim the right to become a Republic with its own legal system and immigration laws.

Now to be fair to the people of this new Republic, they knew in their hearts how wrong and selfish it would be to deny others the chance to enjoy living in such a wondrous and peaceful place, yet they also knew that too many casual visitors, tourists and would-be settlers could easily ruin the idyll that they had founded. To find an answer they called together every wizard, warlock and witch in the village who in collaboration with the local magic folk concocted a spell to surround Pant y Gussett. This spell would not keep the village hidden, nor would it conjure demons and apparitions to scare people away, it merely made the village seem unimportant. Passers-by would do just that, pass by. People knew it was there but seldom took the trouble to look. A bit like one of those leaflets found between the pages of a newspaper, you're aware that it's there but you seldom read it.

So effective was this spell that many years later when the A484 between Swansea and Llanelli was constructed it included a roundabout with an unposted turning that led to the car park just outside Pant y Gussett that many a driver mused, " I wonder what's down there" but seldom did they feel the need to explore.

2. TO THATCH OR NOT TO THATCH?

Pant y Gussett is truly situated in an idyllic location, surrounded by beautiful stretches of coastline less than a short cart ride away on one side with beautiful woods, forests and mountains on the other, where the abundant wildlife scampers around the tree branches, feeding on a great array of nuts, seeds and flowers and nesting under the protective shelter afforded by the abandoned supermarket trolleys and cola cans littering the ground, a sure sign of the advance of civilisation.

Pant y Gussett is truly a magical place, home to dragons, ogres, witches and many other followers of the old ways, all brought together by the wonder of the area, where they can feel accepted, whether they be winged, horned, blue, green, labour or conservative, all also benefiting from the convenience of the nearby M4.

The main residential parts of the village are, on the whole, inhabited by ordinary folk who fall into two very different categories. The majority are those with long family ties with Pant y Gussett, who can trace their lineage to the original settlers many of whom were refugees from the great ogre wars of ancient times. These people try not to have anything to do with the modern world, often shunning the advantages of electricity and indoor plumbing, holding to the belief that such "dirties" should be consigned to outdoor sheds or the Ty Bach (Little House) as they're known in Wales.

Others, although loving the Olde Worlde charm of the village, embrace modern living and all its accoutrements, employing generators to power their TV's and computers and emigrate weekdays from the village to jobs in such cosmopolitan and sophisticated locations such as Swansea and Llanelli.

The traditionalists like to hang pans of burning charcoal for illumination (given the shortage of street lights) near their front doors for visitors calling at night. So, walking down any street it is easy to tell if it is owned by traditionalists or moderns by whether or not they have a satellite dish or a set-alight dish outside.

Architecturally the village has a very "Dickensian" feel, although over the centuries the buildings have evolved from simple mud and straw construction to wooden cabins, many examples of which can still be found in the surrounding areas. These are usually inhabited by the more magical or indeed downright weird members of the community, such as hermits, lay preachers and even a hedgewitch called Malifi, whose dubious personal hygiene coupled with hell-spawned halitosis was the reason that she was not particularly welcome in the village.

It would be fair to say that the main streets of Pant y Gussett look like a cross between a set from "Oliver Twist" and the quainter parts of Shrewsbury. This building style was adopted as it was considered by most to be the first type of construction people felt safe for erecting two or more storeys on. Over the years this was what a lot of the locals did as their families grew, with a very limited choice of finding larger housing to move to, and leaving Pant y Gussett being an almost blasphemous idea to any villager, the only way left was up. Unfortunately, a lot of these extensions were often done by residents with more confidence in their DIY skills than they had ability or by several rough looking characters met down the pub who were short on credentials but all had the same mantra

"No problem guv me and the lads can do that for half the price".

The upshot of this was that it was nigh on impossible to

find a straight wall or window in the entire village, indeed to date most of the houses only remain standing through a little bit of magic and a great deal of hope.

Benefitting from a lack of an official planning department, and often to the frustration of visiting historians, many of the properties were fitted with all manner of PVC double glazed windows, doors and guttering only some of which matched. Those with sizeable back gardens also had all shapes of conservatories crammed into whatever space they could afford overlooking the lawn where families have the seemingly obligatory mesh caged trampoline, unused and rotting since the first sugar fuelled incident leading to a mild concussion between overly-excited, youthful siblings.

To thatch or not to thatch was a question faced by homeowners. Many liked the insulative and aesthetic properties of a good thatched roof while others preferred the relatively maintenance free option of Welsh slate or tiles. Such a choice was not an option for the Fat Wizard; FW as he was most commonly known, his real name so little used that he had trouble remembering it himself, learnt at an early stage in his career the danger of a combustible roof covering when most of your days were spent tinkering with volatile chemicals and little known herbs and roots. This was exacerbated by his eldest daughter's love of hatching and rearing abandoned dragon's eggs where she helped to teach them to control their fire breathing abilities, prior to release, which also fired the kilns for the Fat Wizard's good lady's pottery business.

With such an increasing number of call-outs for the local fire brigade he became on first name terms with all the firemen; but when he found himself being invited, one year, to their annual Christmas party it occurred to him, somewhat reluctantly, that it was time to replace the thatch with tile, resulting in a hearty round of applause from a relieved fire station.

The Fat Wizard was quite a traditional looking wizard; he had a tall, slightly wonky hat and matching long flowing, blue velvet robes. It had voluminous (easy to hide things in) sleeves, a Velcro fastened front and neckline, which were edged with gold silk that Mrs FW had embroidered with mystic runes and a woven sash come belt. The whole majestic ensemble was only let down by the Fat Wizard's habit of wearing open toed sandals over stripey socks. To complete the image the Fat Wizard had long greying hair, an almost as long greying beard, and a pair of gold coloured glasses that he only wore to see.

The Fat Wizard's (slate roofed) cottage sits on a large corner plot on what passed for a main street leading to the village square. The third floor contained the three bedrooms, the largest one naturally being for the Fat Wizard and the lady of the house, while the other two rooms belonged to their two daughters, Rebe, the aforementioned dragon hatcher and Kayls who had left her beloved family home after developing an almost obsessive love for computers as well as listening to and performing punk rock. Neither of these passions were particularly well catered for in Pant y Gussett so she relocated to the bright lights of the metropolis of nearby Bridgend. Here she honed her craft as a performer, eagerly waiting for her first number one hit, or as FW likes to call it "my retirement plan".

The Fat Wizard's bedroom was simply decorated with a large king size bed in the centre of the room to the left of which was a large oak wardrobe and matching dressing table, while on the right lay what can only be described as a hillock of clothing, a mix of clean, dirty, and partly singed laundry dominated by odd socks. The average married reader would not have to train as a modern day "Sherlock Holmes" to deduce who slept on which side of the bed.

Rebe's bedroom hadn't changed much from her teenage years with all four walls festooned with posters depicting such diverse subjects as cute kittens (just keep hanging on) to a plethora of different species of dragons, David Bowie (the Aladdin Sane years) and some Dutch heavy metal bands whose music the Fat Wizard reckoned he could replicate by tying a dozen stray cats and a dustbin to a piano then throwing the lot down a very long staircase. To add to the ambience of the room every square foot of floor space was taken up by the usual paraphernalia such as a TV, a computer, several game consoles, a tray with an old, curled up ham and pickle sandwich with an empty crisp packet on the side and a large tank housing her pet snake, non-venomous of course, FW thought there were enough hazards downstairs for one household. Any other spaces were taken up with books, dragon books, did I mention Rebe's love of dragons?

Kayls's room however was completely different as she took most of her belongings with her leaving only a couple of Blink 182 posters and an old guitar with a warped neck and a broken string up on a wall. This facade of tidiness went to pot after every visit.

As commonly found in these houses, the narrow staircases, so beloved by house removal men the length and breadth of the country, had the appearance of being built long before the invention of the spirit level. So much so that should the roof ever leak there was never any danger of the water pooling on the stairs. Following the rough geometry of the staircase are a staggered line of paintings following the Fat Wizard and family's ancestry, with the Fat Wizard himself in all his robed and portly splendour, marred only by his wand seemingly caught up in his beard. Next was the portrait of Mrs FW, no longer in the first flush of youth but considered by many, despite her slightly stern and headmistress like demeanour to be well out of the Fat Wizard's pay grade, not that they would mention it out loud, the Fat Wizard was a wizard after all. Then came Rebe with a slightly unusual hairstyle due in part to an unusual sense of fashion, but mainly thanks to a particularly mischievous Ddraig Goch, a species of dragon that inspired the Welsh flag (which incidentally is considered by many to be the oldest national flag still in use) who objected to having to stay still and pose for the painting. Kayl's picture was typically obscured by her insistence on wearing headphones over her ears with a microphone in front of her mouth and a bass guitar strung around her neck.

As you go further down the stairs are the portraits of the ancestors, many of which were noted wizards and warlocks of their day; some were military men and women, some were seamstresses and tailors with one very attractive lady adorned with a very fine dress, heavy make-up and extensive gold and pearl jewellery. Not much is known of her except that she ran some sort of boarding establishment and it remains a mystery to this day how she made so much money.

Consigned to the broom cupboard is a picture of great great Uncle Silas' on FW's side. He was a bank manager in Gorseinon. The family never speak of him.

The second storey is where the family lives, comprising of a simple living room with a comfy sofa, an occasional table (it was made by the Fat Wizard so sometimes it preferred being a chair) and an old large recliner by now heavily contoured to accommodate the less than ballerina like frame of FW, all facing a large log fireplace with the TV adjacent. The walls are all framed with bookshelves crammed with such titles as "Apothecary through the ages", Spelling (for ages 40 and upward), "Advanced Pottery Skills" and of course a veritable library of titles about dragons. (Wonder who they belong to?). Next to this is a large kitchen come dining room fitted with all the white goods a family could wish for. Mrs FW was a keen and enthusiastic cook which goes a long way to explaining why it wasn't just tradition that kept the Fat Wizard in flowing robes rather than the restrictive britches so favoured by most villagers.

Down the hall is the WC and bathroom though the

shower was on the ground floor next to the workshops as emergency showers are all too often an imperative as everyone in these sorts of professions would testify. Apart from the shower the ground floor consisted of a huge back room which always felt unnaturally chilly, dark and gloomy surrounded by row after row of shelves, holding a seemingly endless array of glass jars, pots, cauldrons, test-tubes and mugs, all containing weird and wonderful herbs, roots, spices and pickled bits of obscure animal parts, some suggesting a sinister purpose, some moving. Maybe not all of them held items required for the ancient arts. The mugs contained half-drunk tea abandoned and forgotten by the Fat Wizard when one or other of his many experiments carried out on the huge, battle scarred table that dominated the workshop, appeared to be going critical.

On a shelf under the table and well within easy reach sits an abnormally large first-aid box with a quick release lid. This contains every branded skin cream, burn ointment, eye wash and painkiller known to man, as well as many industrial remedies made by the Fat Wizard himself which would be considered illegal throughout most of Europe and the U.S.A. These contents had to be replenished often. The front room, which faced the street, was the shop where Mr and Mrs FW shared shelf and display space. This, in the past, had led to some quite heated arguments as to who portrayed their wares where, but after a long discussion and the threat of "no dinner" it was decided that the Fat Wizard could have all the floor shelves and the very high ones for his potions, while Mrs FW settled for all the easily reached shelves, the counter display and the window space for her pots. She did, however, concede to letting him keep his beloved sign above the door. "The Fat Wizard" and underneath "come in for a spell".

To the side of the cottage there is a large garden, partly laid to lawn but heavily bordered by a stunning variety of bushes, herbs and wildflowers, with one section including a small greenhouse dedicated to his prize-winning blooms. All were lovingly tended to by the Fat Wizard himself. This meant that much as he enjoyed spending a great deal of his time exploring all the paths and hedge ways surrounding Pant y Gussett in search of exciting new ingredients, whose magical properties might be able to be put to good use in spells as diverse as, protection from a striped shirted, mask wearing, swag bag carrying, nocturnal intruder to instant treatment for ingrowing toe nails, the convenience of having a constant supply of home grown, common ingredients saved a lot of time. Another advantage to his horticultural endeavours was that a well cultivated garden attracted a certain species of tiny elf that the Fat Wizard had a soft spot for, even leaving food and nest boxes out for them to take shelter in on cold damp nights. Now these elves had a passion for fashion and made all their own clothes, everything from hats, gloves, dresses and even shoes out of the prettiest petals they could find. Unfortunately, the thought of stealing petals caused outrage amongst the members of the "Pant y Gussett and District Garden in Bloom and Annual Flower and Beer Festival" Society, who actively chased off and sprayed with foul chemicals, any poor elf caught within miles of their gardens. These green-fingered yet short sighted "sons of the soil" never cottoned to how the Fat Wizard came away from every competition with armfuls of cups and rosettes for "Best in Bloom, best petunia, best hyacinth etc while their own exhibits looked decidedly dog eared at best. So jealous did they become that, one year they insisted that FW's blooms be tested for magical enhancement; that really brought a smile from FW.

The back of the property boasted a very large garden dotted with various outbuildings, the largest of which housed a fancy, large potter's wheel, surrounded by a range of racks and shelving which sported all manner of pots, urns, dishes and tea sets in various stages of construction. Some were drying, some were waiting for paint and decoration and some were waiting to be consigned to the bin. Well as good a potter as she was, Mrs FW was as prone to the occasional, momentary lapse of concentration as anyone else, as attested to by the many globs and spears of drying clay hanging from all corners of the ceiling giving her workshop the appearance of an ancient underground cave with well-formed stalactites.

The kiln is a large round chimney shaped building attached, and with access to, the back of the workshop, while a specially designed dragon pen lay at the side of the kiln where baby dragon shaped holes allowed for the young ones to insert their snouts and let rip with impunity with no risk to life for any innocent passers-by. The temperature of the kiln could be controlled by feeding the dragons a variety of different diets. Rebe had painstakingly tested various foods and discovered meals of peppers and spices produced lower temperatures whilst certain, obscenely hot curries (the sort favoured by Neath RFC players after a hard championship match followed by drinking their own weight in beer) produced the sort of heat found on the surface of the sun, or the feeling you get when you spill coffee from a well-known food chain down your lap. The downside of such cheap energy was the eye-watering and toxic cleaning duties endured by Rebe when mucking out the pens the next day.

3. A PINT, A NEWSPAPER AND AN EARTHQUAKE?

Now the Fat Wizard could never be described as a creature of habit, on the whole his day to day activities were often a surprise to himself, except that is for Sundays. As he had been doing every Sunday for as long as he could remember he enjoyed a long lie in then a quick shower, clean robes and with his Sunday best wand tucked into his sock, he kissed his darling wife goodbye, waved vaguely in the direction of Rebe, whose nose was firmly planted in a book, (guess the subject) and he went off to buy the morning paper.

"Be back for lunch by one o'clock" warned Mrs FW with a smile "or the dog will be taking your place at the table". At this, Jasper, the family's pet's ears pricked up as he lay in front of the unlit fire. Jasper was a handsome young beagle cross, though cross is not a word that should be applied to one of the most docile, loving creatures you could ever wish to meet, but he did have one major flaw. No one could ever work out if he was terminally stupid or a canine genius, he could instantly recognise the words "dog" and "lunch" while "sit, lie down" and "leave that it's not yours" were a complete mystery to him, or were they? The family suspected that it was calculated, selective deafness but on the other hand he was just drowsily basking in front of a cold hearth.

As the Fat Wizard left the house he stood on the doorstep and inhaled a deep lungful of the crisp, September morning air, forgetting for a minute that his neighbour, Goodwitch Evans ran her "Fish and Seaweed Pickling Emporium" seven days a week. After a few moments of eye watering, wracking coughing he fumbled for his wand, a brief incantation and a possibly vulgar gesture of the wand and fresh sweet air was returned and he tried again. Suitably fortified FW stepped down on to the cobbled street, which even on a Sunday bustled with people, people with horses, people with horse and carts and less fortunate people with carts and no horses. As he turned left to walk past Miss Evans' house, he noticed a cheeky little robin in a tree on the other side of the road,

"Hello robin" called the Fat Wizard in a friendly, cheerful voice, "tweet tweet" replied the robin.

"Hello Mr crow sang the Fat Wizard to the large black and rather unkempt pile of feathers that alighted on a branch above the robin.

"Caw caw" came the rasping reply from the crow. The bustard and the booby, sunbathing on a nearby thatched roof, were ignored after the unpleasant incident several weeks ago involving the rather hard of hearing "old ma Warwick and her steel reinforced umbrella who had walked past, during this weekly ritual at a very unfortunate moment and laid into an innocent, and bewildered FW, who took the rest of the day to work out what on earth she was so upset about.

A few more doors up and FW reached his favourite spot of his Sunday constitutional, Rose Cottage, one of the few properties on the street that being slightly set back from the road enjoyed a small front garden. Originally called "Dunroamin" or some such, old man Cobbins had moved there over a decade ago and spent his time cultivating roses. As well as having the garden surrounded by rose bushes, he had also trained climbing roses to cover most of the front of the cottage providing an exploding rainbow of colours as well as a very heady fragrance. How he kept these flowers in bloom all year round was a subject of much discussion within the village and indeed the cause of much delight to the Fat Wizard who may or may not have been involved with old man Cobbins' amazing horticultural success.

Amongst the thorned splendour of the garden, and in line with a wall mounted garden tap, was a fully functional well, made of a red brick and white mortar circular construction over which sat a Welsh slate pitched roof giving the effect of looking like it had come straight from the pages of a children's nursery rhyme book. Today was slightly different though, today with old Cobbins there was a small group of neighbours surrounding the well. Nearest the front gate was a tall skinny man called Huw Puw. He was wearing his customary dark pair of trousers and a matching jacket two sizes too big, obviously made to measure but "who?" is the question. His head was almost bald save for an unkempt thatch above both ears which, with his overly long hooked nose and beady little eyes framed in what looked like wire swimming goggles, gave him the appearance of an upset buzzard. Huw was a retired civil servant who had spent his entire working life pushing pens and paper around a desk (for no discernible reason) in the Llanelli town hall and who now devoted his life to a single-handed neighbourhood watch scheme. A part of Huw's perceived civic duties would often see him donning an old bus conductor's cap he had found in a car boot sale and patrolling the streets of Pant y Gussett, with his buttons polished to a mirror finish, the peak of his cap so low it was a wonder he could see where he was going, he looked like one of Scotland Yard's finest after another crippling budget cut. This image was not improved by the short length of a broom handle, painted black, with a string handle that he would swing in time to off-key whistling while he was "patrolling" on the beat.

Alongside him, bearded and bicep bulging, stood the

imposing figure of Griff the Hammer, the local blacksmith and his not so imposing and slightly effeminate, brother David who worked in a gentleman's outfitters in Carmarthen who Griff teasingly named "Dai the Cloth". Completing this colourful line-up was Downwind Jones the village road sweeper, a hairy little man of, let's say, "casual" appearance who had a side-line of supplying horse manure to anyone willing to pay the price of a pint for a bucket of equestrian gold.

The five of them were all mumbling to each other and peering intently into the depths of the well. Some of them were holding their caps in one hand while demonstrably scratching their heads with the other.

"Hail good neighbours" the Fat Wizard cried out, "what's the problem",

"Oh, hi FW" replied Dai, "The well has run dry",

"That's not all", Huw pitched in, "There have been funny rumbling noises coming from it all night, and Jones here reckoned he heard voices",

"Heard voices" said Griff chuckling, "that mad old bugger has been hearing voices since he discovered the drink",

"Oi what are you implying" snapped an indignant Downwind Jones.

"Gentlemen, gentlemen" the Fat Wizard interjected, before this escalated into a heated debate, the people of Pant y Gussett did enjoy a good argument if they could find one. "I'm off for my Sunday paper, please ask old man Cobbins to call me if anything else happens" and with a fleeting glance of concern on his face, the Fat Wizard carried on his way.

You may, dear reader, be wondering at this point why it was such a "mission" for the Fat Wizard to buy his Sunday paper. The truth is, it was not just the paper that made Sunday mornings so sacrosanct to the Fat Wizard, but more to do with the fact that he retired to his specially reserved Sunday morning table in the local pub to read it over a couple of pints of mead before walking home (slightly unsteadily) to enjoy a full roast dinner before falling asleep in his favourite comfy armchair while watching some oft repeated rom com or an all American Hero war film.

Church on a Sunday was not an option for the Fat Wizard as he was of the strong opinion that should a deity really wish to be worshipped then they should take the trouble to visit from time to time.

A few more yards down the road (Pant y Gussett hadn't converted to decimalisation and the metric system yet as the villagers didn't see the point) and the Fat Wizard finally arrived at Dodd's paper shop, the last building in the row occupying one corner of a large crossroads.

Of course, it wasn't actually a paper shop, it was constructed of brick, mortar, wood and thatch as were most of the village shops. Though a visiting crone from Aberystwyth once had a dalliance with a sweet shop, unfortunately she underestimated how sweet a tooth goblins have and after a week oddly enough all that remained of the establishment was a large, child sized oven.

In all honesty the shop wasn't always so conventional, when, many years ago a young Mr Dodd's bought the empty plot where the shop now stands, and being full of entrepreneurial spirit and ambition, he decided to build his new " Newspaper and Novelty Goods Emporium (keys cut while you wait)" completely out of paper, reasoning that such an original idea would bring lots of custom to his genuine paper shop, truly a ream come true. For a while it was a great success until eventually it caught the attention of some of the local youths. More out of a sense of mischief rather than malice, it became their favourite pastime of a Saturday night to lift the entire shop and relocate it to other parts of the village, leaving poor Dodd's the frustrating task every Sunday morning of finding where they had left it. Several weeks of this

"Shoplifting" was enough to convince him to rebuild with far heavier materials.

As the Fat Wizard entered the shop, there on the right hand side stood Mr Dodd's behind the long counter displaying every conceivable confectionary imaginable from sherbet dips, boiled sweets, to luxury boxes of chocolates with picturesque images on their lids, the apology of choice for so many errant husbands (even if they had no idea what they had done to upset their beloved spouses).

"Morning" said the Fat Wizard to the always friendly Dodd's, who was as always resplendent in his white tunic which he always wore as a sign of professionalism. This incidentally matched his snowy white hair and a handlebar moustache so heavily waxed it looked like his nose was sitting on a shelf.

"Good morning FW" said Dodd's chuckling as he sorted through his new line of anti-greeting cards bearing unpleasant messages such as "I thought you were dead", "Long time no see, let's keep it that way!" and "I wish you were here, it's awful", before displaying them in one of those demon spawned card carousel contraptions that see to it that for every card you look at four more will fall off leaving you feeling obliged to buy the ones you have accidentally trodden on as well as the one you actually wanted.

To get to the massive newspaper and magazine racks that lined the complete left hand side of the shop the Fat Wizard had to negotiate his way through the other customers which included other people looking for a newspaper, some harassed mothers struggling to control their kids who were all dribbling all sorts of sticky stuff down their Sunday best blouses and a handful of, hard looking, yet surprisingly shy, axe and shovel carrying dwarves (for whom Sunday was the only day off from working in the quarry), who were awkwardly shuffling their feet and staring, both frustratingly and longingly up at the highest shelves of the rack.

As the Fat Wizard bent down to get the "Pant y Gussett Times Incorporating the Pant y Gussett Herald, the Pant y Gussett Echo and Knitters Weekly, Sunday Edition" he was overcome with a strong, shaking sensation more akin to how he felt leaving a pub than before he got there. As he was pondering this strange malady, he noticed the other customers in the shop. The kids were crying and wrapped in a tight embrace with their mothers, women were holding each other, the men of course were far too masculine for that nonsense so all stood in the middle of the shop in a pose that looked to all the world like they were either astride an invisible horse or were about to perform some fancy trick on a skateboard, Dodd's on the other hand stood rooted to the spot with his arms firmly wrapped around the till while an overturned jar scattered mint imperials in all directions, Meanwhile the gleeful dwarves gratefully collected magazines (designed for gentlemen of a discernible taste) that had tumbled from the uppermost shelves.

Then as quickly as they started the tremors stopped.

"Is everyone okay?" shouted the Fat Wizard, wand drawn and ready for action.

"We're okay!" was the general reply which could only just be heard above the frightened sobbing of the kids now clutching their mothers tightly and transferring whatever they were drooling on to their Sunday best clothing.

"Fine, fine," mumbled Dodd's as he panicked frantically trying to herd up his wandering imperials, "an earthquake, in Pant y Gussett, I've never heard the like!",

"No neither have I" said the Fat Wizard quietly as he reached into one of the leather pouches tied to the heavy cord around his waist for his mobile phone. (Yes of course a wizard can communicate using magic but you must admit the convenience of also being able to take pictures and download funny videos of people falling over the cat is always going to be the better option).

"Everything alright there dear?" said the Fat Wizard to Mrs FW, with just a hint of how worried he was for her raising the tone of his voice slightly.

"We're all okay here!" she replied, almost drowned out by Jasper's frantic barking in the background "apart that is, from the dozen pots I had drying in my workshop collapsing and one of your hair restoring potions smashing on the floor of the shop, our lovely tiled floor now looks like a deep pile carpet!", "Was that really an earthquake?".

"Hmmm, seems so, ", said the Fat Wizard, thoughtfully stroking his beard,

"Look pet there's nothing I can do right now, so if you and Rebe are ok I think I'll still pop on down to the pub and see if anything else is going on" and actually remembering to press the "disconnect call" button on his phone, The Fat Wizard left the noisy and excited patrons of the paper shop and crossed the street to the "Cross Inn".

Although known as the Cross Inn by the villagers for the last few months it had been trading under the name "the Cat and Parrot". Over the last year or so it had endured several different names and themes ranging from "Paddy's Gaelic Bar", "Pirates Rest" to "The Philosophers Stone" and the thankfully short lived "Put it Inn". The reason for all the name changes was the fault of the current landlords, Justin and Jason.

Justin and Jason were two young lads who were in their late twenties when they met while working for a large hair salon and nail bar in the centre of Cardiff. Both were tall and slim and shared the same hairstyle, long blonde and curly looking a bit more like brothers than lovers. Within a year they were married and decided that as they enjoyed working together so much that they would go into business for themselves. Fortunately for Justin (not so much for his dad) Justin's father, who owned the Cross Inn, had tragically died during a lock-in one balmy Friday night whilst playing a game of cheat. Sadly, the other players were playing poker.

Upon hearing of Justin's inheritance the pair of them packed up and moved to Pant y Gussett, heads full of ideas of modernisation: a fashionable wine bar perhaps, maybe a gastro pub serving portions of pretentious sounding food, too small to sustain an elf, at prices that that could relieve the national debt of Poland, but in the end they settled on theme pubs.

Now as you can imagine a community as diverse as Pant y Gussett is completely tolerant of people from all walks of life whether it be members of the LGBT community, giants , dwarves, black, white or even the French would not cause even an eyebrow to be raised, but fiddling with their local watering hole was hard for them to understand and accept. For example when preparing to turn the pub into an Irish theme bar, Arthur, the wizened old man sporting a flat cap and an ancient stained military style tunic, who had his own chair and tankard and would regale anyone who bought him a half of stout, with stories of the war (used to be that every pub had an "Arthur") upon seeing the green paint being applied to the walls remarked,

"Duw that's foul, undercoat is it?" followed by, "and what's with all these sacks of potatoes dotted around the place, opening a chip shop next, are you?"

Neither did the boys fare any better on theme nights. After a heavily advertised seventies night they were perplexed when the customers turned up in all manner of Victorian clothing, only finding out later that everyone presumed it was an eighteen seventies night. Things did not improve a month later when the bar filled up with octogenarians with Zimmer frames. Perhaps they should have been clearer when promoting Eighties Night.

What happened to the local poultry on cocktail hour is best left unmentioned.

Undaunted the boys carried on, although this current "Cat and Parrot" concept would have to be reviewed following last night's chaos after Downwind Jones, celebrating a particularly profitable day collecting street "pancakes" let all the pubs newly acquired parrots out of their cages, much to the delight of the stray cats who had been encouraged in for ambience.

The one stabling influence that kept the pub in business throughout all this turmoil was the long-time barmaid Debbie Dee. Known affectionately as "Double D" for two reasons that are amply obvious. Double D's long dark hair, piercing blue eyes and winning smile was a massive draw for the pub though this might have been aided by her preference for low cut white blouses. Unfortunately, when it came to her "Assets" Double D was very lacking in spatial awareness. You could always tell between the regulars and the occasional visitors drinking at the bar as the regulars always held their drinks in their hands while talking, the less experienced visitors would happily leave their tankards on the bar as they talked, only for them to get swept away every time Double D's ponderous protuberances glided over the bar when serving.

She was also invaluable when it came to quenching the fires of the often alcohol fuelled arguments that rise up in every licensed premises, usually over very inconsequential things such as. "You looking at me", "I saw you looking at my missus" and the heinous "It's your round". Double D could usually stop these little altercations in their tracks by employing the common feminine wiles, a change of subject, a large smile, a flutter of the eyelashes, even a peck on the cheek if necessary, but if all that failed then she was quite adept at escorting any miscreant to the door of the pub and using a forward body slam eject the offender out onto the cobbled street outside. Double D was in charge of security, the pubs "bouncers" if you like.

Even a bright sunny day like this could do little to lighten the shadowy gloom of the interior of the pub. Between the small cottage windows each side of the main door and the walls of the pub coupled with the low lying cloud of tobacco smoke that seemed to be permanently present, sunlight never had a chance. Even the always burning log fire opposite the entrance did nothing other than to cast moving shadows. That is not to say that the pub was unwelcoming, far from it, it had a really cosy homely feel, though calling it romantic would be a stretch.

A great variety of mis-matching wooden tables chairs and benches were crammed into the pub, all heavily patinated with beer and wine stains, tobacco burns, crude (and rude) carvings and slightly worrying dried streaks and splatters of what looked like blood, probably a remnant of pre-Double D days. The floor was laid with huge black slabs of slate with what a lot of customers thought of as a non-slip surface. The truth is this apparent non-slip surface was more down to a decades, long build-up of spilt ale due to an ancient cleaning lady with an ancient mop for whom any enthusiasm for the job had long since waned, as attested to by the surprising amount of colourful tropical feathers currently residing in every nook and cranny.

The clientele was quite typical for a Sunday morning, a group of gnomes with their tall pointy hats had taken over one table, one was playing cards another had a drink in one hand and a fishing rod in the other while the last one was sharing his holiday snaps from an unwitting tour of Europe some wag had taken him on. Next to them an unkempt sallow looking youth was struggling with a pint of the universally accepted restorative, "hair of the dog". On the other side of the room sat a middle-aged married couple, Ivor Williams and his wife penny. Ivor was a sturdy fellow with short rapidly greying hair and a heavily wrinkled brow portraying a man who had worked hard all his life, Penny on the other hand was tall and thin, she wore a long kaftan and multi-coloured beads, with her (also greying) long hair in braids and a smile that made her look like she was eternally optimistic, a remnant of her hippy heritage.

They were an interesting couple in that he was a very able man who could turn himself to most things from carpentry, building and other trades to sculpting and painting, unfortunately he suffered from a complete lack of imagination and original thought. Penny was the opposite; she was a dreamer with a sharp and inventive mind but an absolute calamity when attempting any practical task. They both shared a burning sense of ambition to make it big in Pant y Gussett.

You could be excused for thinking that such a pairing would be a match made in heaven for a couple wishing to have their own business but the reality is that not unlike the old joke when someone was elated to find both a Picasso and Stradivarius in the attic and then learnt that Picasso made awful violins and Stradivarius couldn't paint, their individual talents brought out the worst in each other. After yet another failed venture, this time brewing non-alcoholic red wine suitable for vegetarians, as well as being sugar free, gluten free, fruit free and taste free, turned out to be a product that none of the villagers could see anything in. As was customary with the Williams's they retired to the "Cross" to drown their sorrows and waited for Ivor's next strike of inspiration, which was normally after his third pint.

There were quite a few other characters in the bar that morning. Some were crying into their beer; some were chuckling into their beer one poor unfortunate was even sleeping in his beer but that was a regular occurrence with him and he hadn't drowned yet so the locals let him be. There was however one very incongruous looking group seated at a large table at the very rear of the pub. Two of them were wearing properly tailored and very expensive looking dark pin-striped suits. Both were obviously not young but were of the indeterminable age that only money and a Harley street surgeon could arrange. One was short and round but more through muscle than fat with cropped grey hair matching stubble while the other was tall and thin, clean shaven but with a shock of curly blonde hair with grey highlights cascading down his back. A look that would seem scruffy on most men but made a statement of wealth on such an immaculately manicured and sartorially gifted man. Between them sat a young woman, late twenties with her raven black hair tied up in one of those painfully tight looking buns with what looks like a porcupine quill through it. She wore a slightly too tight (which only her buttons complained about) matching grey skirt and jacket, a string of pearls and a pair of horned rim glasses, the type often found on secretaries all over the world who fervently believed (and often rightly so) that the company could not manage without them. In contrast opposite to them sat five rough looking men in work boots, high vis jackets and white hard hats supping ale and nervously glancing around the room.

The people of Pant y Gussett were infamous for their curiosity, always sticking their noses into other people's business and you might well be amazed that the patrons hadn't made a beeline for the suited and booted strangers, but you must take into account the unwritten code of pubs throughout the UK. Unless invited to join them people with a drink can be nodded at or a given a little wave, maybe even a quick "hello" but other than that they should always be left alone.

"May peace and good fortune come to all here" bellowed the Fat Wizard as he walked into the bar.

"Shut that ruddy door! you're letting the fresh air in", growled Ivor as his jaw dropped in horror when he looked up and realised who he had just snapped at, "sorry FW I didn't realise it was you".

"Think no more of it" replied the Fat Wizard with just a hint of a scowl on his face, "but remember, when your down, being rude is hardly the best way to find a hand back up".

"Wise words indeed FW" replied a relieved Ivor. Relieved, because as everyone knew the Fat Wizard was a kind and generous soul who would always go out of his way to help anyone in need, even humans, but to cross him had been known to carry some severe consequences. These ranged from something mildly irritating like an itch in a place that you can't reach to scratch to the punishment meted out to the unfortunate shoplifter who inadvisably chosen to ply his trade in the Fat Wizard's shop. He can still be found living on the lily pads in a garden fish pond behind the pub where all he steals now are flies. (Don't worry the spell will wear off eventually the Fat Wizard is also a very forgiving man).

"Mornin' my lovely" said Double D with her customary warming smile as she finished pouring the Fat Wizards' favourite tipple, a pint of warm mead with just a dash of lemonade, any more than a dash would make it a cocktail in the Fat Wizard's eyes. "I've got your table ready."

"Thank you, good lady," said the Fat Wizard as he went to pay her, carefully selecting the correct pouch from the selection tied to the sash around his waist that prevented his robe from falling open. Like a Scotsman's kilt the mystery of what a wizard wears under his robe should never be revealed.

He often fancied that the different pouches, with their many magical contents, could be compared to a certain superhero's utility belt but with many components derived from real bats.

As he picked up his pint the men from Rose Cottage all poured in, Led by Huw Puw.

"Did you all feel that?", asked Huw,

"Feel what?" one of the nonplussed patrons replied.

"The earthquake"

"What earthquake" replied Penny

"Earthquake was it? Said one of the gnomes, "we just thought the beer was particularly good today".

"Might explain why the pictures on the wall are hanging straight, for a change" mused one of the other regulars.

"Cor blimey" exclaimed an exasperated Huw, "you lot should take more water with it". "Besides that's not all"..., and as the Fat Wizard made his way over to his table with his pipe, pint and paper Huw and his friends went on tell all who would listen about the mysterious "Rose Well incident".

Finally settled at his table by the fireside and after noting the seemingly hurried departure of the suits and boots group from the back of the pub, the Fat Wizard opened his paper.

As was his custom the Fat Wizard always started with the horoscopes and obituaries columns. He knew that as a businessman it was always prudent to keep up with the latest prophets and losses. He then went on to check that they had included his latest advertisement for a new scented candle he had concocted called "Dragon Snot" a sure-fire remedy for a blocked nose that boasted a 5-star rating in a recent "Witch Magazine" survey. Satisfied that the advert was written correctly he then flipped through the local news stories where one particular headline caught his attention, "Pant y Gussett Residents Report Mass Mole Evacuation". As he was pondering over this article he got distracted as a winking Double D, noticing his now empty tankard, brought him a fresh drink.

"Ta love" said a grateful Fat Wizard as moved on to his favourite puzzle section. Every Sunday an anonymous local resident set a "fill in the blanks quiz" where the answers to the clues were all names of people the compiler had argued with that week. The Fat Wizard loved a good crossword.

After "one more for the road" the Fat Wizard said a fond farewell to all as he made his way home for his dinner. He knew that he couldn't be too late as the last time he did Mrs FW served him a religious meal, a burnt offering, or even, as after a particularly late session a few weeks ago, when he arrived home to hear Mrs FW announce

"Your dinner should still be warm, it's in the dog!"

☐

4. MUGWORT, FOXGLOVE AND
DON'T FORGET THE MILK

Monday morning, and another bright sunny day with just enough of a nip in the air to hint of winters approach.

After getting up early the Fat Wizard enjoyed one of Mrs FW's famed "start the week properly" breakfasts that generally included anything that would fit in a frying pan, covered in ketchup, and accompanied by several large slices of heavily buttered toast. With his fast truly broken the Fat Wizard turned to his wife and asked;

"Could you manage the shop this morning dearest? I've been meaning to do some foraging in the woods as I'm running low on mugwort and foxglove. Besides after yesterday I think I'd better have a look around and see if anything else has happened."

"Course I can dear" replied Mrs FW, who then went on to make the request that wives the world over have ingrained into their DNA, "and could you pick up another loaf of bread on your way back?"

"And a pint of milk too?" sighed the Fat Wizard.

"Well now that you mention it" chuckled Mrs FW.

"Fancy joining me for a walk Rebe? you haven't left the

house for a while." enquired the Fat Wizard.

"Busy" a monosyllabic voice said from behind the covers of Dragons Weekly.

Now don't go getting the impression that Rebe was a surly teenager, far from it. She was in her early thirties and generally one of the most cheerful and helpful young ladies (and I use the term Lady quite loosely) you could wish to meet. But she had just encountered an article written by a German Dragon breeder entitled, "Temperature Sex Determination During Incubation and It's Possible Effects on Dragon Species Due to Global Warming" now obviously who would not rather study this than go for a walk in the countryside gathering herbs.

Closing the shop door behind him The Fat Wizard noticed a gangly, awkward looking and acne ridden teenager nervously looking down at his feet trying desperately to avoid eye contact.

"Hello Peter" said the Fat Wizard instantly recognising the youth as a farm labourer and son of a neighbouring pig farmer, "can I help you?"

"Erm, dunno" said Peter "maybe erm, well, look there's this girl I, uh met on the weekend see"

"Ah" said the Fat Wizard, "perhaps you'd better come inside."

As he held the door open for Peter, he could hardly miss the pungent aroma as Peter walked past, an odour that mother nature so cruelly cursed boys of a certain age with, at a time when the urge to impress the fairer sex was at its strongest. This was not helped by the clingy aroma of his trade.

"Let me guess" said the Fat Wizard stroking his beard, "you're wondering if I could sell you a love potion or something similar?"

"Er, well, I suppose" mumbled Peter still studying his feet as if he'd grown an extra toe in his wellies. "But I really love her see, but she doesn't even know I exist" he said forlornly.

Now over the years the Fat Wizard had invented many potions, potions that could cure many ailments, potions that could help people lose or even gain weight, potions that could even help politicians win elections (though let's not speculate about recent events in America) but the one potion that he had absolutely no time for was love potions. There was seldom a winner with a love potion, they either resulted with one unfortunate victim becoming a veritable slave to a partner they would normally abhor or, and quite commonly, the person who had administered the potion would be back after a year begging for a "please get rid of them" potion.

"Right Peter, let's see what we've got" said the Fat Wizard as he bent down to a low shelf and retrieved two small packages. "Now then" he said passing the very fragrant items to Peter, "You've got to promise to use both of these at least twice a day every day, can you do that?"

"Yes definitely" Peter said excitedly "what are they?"

"Lavender and peppermint soap and a wild mint toothpaste"

"Oh" said Peter with a little concern in his voice, "will they work?

"Peter Peter, Peter" sighed the Fat Wizard "there are no guarantees in this life!," and now with beaming smile on his face added "but if you follow my instructions, keep working hard and always be respectful, I can promise you that the girl of your dreams will find you!."

"Thank you, thank you" Peter replied excitedly, "how much do I owe you?"

"Have these on me Peter but promise to let me know how it goes."

"I will, I will and thank you" Replied a grateful Peter as he hurried out of the shop on his way home for his first ever Monday morning bath.

For the second time this morning the Fat Wizard closed the door of his shop and stepped down onto the cobbled streets of Pant y Gussett.

"Morning FW", called out a scruffy small figure from the opposite side of the street as he parked a hand drawn cart heavily laden with buckets.

"Morning Dai" replied the Fat Wizard, "just finished for the night, have you?

"Aye" Dai replied with his arms windmilling in a futile attempt to shoo off the inordinate number of flies that were congregated among the buckets that had now turned their attention to him. "Give us a hand with these doors would you"

"Glad to." said the Fat Wizard as he crossed the road to Dai's small cottage which had a large barn attached to the right-hand side. The barn was fronted with two huge and rather unwieldy, heavy sliding wooden doors. Above the doors hung a large, crudely painted sign pronouncing,

"Dai the Dwarfs Night Soil Collection Service" and underneath in much smaller lettering, "best prices paid, EST 1979"

Dai the dwarf had had to retire young from the mining industry after an unfortunate mishap with a poorly attached pickaxe handle, this on a day when he had experimented with a pair of trainers instead of his usual heavy-duty leather boots. Despite, thankfully, not receiving any long-term injury he developed a phobia of all things sharp so he decided on a career that involved working with all things soft.

"Did you notice anything odd last night" enquired the Fat Wizard" as the doors succumbed to their combined effort.

"Odd, what do you mean odd? Said Dai.

"Oh, I don't know" said the Fat Wizard "tremors, or the ground moving sort of thing"

"I saw a lot of "movements" last night" Quipped Dai "indoor plumbing hasn't affected business yet, but apart from that nothing."

"Ah well, thanks anyway" said the Fat Wizard, and after helping Dai manoeuvre the cart into the barn and wrestle the doors closed, The Fat Wizard went on his way.

Now the more observant of you might have realised that the Fat Wizard lived very close to a night soil collection service and a seaweed and pickling emporium, and justifiably wonder why, when location, location, location, was such a common buzzword, would he remain in such an olfactory offending place. The simple truth is that this location, location, location, meant, that for remedies or not, he enjoyed a very high turnover in his homemade scented candles.

Leaving Dai to attend to his night's bounty, the Fat Wizard thought to himself

"I wonder what Dai actually does with all that sh….stuff," but being too polite to ask he carried on walking up the street.

The street was now getting much busier as the good people of Pant y Gussett roused and set out to embrace the start of a new week, it seemed the Fat Wizard could not walk a few paces without a cheery hail of,

"How are you FW", or a hearty "good morning FW" from the throng of shopkeepers, shoppers or people hurrying by on their way to whatever work they were inevitably late for.

The Fat Wizard was a very popular character among the locals, very few of them had not at some time employed his services whether it be for a treatment for an unpleasant malady, to a detergent to rescue an expensive frying pan from the carnage of a drunk spouse trying to cook sausages.

Just like on his side of the street there was a selection of shop fronts interspersed between the various cottages and houses. Most of the shops were typical small family enterprises not unlike The Fat Wizards' own place where the front room had been converted into a shop front. There was a wool shop, a cobblers' which was famed for its rapid overnight repair service, and a large, double fronted bakery run by Mr and Mrs Crumble. Mrs Crumble had gained quite a notoriety for her traditional Welsh fare with a twist. She had invented "the cockle cracker," minus the shells, "the miners pasty" which was encased in a really black pastry so the miners wouldn't be put off by sooty fingerprints and the "welsh cake" (Ok she didn't invent that, but she does claim to be the first to put jam on them.) But most famous of all, was her seaweed, peppers and chilli stuffed bread roll, where the filling oozed out from the top of the crust when you cut into it. This "lava" bread was a particular favourite with trolls and ogres as the spicy flavour excited even their unrefined palettes.

"Must remember to call in there on the way back." mused the Fat Wizard remembering Mrs FW' instructions. So, summoning up the willpower the Fat Wizard walked on past the Crumbles' window, for as we all know passing a bakery is as hard as passing a "clearance sale, everything must go!" sign or a basket of puppies.

At the end of the street, at the crossroads, directly opposite the pub was a huge imposing building, constructed in a very gothic style that wouldn't have looked out of place in a "Hammer House of Horror" production. The building had dark stone walls and arched stained glass windows, topped with a tower with a large clock face visible on all four sides, each of them displaying a different time, and indeed had done in most of the residents living memory. On top of the tower was a comically overly-large and very twisted tiled roof. Despite the very church like appearance of the building there was not a religious icon in sight. There were no crosses, upright or otherwise, no stars, moons or pentagrams, not even a lucky horseshoe. This is not because the people of Pant y Gussett were a bunch of atheists, far from it, most of the villagers believe in a greater divine being but they also understood that most of the theologies were very similar to each other and so not worth arguing, or even warring over what each belief system should be called.

This was the undertaker's, as proudly proclaimed on a brass plaque to the right of the heavily varnished oak doors'

"Cribbens And Sons Funeral Parlour" and underneath

"EST 1920" which some wag had scratched out the "EST" and had etched before it, "putting the fun in funerals since...."

It wasn't a very busy funeral parlour, partly due to the natural longevity of the magical folk and partly due to the rude good health that the villagers enjoyed thanks to the clean air, the peaceful way of life in Pan y Gussett and not forgetting to mention the Fat Wizard's many cures and potions.

Mr Cribbens took his position very seriously. Seldom would he be seen in public not wearing his black trousers, long tailed jacket and top hat. He always spoke in the slightly hushed and sympathetic tone that he used with bereaved partners and their families, and even on the rare occasion when he visited the pub, where he always had a single whisky then went home. Not surprisingly such an austere lifestyle meant that Cribbens was a confirmed bachelor and pretty certainly the last of the Cribbens' funeral parlours descendants.

That is not to say that Cribbens was an unhappy man. Coming from a long line of undertakers he had never known any other sort of life and being a naturally quiet person, it suited him. Neither was he lonely, he had two live in employees, Wilf a semi-retired carpenter who obviously now specialised in boxes and his aptly named gravedigger, Douglas. Dug, as he liked to be called, was as far removed from Cribbens as fairies are from trolls. Where Cribbens enjoyed the formal trappings of his profession then so did Dug wallow in his grimy tan baggy trousers held up with bright red braces, chequered shirt with permanent pit stains, a faded yellow neckerchief and a grey flat cap. Not afraid of hard work, much as people with a phobia of heights don't climb mountains, Dug liked to let all in earshot know how busy he always was, often reciting the old cliché "and if I had a broom I could stick that somewhere dark and sweep the floor at the same time!" while the truth was that had he spent half the time digging instead of complaining about how put upon he was he'd finish work by lunchtime most days.

Cribbens had inherited Dug from his father when he inherited the family business and just didn't have the heart to let him go, though he did come close a few years ago when after a few days of heavy rain people had complained that some of the recently interred were floating out of the very shallow graves that an unsupervised Dug had dug. On inspecting this shocking debacle, the stress caused Cribbens to have a near fatal coffin fit and although it was against his nature, he gave Dug the dressing down of his life.

Most evenings would find Dug enjoying a pint or two with his best friends, Downwind Jones and Dai the dwarf, before his nightly rounds, usually standing by the door or an open window as insisted upon by Double D.

Rounding the corner, the Fat Wizard passed along the workshops behind the funeral parlour where Wilf was struggling to hammer some huge industrial nails in the lid of the most-heavy duty casket the Fat Wizard had ever seen.

"Hi Wilf, what you got there?" asked the Fat Wizard.

"It's the old Count, the one who never came out in the day" said Wilf.

"Oh" said the Fat Wizard slightly puzzled, "so what's with all the extra fortifications?" the Fat Wizard enquired.

"Buried the bugger three times last month, this time he's staying down!".

Hastily the Fat Wizard moved on down the street, the further he went the more ramshackle and rustic the buildings became before the cobbled road became more of a wide, hard packed dirt track which led to the Pant y Gussett car park. The people of Pant y Gussett had decided a long time ago that all motorised vehicles, including steam driven, would be banned from the village. They had reasoned that such pollution and risk of serious accidents was not something they would tolerate so the many residents who commuted to the "outside" (as it was commonly called) had to endure having a two-mile walk or pony ride added to their journey.

The closer you got to the car park the fewer buildings there were, and those were not much more than small log cabins, usually inhabited by people who liked their privacy and grew their own food, which if they had any surplus they traded in the village.

About half a mile from the car park the buildings completely petered out. It seems nobody wanted to live in sight of anything that reminded them of the outside world unless, like a washing machine it was really convenient.

Just before you got to the car park there was a deep gully with a large fast flowing stream at the bottom. This was spanned by an ancient stone bridge and, like many old bridges found all over the world, this one attracted a resident troll. Now trolls, despite being huge almost cave man-like creatures often seen carrying a large wooden club, generally lived quite secretive lives keeping themselves to themselves and apart from unintentionally scaring the few children who leave their computer consoles long enough to explore the real world like a modern day "Indiana Jones" they are seldom seen. However, Eric, (as the locals had named him) had taken it upon himself to be the unofficial car park attendant and reasoned that if he was going to look after all the vehicles in the car park then he should be paid. Eric was often left bemused when newcomers to the village, after being confronted by this 7ft apparition with his hand held out expectantly, often fumbled for their wallets or purses and panic stricken, emptied their contents into his hand. All he really wanted was a nice shiny apple or a packet of crisps.

"Hi Eric, you there?" called the Fat Wizard as he approached the "Troll Bridge"

"Ugg" replied a deep baritone voice as Eric lumbered up the bank.

"Don't suppose you noticed anything odd happening yesterday? Asked the Fat Wizard, craning his neck to look the behemoth in the eye.
Eric shrugged his shoulders, not an insignificant movement in one so big, but after a moment of contemplation, which was an obvious source of some discomfort to him, he added.

"Water smelled funny" which stretched poor Eric to the very limit of his vocabulary.

"I see" said the Fat Wizard, "thanks for that." and knowing that that was as much as he could expect from him, he handed Eric a boiled sweet from one of his pouches, even though he was heading to and not from the car park, he had always had a soft spot for Eric as indeed he had for all creatures of great strength that never intentionally hurt anyone.

5. WHO'S AFRAID OF CATS AND LAWNMOWERS?

Being a weekday there weren't that many cars in the car park. There was a silver VW golf, a couple of Japanese four-wheel drive, all terrain, jungle ready explorers, who had never gotten their wheels muddy and the standard rusty Ford Transit van with at least one axle up on bricks waiting to be repaired. This one was a remnant of one of Ivor and Penny's former commercial ventures. Parked next to this was, in pristine condition, a 1974 Austin Allegro 1.3 in faecal brown with gold pinstriping. Now the Fat Wizard generally knew who owned what, having a passing interest in cars despite not owning one himself, but funnily enough no-one had ever admitted to owning the Allegro.

Shielding the far side of the car park was a small but dense woodland where the link to the main road meandered through, hiding it from view of the relatively close A484. It was from this side of the car park where the main tracks and lanes for the more magical areas of Pant y Gussett were located.

What immediately caught the Fat Wizard's eye were the two vehicles parked right at the entrance to the car park next to these paths. One was an obviously new glossy black panel van that lacked any sort of sign writing or advertising on it, not even a "How's my Driving call 0800……" plate on the back. Parked alongside this was an equally black and glossy huge Mercedes Benz, of the type normally only afforded by royalty or footballers, which upon closer inspection carried private number plates A5 OIL. Seeing no-one inside either vehicle the Fat Wizard passed them by and chose the path that would take him around the footholds of Brakin Wind.

The Fat Wizard loved walking this path, he was surrounded by trees and hedgerows and the stunning cascade of colours from the bluebells, snowdrops, primroses and of course daffodils. All busily frequented by shiny metallic beetle, bees and butterflies and all manner of other creatures beginning with "B" who together produced an almost tuneful hum as they went about their business.

Now before you reach for your pen to compose a letter of complaint about the inaccuracies of what blooms in September, I would like to remind you that Pant y Gussett is a magical place that might not break the laws of nature but has no problem with bending them now and again.

Straying off the main path the Fat Wizard climbed a small bank where he knew that in the dip just behind it was his favourite stand of mugwort. Ever careful to take no more than he needed he started to pick some of the sturdier leaves and carefully fold them into one of his pouches.

"OI WATCH WHERE YOU'RE SSSSTANDING! Exclaimed a voice with an extreme lisp.

"Oh sorry" said the Fat Wizard looking down at his feet where a young grass snake was looking up at him reproachfully. "Didn't see you there"

"That'ssss ok" replied the snake, "good to know the camouflage isss working I sssupossse"

"Hey you haven't noticed anything odd happening out

here, recently have you?" enquired the Fat Wizard.

"Thisss isss Pant y Gussssett mate, there's alwaysss sssomething odd happening, but I have notissed the ground trembling a bit of late. Been wondering about moving to the outssside where all I have to worry about are catsss and the occassional lawn mower."

"Thanksss, I mean thanks for that" said the Fat Wizard stroking his beard thoughtfully. A habit that you've probably noticed that he had whenever he pondered. "See you around."

"I hope ssso" replied the snake who added cheekily, "you aint half got big feet" and with whatever passes for a smile in the reptile world, he slithered on his way.

"Cheeky sssod" mumbled the Fat Wizard with a smile as he turned to head back to the main path. As he started to climb out of the dip he could hear voices coming down the track. Not normally shy about meeting people, instinct told him to take cover and not be discovered by whoever was heading towards the car park, so like a very peculiar robed commando he crawled up to the top of the dip on his belly. No mean feat for a man of his considerable girth. Carefully parting a clump of tall daffodils, the Fat Wizard recognised the gang of workmen led by the two suited men; who now had their expensive trousers tucked into the same industrial boots as the other men, the same group that were in the pub yesterday. As they approached his vantage point, he could just make out one of the suits speaking quietly over his shoulder to the workmen,
"And remember when you come back tonight be discreet, we…" and with that they moved on out of earshot.
After waiting enough time for the group to disappear round a bend, the Fat Wizard grunted as he got to his feet and climbed back down to the path.

"How curious" he mumbled to himself as he carried on on his way. Half an hour later as he approached the gentle slope that was the start of the climb to the steepest part of Brakin Wind he came to a crossroads. The left-hand path would take him to the old mines and quarry still worked by the dwarves who eked a living digging for the copper and tin that used to be such a major industry in Wales. Straight on was the quickest route to the top of the hills. There the different species of dragons liked to roost. They were more than capable of taking off from the ground but enjoyed the energy efficient method of jumping off a promontory and gliding to gain enough speed to fly, something that is copied by birds of prey to this day.

Just as he was about to choose the right-hand path, he noticed to his left that some of the grass to the side of the path had been flattened, as if something quite large and heavy had been dragged over it.

A few more strokes of the beard as he inspected the damage and the Fat Wizard turned back to the right-hand path, where he knew a bit further on, he would find the foxgloves he had originally set out for.

It was a good half an hour before he came to a patch of the tall flower laden spikes that he had been using to make heart remedies, long before doctors had discovered the benefits of digitalis. Collecting what he needed the Fat Wizard decided to return home. As he stood up he heard a heart rending sobbing sound. Praying he hadn't stepped on a grass snake he searched through the undergrowth where, under the white spotted red cap of a large toadstool he found a small girl fairy clinging to the toadstools stem crying uncontrollably.

"There, there, little one," said the Fat Wizard gently, "what are you doing out here all alone?" noticing that she was so young her wings hadn't started to grow yet.

"I, I'm lost" came the pitiful reply.

"Can you tell me your name" asked the Fat Wizard gently

scooping her up with one hand.
"Elspeth" she sobbed,

"Elspeth, what a lovely name, now tell me Elspeth how on earth did you get here?"

"I was in my home tree chasing my pet butterfly across a branch when everything started to shake and I fell off"

"Oh dear" said the Fat Wizard, were you hurt?

"No no" said Elspeth "I landed on something soft, it was a rabbit who was hopping past the tree, Peter, I think he said his name was. I begged him to stop but he said he was running away from a loud noise and had to keep running. I held on for as long as I could but I fell off and now I don't know where I am."

"And when did this happen?"

"Yesterday morning" replied Elspeth breaking into floods of tears again.

"What! You've been out here on your own all night" gasped the Fat Wizard.

"Yes" said Elspeth peering up at the Fat Wizard with her piercing blue eyes and golden locks just visible under her bluebell bonnet, "I walked around for hours and when it started to get dark, I hid under that toadstool".

Looking at her fluffy white dress made from dandelion seeds, the blue cap and the trademark blonde hair and blue eyes, he said;

"You must be from Queen Megan's clan They must be worried sick about you, but don't worry pet I know roughly where Queen Megan's tree is. I'll take you in that direction and I have a plan so that they will find you quickly," and with that he lifted her up and sat her on the brim of his Wizard's hat. "Now hang on and enjoy the view. We'll have you back with your family in no time"

"Thank you, thank you" replied a considerably more cheerful Elspeth, feeling a lot safer now she was off the ground.

As he had expected the Fat Wizard had hardly gone more than a few paces when a small dark cloud suddenly descended from the sky above them. Stopping a few feet from his face the Fat Wizard could see that they were fully winged fairies. He also recognised the plain grey uniforms worn by the squadrons of Queen Megan's personal guard, The Resolute Ariel Fairies, or as we mentioned earlier, the RAF.

"Praise the trees" exclaimed Captain Riser from the head of the squadron all hovering at the Fat Wizard's head height,

"You've found Elspeth. We've had every able winged fairy out looking for her since yesterday. We were starting to fear the worst, thank you! FW thank you!"

"My pleasure Riser, I had a feeling that you would find it easier to spot her on my hat than under fungus" grinned the Fat Wizard.

"True" said, Riser "My people owe you a great debt."

"Think nothing of it" replied the Fat Wizard "Glad I could help, oh just one thing I don't suppose you know what caused the tremor yesterday do you?

"Not yet, but we have some of our woodland allies looking into it. I'll keep you posted" and with that Riser flew over and retrieved Elspeth from the Fat Wizard's hat. But as they started to fly away, he could see Elspeth whispering into Riser's ear and they turned back. Now in front of his face, Elspeth reached out and held onto the Fat Wizard's beard and kissed him gently on the cheek and with a heart melting smile said, "thank you mister". Then clinging back on to Riser the fairies all flew up into the air and within seconds were completely out of sight.

"Right!" said the Fat Wizard loudly to no-one in particular, "That's enough excitement for one day. I'm off home for a mug of hot strong tea, and if my darling wife isn't looking, I think I'll add an extra sugar or two" he thought to himself guiltily.

Trudging back through the car park he noticed the absence of the two black vehicles, confirming his suspicions as to whom they may belong, and a few minutes later he reached the bridge where Eric, with his hand outstretched was blocking his way.

"Hello again Eric, did you see who went into the car and the van at the other end of the car park?" enquired the Fat Wizard.

"People" mumbled Eric in his monosyllabic style holding his hand out further.

"I see" replied the Fat Wizard, realising that any further questioning would be a futile exercise. So, reaching into a pouch he produced another boiled sweet, this time a lime one, you know the ones with a chocolate centre. Tossing the offering to Eric the Fat Wizard bade him a hearty farewell and continued on his way.

He had bought the sweets from Dodd's paper shop although some time ago he had experimented with making his own confectionary to sell in his own shop.

Unfortunately, he had been a bit overzealous with some of his more magical ingredients. His lemon sours were so sour that even one would render people unable to whistle for a week. His sherbet dips left people frothing so badly at the mouth that they started a rabies scare, while his toffees, well actually they were quite nice.

Finally approaching his street, he made a quick detour to a large shop on the corner of the crossroads opposite the funeral parlour, (no not the corner with the pub the other corner the same side as the parlour), to pick up a pint of milk. This massive shop sold a bit of everything, including milk, but specialised in locally made consommé, casseroles and broths, it was known as the Pant y Gussett soupermarket.

One more stop, this time at Mrs Crumbles bakery for the loaf of bread that he dared not return without and the Fat Wizard was, with some relief, home.

6. OLD COWS AND ACCOUNTANTS

At home with a steaming hot mug of tea in one hand and a freshly made ham and pickle sandwich in the other, the Fat Wizard recounted the morning's events to Mrs FW and Rebe.

"My hero!" declared Mrs FW with admiration, and maybe the merest hint of sarcasm in her voice. "But who do you think those cars belong to?"

"I have no idea" said the Fat Wizard, accidentally spraying crumbs over Jasper who, sitting at his knee, had been following every movement of the sandwich in anticipation of just one unguarded moment. "But I think I know how to find out, pass me that, 100 Most Popular Spells, Volume 1 off the big bookcase would you dear?"

"Certainly, my dear" she replied as she struggled to retrieve the weighty tome from the top shelf, adding "but you don't really expect to find a spell to tell you who owns what car, surely?"

"Course not silly" sighed the Fat Wizard, who with a momentary lapse of concentration when accepting the book, let the crust of his sandwich slide off the plate. It was never destined to make it to the floor thanks to an eager Jasper, ecstatic because his patience had finally paid off.

Opening the front cover of the book he smiled saying;

"I thought I'd left that there" as a business card, titled "Brian Jones ACCOUNTANT" ICAEW, ACCA, FiBAc.", slipped from the page onto his lap.

Brian was an old friend of the Fat Wizard, an unlikely pair being as different as chalk and cheese. Where the Fat Wizard was, well, fat and bearded then Brian was tall skinny and close shaven. They first met at wizarding school, not that it was a school as such Being a wizard is something that some people just are, but years ago some senior and respected wizards joined together to form an official council in order to control some of the, would be, practitioners of the magical arts. Their goal was to prevent some of the more unsavoury characters from practising the darker side of the craft. The sort of people who might use magic to aid them in political ambitions or even experiment with forces more powerful than they could control and could threaten life as we know it. It's a shame really that such an authority doesn't exist for some of our modern scientific bodies. This council of wizards, or "the Old Cows" as they were known behind their backs, would watch over an emerging wizard's spells and potions, in order to monitor and advise them to keep each candidate on the correct path. Once they were satisfied with their character, each participant was summoned to the wizards council's great boardroom (in truth a rented office above a tattoo parlour in Swansea) and asked to produce a unique spell or potion of their own devising for judging, which if successful meant registration with the council of wizards, also a £50 book token from a major bookseller and a framed certificate declaring the candidate as an "Official Fellow Of The Council Of Wizards. More importantly such status meant that the wizard was now eligible to purchase Public Liability Insurance, an absolute must in today's society.

For his certificate the Fat Wizard entered one of his specialty remedy scented candles. This one had amongst other ingredients grated dragon scales, (these were naturally shed, there were absolutely no dragons harmed in the writing of this book) that served to promote good feelings and dispelled negative thoughts. How much the "old cows" were swayed by the slightly euphoric effect of the candle is a matter of some conjecture.

Brian however, despite much private tuition from the Fat Wizard had displayed little ability with magic. Even his qualifying masterpiece, a potion to instantly relieve heartburn even after a garlic infused curry he boasted, reduced the council to an embarrassing cacophony of belching and flatulence.

After opening the windows, a red-faced Gerald, lead spokesman for the "Old Cows" turned to Brian and said;

"I'm sure that you must agree that maybe a career in wizardry may not be the best course for your future, however" he added kindly "it has not gone unnoticed that you seem to have an almost magical affinity with numbers. Despite the results we have observed the great skill with which you have mathematically calculated formulas, weights and ratios in your endeavours, so may we suggest that maybe a career in the finance industry would be beneficial for all of us."

Reluctantly, Brian had to concede that there might be some wisdom in the council's suggestion.

"But wizardry is all I know; how would I get into commerce?" said Brian with a slight tone of desperation.

Gerald turned to the rest of the council and after some whispered consultation declared,

"We have unanimously agreed that although you are not true wizard material, your unnatural ability with numbers cannot be ignored. So we have decided to grant you "Associate Member of The Council of Wizards" status, and with that in mind will arrange an interview for you with a large accountancy firm based in Cardiff, that just happens to be part owned by one of our members."

Expressing his gratitude, Brian caught himself actually bowing as he left the boardroom.

His interview with Messrs Pinkerton, Aristotle and Smith was far different from anything he had imagined. All the candidates were told to meet in a basement office in the firm's headquarters in Cardiff. Lit by a single dim bulb and smelling like a neglected library, the office was lined with wall to wall stacks of files and ledgers. The only furnishing was a single desk, the sort that would have been keenly sought after in one of those antique hunting TV programmes.

All seven of the candidates had been instructed to line up and face the occupant of the desk who was frantically scribbling something on to a huge leather-bound book. Without looking up the skinny old man with a shock of long white hair and a pronounced freckled bald patch announced himself as William, the chief clerk.

"You" William said gruffly, pointing to the first in the line with his pen, though with his demeanour a quill wouldn't have looked out of place. "what's two plus two?"

"Four" stammered the first victim, perplexed.

"Next!" demanded William," with an officious growl, "What's two plus two?"

"Well, four" said the next candidate determined not to be outdone.

"You" demanded William aiming his pen at the next in the row, "What's two plus two?" with a slight hint of exasperation entering his voice.

"Four of course" said the next interviewee puffing out his chest in an attempt to show confidence that he didn't really feel.

And so it went on until he finally reached Brian at the end of the queue.

"What's two plus two?" enquired William with a resigned sigh.

Unable to contain himself with this bizarre process, Brian blurted out, cheekily.

"What do you want it to be!"

"You're hired!" said William, nonchalantly, "pick up your contract from the third floor, you start next week," and without looking up he returned to scribble in his ledger.

And so Brian embarked on his illustrious career as an accountant. He quickly worked his way up the corporate ladder and within a few short years had become chief accountant with Messer's Pinkerton, Aristotle and Smith. Not content with this he had decided to go out on his own and had now become a freelance accountant to anyone who could afford him, and indeed the many who couldn't afford not to use him. Today he rubs shoulders with all manner of pop stars, premier football players and even the occasional royal, but he never forgot where he came from and never missed attending the "Council Of Wizards"

Summer Ball. They called it the summer ball but it was usually held in October and consisted of past and present council members sitting at food and drink laden tables trying to outdo each other with boasts of their latest spells and potions.

It was at the last such event that Brian had given the Fat Wizard his current business card and told him;

"If there is anything I can do for you, just call. I'll never forget how much you tried to help me."

And so here we are almost a year later with the Fat Wizard attempting a task, that anyone born after the late nineties seemed to manage effortlessly, of holding a card in one hand and tapping numbers on to a phone with the other. Several misdials later, including one that somehow reached a speaking clock in Serbia and another, an old man living in Slough, proclaiming that he didn't have PPI, the Fat Wizard finally heard a familiar voice.

"FW! How are you? Long time no see" said a jubilant Brian.

"Fine fine" said the Fat Wizard, gratified that Brian seemed so genuinely pleased to hear from him. "How's the big city and all that money treating you" he teased.

"It's a struggle but the penthouse suite overlooking Cardiff bay, the gorgeous women and the Porsche help me get by." Brian chuckled, "and you?"

"Much the same," said the Fat Wizard, adding "but the little cottage, a gorgeous wife and the use of a neighbours donkey keep me sane" he replied just as jovially.

"Well I know that I'll be seeing you at next month's summer ball so come on, out with it, what can I help you with?" enquired Brian sounding slightly concerned.

"Straight to the point as always" a trait the Fat Wizard had always respected in Brian. "I was hoping to ask a small favour" he asked, "it's probably nothing but I wonder if you had any contacts that could trace car registration plates?"

"As it happens I've just helped a famous comedian out of a sticky situation regarding a rather hefty income tax bill. His brother is a chief inspector with the police and is rather grateful that I've saved him from the embarrassment of having a felon in the family, but why, what's up?" asked Brian, sounding even more concerned.

"As I say it's probably nothing, but some strangers have been visiting Pant y Gussett and they're making my beard twitch" said the Fat Wizard trying to keep the conversation light.

"Beard twitching eh, sounds serious to me, ok let me make a call, text me the registration number and I'll get back to you as soon as I know anything." said Brian.

"Thank you my friend" said the Fat Wizard "I'll buy you a few pints when we meet at the ball."

"You know the drinks are free there" said Brian.

"Yes, yes I did" Laughed the Fat Wizard.

Sitting back in his chair the Fat Wizard was about to put his feet up on the dog and have a snooze when the apple of his eye tapped him, quite roughly, on the shoulder and said.;

"Oi! Don't get too comfy, you're manning the shop this

afternoon, teapots don't make themselves you know."

"Fair enough" sighed the Fat Wizard, and slowly made his way downstairs to the shop.

7. DRAGON EGGS AND BINGO.

Monday afternoons were never a particularly busy time for the shop but there were enough customers to keep the Fat Wizard's mind off his expected phone call. Ivor and Penny had called in to once again apologise for Ivor snapping at the Fat Wizard in the pub yesterday, and also to pick up a hangover cure. It appears inspiration did not arrive after all yesterday, but they had doggedly stuck it out, just in case. After they had left, the Fat Wizard had a slightly embarrassing mix up with a nervous and rather unhappy looking farmer who had had come in mumbling something about needing lead for a pencil. To which our intrepid hero suggested that he try the stationers up the street and around the corner. With the bemused farmer looking up at him, imploringly, the penny dropped and the Fat Wizard unlocked a metal strongbox that was under the counter and produced a small box of pills.

"Just take one of these about half an hour before you spend some alone time with your wife." instructed the Fat Wizard.

"Oh, I'm not married." said the farmer.

"OK" said the Fat Wizard, not one to judge, "half an hour before you spend some alone time with your partner then."

"Actually, I'm single" said the farmer.

"I see," said the Fat Wizard with a growing look of concern on his face.

"No… No" said the farmer, they're not for me they're for me prize bull, "he's not been performing, if you know what I mean."

"Thank heavens for that," said the Fat Wizard obviously relieved, "in that case give him two of these pills, but whatever you do make sure you get out of the field within half an hour!"

"Will do" chuckled the farmer paying for his medicine but as he turned to leave the Fat Wizard stopped him and asked,

"Any idea why your bull should be falling down in his duties, so to speak?"
"Not sure really" said the farmer "but I keep my herd in a field the other side of the car park, and for the last week or so there have been some funny noises coming from one of the abandoned mines late at night and he's been acting all nervous like since.".

"I see" said the Fat Wizard starting to stroke his beard again, "and have you seen anything odd out there?" queried the Fat Wizard.

"I fancied that I saw some lights on the hill, but it was quite late so I put them down to one of those annoying sprites that pass through from time to time, you know the ones who like to leave gates open, or knock the door and run away when you're in the bath or even worse, deliver leaflets advertising double glazing and the like!".

And with that the farmer left, politely holding the door open for the rancid odour that always preceded the arrival of Downwind Jones.

"Afternoon FW" said Downwind "have you got one of my favourite bars of soap, you know the one with the bits of grit in it?"

"Good grief," September already is it?" said the Fat Wizard painfully aware of Downwinds' hygiene protocol, "Yes I have, and as it happens Downwind, you're just the man I wanted to see."

"Uh?" said Downwind looking up suspiciously, he wasn't used to being a man that someone wanted to see, unless he owed them money.

"Do you want to earn an easy twenty quid?" (that's a slang term for pounds for those readers outside of the UK).

"Twenty pounds!!" (See, I told you) "I'd love to, but I won't do anything really dodgy, well not for less than thirty pounds anyway. said Downwind.

"It's nothing bad, all I want you to do is to spend a couple of hours late tonight wandering around the paths near the old quarry and the mines and report to me tomorrow."

"What am I looking for?" queried Downwind.

"Anything odd or unusual" said the Fat Wizard.

"What, in Pant y Gussett?"

"I mean anything particularly odd or unusual, will you do it?"

"Cash up front?" asked Downwind, hopefully.

"Cash up front" sighed the Fat Wizard, handing Downwind a couple of tenners from one of his pouches. He reasoned that it would be easier to pay Downwind out of his pocket money than justify a discrepancy in the till to Mrs FW, who kept a very tight rein on the books.

"And you'll chuck in the soap for free?"

"And I'll chuck in the soap for free" resigned the Fat Wizard, but he added, with a marked tone of warning in his voice, "I'd better see you first thing tomorrow."

"I'll be here, don't you worry 'bout that, see you tomorrow."

"Make sure you do" replied the Fat Wizard, still with an air of menace in his tone, and as he watched an excited Downwind leave, repeated quietly, "make sure you do."

The last customer of the day was Dorcas Edwards, a stern looking woman who always wore a full-length black coat and matching black hat whatever the weather. Her wrinkled long nose and permanently pursed lips gave the impression that wherever she went, something smelled bad. Which considering Downwinds' earlier visit, might, this time, be justified.

"Ah Mrs Edwards" greeted the Fat Wizard with a warm smile, that in another profession would have had him nominated for an Oscar, "How can I help you today?"

"I'd like another of your good lady wife's crockery sets please, the plain grey ones without any pictures of birds or flowers on them." said Dorcas in the same tone she reserved for all tradesmen.

"Certainly" replied the Fat Wizard through slightly gritted teeth, "Bill home late from the pub again last night?" he added.

"His name is William" Dorcas snapped coldly "and if you would be so kind as to keep your nose out of other people's affairs and just concentrate on what you're paid to do, the better for all of us.

If you only knew what Bill had once requested of me, for the better of all of us, you wouldn't take that tone with me! thought the Fat Wizard to himself, now reconsidering his denial of Bill's wish to turn his beloved into a "Stepford wife" style automaton with a remote control and mute button.
Carefully wrapping Dorcas' plates and saucers to her begrudging satisfaction, the Fat Wizard closed up shop and walked over to the pottery workshop to collect Mrs FW, who, he knew, would be in a world of her own throwing clay and be totally unaware of the time.

"Brian rung yet?" enquired an attractive pair of blue eyes out of a body so covered in wet clay that she was only several hours away from becoming a statue.

"No not yet, but he did say it might take a day or two. You've been busy "said the Fat Wizard admiring a large range of teapots and saucers, sitting in racks waiting to go into the drying room.

"Well Rebe seems to have quite a few dragon eggs about to hatch so I thought I'd make the most of all that extra free energy."

"How come so many eggs?" queried the Fat Wizard

somewhat afraid of the reply.

"I don't know" said Mrs FW distractedly while attaching a handle to a just finished teapot, "ask her, she's in the hatchery."

Crossing the garden, the Fat Wizard came to a large outbuilding with a large sign on the door, "KEEP OUT, RISK OF INCINERATION". Opening the door carefully lest anything flying about should escape, the Fat Wizard walked to the end of the brightly lit brick building where Rebe was busy tending to row after row of eggs. She had worked out years ago that there was a higher percentage of successful hatching if you increased the air circulation by making sure that the eggs were placed singly, and not touching each other, It was one of her proudest moments when she submitted her findings to "The Dragon Conservation Society" and they printed her paper on the inside front page of their monthly newsletter.

"Hi pet" said the Fat Wizard affectionately. He had always admired his eldest daughters' dedication to the welfare of her charges.

"Hi Dad" she replied, looking up only briefly before wiping away a spot of fungus that was starting to attack a rather sad looking egg, considerably wrinklier and smaller than the others.

"Oh dear" said the Fat Wizard, "that doesn't look very healthy, will it make it?" he asked.

"Well I've done everything I can, it's up to her now".

"Her?" queried the Fat Wizard.

"I consider all the eggs female until they hatch. Don't

know why I just do" said Rebe.

"Your mother says that you've got a lot of eggs here at the moment, any idea why?
"I dunno" said Rebe, "as you know I usually just come across nests that inexperienced mothers have made, and then forgotten where they left them if they get startled by something and fly off. Recently though even the more mature dragons, who normally guard their eggs aggressively, seem to be abandoning their nests. Something is spooking them."

"What could scare a mature dragon? They don't have any natural predators round here, do they?" he said, as much to himself as Rebe.

"None that I can think of" said Rebe, "do you think it could have anything to do with that little earthquake we had on Sunday? Is it possible that there were more tremors up on the hills where they nest that we didn't notice?

"Could be, could be," mumbled the Fat Wizard starting to stroke his beard again, "course it could be just a coincidence."

"Come off it Dad, I know, you, you're more likely to believe in honest politicians than you are coincidences."

"Very true, look keep me posted if you notice anything else unusual happening with the dragons."

"Define unusual, this is Pan….."

"Anything particularly unusual" interrupted the Fat Wizard, "even for Pant y Gussett." he said slightly exasperated, "and don't be too long fiddling about down here. You promised to help Mam with dinner."

"Fiddling about!" exclaimed Rebe indignantly, "'I'll give you, fiddling about," as she light heartedly threatened the Fat Wizard with her pump action, dragon egg, water spray bottle.

Beating a hasty retreat, he quickly exited the room and went to water all his herbs and plants in the garden before heading back to the cottage.

As he walked into the living room he was greeted by his now, freshly showered, and dressing gown clad wife.

"I didn't wait for Rebe, I thought I would do you one of your favourites, toad in the hole."

Now for those of you unaccustomed to British culinary delicacies, toad in the hole consists of sausages in batter and covered in gravy. (not a single toad was harmed in the writing of this book, although, already dead ones might be harvested for magical purposes).

"Lovely" said the Fat Wizard as he kicked off his sandals and sprawled into his favourite chair at the head of the dining table.

I should add, there was nothing sexist about the seating arrangements, it was merely due to the fact that his seat was in a draft, and being the gentleman that he is he thought his robes afforded him the best protection.

As always he sat there mesmerised by Jasper's ability, despite a frantically wagging tail, to keep exactly one nose length's distance from Mrs FW's hands as she ferried items from the stove to the table.

Finally joined by Rebe the family sat down to their evening meal.

"I hope you don't mind" announced Mrs FW "I've arranged to meet the girls for a game of bingo at the Cross, or Carrot, or whatever it is they're calling themselves these days."

"Course we don't mind love" said the Fat Wizard, "Girls, you say, they have a collective age of at least two hundred and fifty between them! He chuckled to himself, "I fancied a night in front of the telly anyway." he said, "what about you Rebe, fancy a night in front of the box like we used to?"

"Sorry Dad, would love to," said Rebe, sounding genuinely disappointed, "but I've got at least three eggs about to hatch and you know I like to be there for them."

"Fair enough. An evening of quiz shows and American sitcoms for me then methinks."

"They're calling for me at half past seven so put your sandals back on, and comb your beard, I don't want them getting the right impression!" said Mrs FW, "and try and play nice this time, no pretending that I beat you and keep you prisoner."

"Sorry dear, but you must admit, they are pretty gullible"

"That's not the point" said Mrs FW, struggling to suppress the laughter in her voice, "do you always have to embarrass me in front of my friends?"

The Fat Wizard tried to look serious as he said "well I don't have to but.."

"Just this once" she implored "please".
"OK" he said affectionately, "but just this once" he added with a mischievous grin.

An hour or so later the Fat Wizard found himself answering the door to a gaggle of housewives looking him up and down reproachfully, enquiring is she ready yet? In a tone that suggested that if he was in anyway hindering her escape then they would incite the wrath of a thousand demons on his soul.

"She'll be down now" he said, but couldn't contain himself from adding, "she's just looking for her wig and putting her new teeth in."

"Well really," came a collective gasp. And with that Mrs FW appeared with a cheery, "Hello Ladies." her smile quickly fading as she surveyed the look of annoyance on the faces of the gathered women. Turning to her husband she said through gritted teeth,

"What have you done this time!"

"Nothing dear" he said with a broad grin on his face, "now off you go and have a good evening, I'll see you later".

With the ladies gone the Fat Wizard settled down in his comfy armchair with a cup of tea in his hand and Jasper asleep on his lap. After watching a particularly high brow quiz show, to which he found himself answering all the questions before realising it was a repeat, the Fat Wizard, in common with most men, magical or not, of a certain age drifted off to sleep.

It was about nine thirty when all hell broke loose.

As the tremor started Jasper barked and leapt up from the Fat Wizard's lap knocking his mug out of his hand and in the process smashed it on the floor. Pictures started falling off the wall, books slid off the bookshelf even the furniture vibrated across the floor in what appeared a futile attempt to escape. Then, just as the lights started to flicker, all went quiet, until Rebe burst into the room yelling,

"You OK dad? that was bad"

"I'm OK pet, you'd better go check on the dragon sheds. Check everything is intact. I'm going to run up to the pub and check on your mother and see if anyone needs any help."

Hastily donning his sandals, the Fat Wizard flew out of the shop, where on the street he was greeted by a throng of scared and confused neighbours all asking "what happened?", "anybody hurt?" and "where's my bloody horse gone!"

Seeing no signs of physical injury among them the Fat Wizard ran as fast as he could to the pub. Vaulting over flower pots, overturned dustbins and for some reason a supermarket trolley, the Fat Wizard could see his good lady and the rest of the patrons from the pub standing outside the doors and pointing excitedly at the roof of the funeral parlour, while the street was littered with all sorts of shapes and sizes of shiny metal bits.

"You OK love?" asked the Fat Wizard hugging his beloved.

"I'm fine" she said, "but you should have seen it! we all ran outside the pub for safety when the shaking started, and then the bell in the funeral parlour steeple made a horrendous clang. It must have come away from its fixings and fell into the clock mechanism."

"Aye that's right" said Huw Puw joining them, "then all these flying rodents and bits of clock started spewing from the tower, raining bats and cogs it was!"

"I see said the Fat Wizard looking round, "Anybody hurt? he shouted.

"No, I think everyone's OK, but the laundrette is going to

be busy in the morning!" some wag from the crowd shouted.

Fair play to the locals, they tended to keep a sense of humour even in a crisis.

It was then a dazed Mr Cribben appeared at the door of the funeral parlour, supported by a visibly shaken, Wilf and Dug.

"Are you hurt? "Enquired the Fat Wizard.

"Hurt" replied the undertaker, even paler than usual, "I've got two smashed caskets and a ruined suit, I'll say I'm hurt!".

"That's not what I meant, oh never mind" said the Fat Wizard who turned to Huw and said, "Can you see that everyone gets home safely. We can't do anything else here at the moment."

"Certainly FW, leave it to me." said Huw puffing his chest out, proud that his unofficial guardian status was finally being given official approval. "Right you lot, nothing to see here, let's be having you off home" he said in the authoritative tone that policemen the world over always resort to in difficult times.

Ignoring Huw, as one the crowd returned to the pub.

"But, but" he said crestfallen, "Oh sod it!, mine's a pint of witches finger" he cried as he followed them in.

Even from outside the Fat Wizard could hear raised voices shouting "another earthquake, what's going on", someone else shouted, It's the end of the world, I saw it on the telly! And even "I blame the Russians I do!" and he thought to himself, I suppose I'd better see if I can calm them down.

With Mrs FW in tow the Fat Wizard entered the pub and

using a magically enhanced booming voice that he normally reserved for cheering Wales at rugby matches, he said,

"Bless all in this place!"

The entire bar went immediately silent, until Double D, piped up,

"Hello dear, pint of the usual? and how about you Mrs FW"
"My name is Jean, as you well know!" replied Mrs FW in the tone that most married women reserved for attractive barmaids.

"Sorry Mrs F... I mean Jean, a half for you is it?" said Double D, her smile not wavering for an instant.

"I may as well, I think Mr FW has something to say to you all".

"Right, thank you dear. Now as you are all aware there have been a couple of frightening tremors over the last few days and you've all probably heard of the "Rose Well" incident. I can also confirm that there have been some strange things going on in the outskirts of the village that's affected some of our magical neighbours. I don't know what's the cause of all this but I promise you that I am investigating it and I hope I'll know more in the morning. In the meantime I beg you all to stay calm until I've found out what we are dealing with. As soon as I have some information I'll call a meeting in the town hall and explain it all."

The pub erupted with cries of "hear hear" and "FW won't let us down" and just before they all prepared to sing, "for he's a jolly good fellow" the Fat Wizard felt an urgent tugging on his sleeve where he looked down to see a gnome excitedly remark,

"But we don't have a town hall!"

"I mean I'll call a meeting here!" announced the Fat Wizard feeling ever so slightly embarrassed.

And, with the villagers feeling slightly more at ease with someone as powerful and trusted as the Fat Wizard on the case, they turned their attention to their favourite pastime of trying to drink the pub dry.

8. A STREET CART CALLED DEE'S HIRE.

Tuesday morning arrived as most Tuesday mornings did, last weekend a distant memory and next weekend an age away. The only thing of note was that for a third day in a row it was bright and sunny, more than you would expect to get from an August in Wales.

The Fat Wizard was up bright and early, keen to man the shop while he awaited the arrival of Downwind Jones or a phone call from his mate, Brian.
He looked up expectantly as the little bell above the door chimed heralding the entrance of a visitor, trying to mask a look of disappointment he said,

"Morning Tom, how can I help you this fine day?"

Tom was one of his regular customers, probably a good looking fellow in his day but time had not been kind, and he had that worn-down countenance of a man living on the edge. You could imagine that if he were a rabbit he would be perpetually caught in the glare of an eighteen wheeler, driven by a drunken roadkill gourmet chef.
Married young to his childhood sweetheart Mable, rather hastily, if the rumours are to be believed, people always felt that Mabel had always blamed him for her lost youth and

had made it her mission in life to see that he paid for it.

"Actually, I'm OK at the moment" said Tom sounding slightly confused, "it's just that you said down the pub last night to tell you if we noticed anything odd, odd for Pant y Gussett that is."

"Yes, go on" said the Fat Wizard rubbing his temples wishing Tom hadn't reminded him of his impromptu visit to the pub last night.

"Well it's just that Mabel has been acting a bit strange these last few days"

"Strange, how?" said the Fat Wizard, his interest piqued.

"Well she's been sort of nice to me recently"

"What do you mean, nice?"

"Well take last night for instance. There we were having dinner then, out of the blue, she gave me a tenner and said, go on you, go and have a pint with your friends on me. And then this morning she started singing while cooking breakfast, singing! I don't mind telling you, I was scared. Do you think this might be connected to the strange goings on in the village do you?".

"Singing you say hmm. Look Tom, we've known each other for a long time now" said the Fat Wizard, awkwardly, and lowering his voice to an almost conspiratorial tone, continued "remember, a couple of months ago how you concreted over your large back garden so you could have more room for your cart and carriage renovation business?"

"Yes, said Tom, I've got the height to do MOT's now you

know, Mounting Overhead Tarpaulins." wondering where the Fat Wizard was going with this.

"Well" continued the Fat Wizard obviously uncomfortable, "didn't it strike you as odd that a couple of weeks ago Mabel employed young Ned, Griff the blacksmith's son as a part time gardener?"

"Now you mention it, that was a bit strange now we don't have a garden, Hey!" Said Tom with the penny finally dropping, "you don't think, I mean, could they?, would they?" and with a grin from ear to ear added, with a slight growl, "When they run off together they're not taking the bloody dog, I'd miss him!" and with a cry of "Oh happy day. Thank you, FW, cancel my weekly order of nerve tonic if you don't mind, I'm not going to need it anymore!", he flew out of the shop to confront his soon to be, ex-wife.

"Well that turned out better than I expected." mused the Fat Wizard and with the shop now empty, started to worry about the non-appearance of Downwind Jones.

By mid-morning the shop had had its fair share of customers buying the sort of goods that were bread and butter for the business, such as cough syrup, athletes foot balm and, headache pills along with some crockery and vases, sales of which have been noticeably increasing since the tremors. But still no sign of Downwind, Now getting really worried, the Fat Wizard called for Rebe to mind the shop while he went out to look for him.

Racing up the street the Fat Wizard enquired about Downwind to everyone he met but unfortunately, Downwind was just one of those characters that, apart from the odour, nobody seemed to notice unless he was actually wanted for something.

Having covered most of his usual haunts, including the pub, behind which was where Downwind usually parked his handcart, upon finding it still there and with the broom and shovel obviously not freshly used and Downwind still nowhere to be found, the Fat Wizard felt a rising sense of panic as he was starting to fear that something awful had happened to Downwind while carrying out the Fat Wizard's errand. Reasoning that Downwind must still be up near the path by the mountain, the Fat Wizard decided to extend his search. But concerned over how long he'd been missing and in order to save time he hailed the taxi.

Yes, I did say THE taxi, there was only one. As I mentioned earlier the trip to and from the car park was quite lengthy by foot, so a couple of years ago Double D's brother Ed, who used to be a minicab driver in Llanelli, decided to set up on his own in Pant y Gussett. He saved up enough money to buy a sturdy horse and a carriage, that he paid Tom to convert into an eight-seater and started a ferry service, four times a day, for people to get back and fore to their vehicles. He also branched out into "party bookings" offering guided tours of Pant y Gussett which he advertised by installing a large billboard with "Dee's Hire" in bright letters above the carriage.
Ed did blanch somewhat when the Fat Wizard commented, "Oh look, a street-cart named Dee's hire!".

Getting off the taxi at the carpark, and after verifying that Ed hadn't seen Downwind while on his travels either, the Fat Wizard went to open his pouch to pay him.

"Your money's no good here" said Ed, "not after you sorted out my, erm, little problem."

"The ointment still working then?" said the Fat Wizard.

"Like a charm, no pun intended. Never realised how comfy the driver's seat of a Peugeot 504 was until I had to make do with a wooden bench instead" Ed chuckled, as he reached into his pocket for a pear drop to pay Eric with on the way back. "Hope you find him; I'll be back in a coupla hours if you want a lift.".

"Cheers Ed." said the Fat Wizard as he started to half jog up the path that led away from the car park. After what felt like an eternity, he eventually reached the crossroads, where, now gasping for air and his wizard's hat all droopy from the weight of perspiration, he decided to stop for a breather while he considered his next move.

Having regained some wind but with his calf muscles on fire he turned left to follow the path to the mines. Walking considerably slower now and muttering under his breath something about "no more cream cakes" and "I wonder if my gym membership has expired yet?", he continued on his way. Normally he would enjoy the majesty of Brakin Wind on his right while on his left the trees and bushes gave way to scenic green fields and pastures, where sheep and cattle spent their day quietly grazing, but not today. All he felt today was a rising trepidation as to the fate of Downwind Jones. A few more yards and his worst fears were realised. There just in front of him was a muddy boot with a hole in the sole sticking out of a ditch in front of a field. "Oh No!" cried the Fat Wizard as he ran forward and found that the boot had the rest of Downwind Jones still attached to it lying face down in the ditch.

☐

9. RESPECT YOUR MINERS.

"What have I done" Cried the Fat Wizard, almost hysterically, "I didn't mean for this to happen." and as he bent over the prone body, he caught a whiff of something other than Downwinds' normal familiar odour. Not too gently the Fat Wizard rolled Downwind over onto his back to reveal him still clutching an empty, grey porcelain jug with three X's boldly printed on the front.

"Ooh where am I," groaned Downwind with breath so sour that the Fat Wizard had to summon all his willpower not to retch.

"I'll tell you where you are," growled the Fat Wizard, "you're in my bad books, and that's not a place you want to be. Now tell me, what happened!".

"Oh!" said Downwind desperately holding on to some long grass in an attempt to not fall off the ground, "it's like this see, well it was a beautiful evening last night, so like you asked I came to have a look around, but being such a fine evening I thought I'd come a bit early and enjoy the view. Well as I had some money, I thought that maybe I should I bring a jug of brandy with me, just in case it got a bit nippy later on you understand.".

"I understand all right" shouted the Fat Wizard, "If you brought the brandy here then you wouldn't have to share it with Dai, the Dwarf and Dug, the grave digger am I right?"

Suffering under the volume of the Fat Wizards retort; "No, it was nothing like that FW, purely medicinal, honest!". Pleaded Downwind.

"Likely story! So, what happened next?

"Well I sat on that stone over by there and thought I'd just have a little drop, to keep my energy up you understand, when I started watching that old bull in the field there. I've never seen anything like it. Well he went from cow to cow and back again, at one point they tried jumping the hedge but he pulled them back in. Well with such a spectacle I didn't notice how much I'd drunk and the next thing I know you're here shouting at me."

"Do you remember anything else about last night?" asked the Fat Wizard, his voice softening a bit as it seemed to him that one of his remedies might have been a part of Downwinds' failure.

"I remember thinking the ground was shaking, but I really can't be sure of that, if you know what I mean. Oh, I'm sure there were raised voices in the distance, proper angry sounding they were too".

"Coming from the mines?" asked the Fat Wizard.

"Think so, but they were a long way off. Sorry to let you down FW, I'll come back out again tonight to make up for it" said an honestly repentant and hungover Downwind.

"No forget, it I don't think my nerves could take another day worrying over you. Don't worry I'll find some safer errands for you to pay me back with."

"I didn't know you cared" said Downwind in the sort of emotional tone common to a lot of people while sobering up and still not too sure what they did altogether the previous night.

"No, neither did I! Can you manage your own way back?"

"Depends" said Downwind.

"On what?"

"Where I am? Said Downwind pathetically.

All concern now gone for Downwind, the Fat Wizard thought it was time to inspect the mines for himself.

It was a good half an hour before the Fat Wizard was in sight of the first of the many abandoned mine entrances high up on the steep slope. Years ago this would have been a busy industrial area worn down by an army of men, dwarfs and heavily laden donkeys, risking their very lives to scratch a living out of the bowels of the earth, digging for precious metals, ore or fuel that everyone that everyone argued over the price of, but never considered the cost.

Scarred as it was, the Fat Wizard could not help but wonder at how mother nature could so quickly reclaim her land. Through all the shale and outbuildings that still peppered the landscape, greenery had taken over. Nettles, bramble, willow herb and a host of other wildflowers and weeds had all come together as if to remind everyone who really rules.

Our intrepid hero scrambled up the slope to the wooden gate of the mine, and panting, mumbled something about,

Yoga, I could do that, or maybe Jazzercise, I must find out what that is?"

"How curious" he said inspecting the shiny new padlock and chain on the gate, and with one pass from his wand that he retrieved from his sock, the whole lot clanged to the floor in a heap. Despite the new hardware the gate was original, wide enough for men and donkeys to pass side by side. The ageing timbers were just about strong enough to bear their own weight, but probably not for much longer, judged the Fat Wizard.

As old abandoned mines go this one was quite typical, cold, dank and dark with water dripping from the ceiling where also hung some chains. Nobody knows why there are always chains, it just seems to be a feature of these places.

The further he walked into the mine the darker it got, but with one little incantation the tip of his wand glowed bright enough to scare the dark away. Having moved far enough into the tunnel so that the entrance was no more than a dot of light behind him, the Fat Wizard stood still and in a big booming voice, shouted,

"OK lads out you come, it's only me."

And as the echo from his call faded away there was movement all around him. Small little men started appearing from every crevice and hole in the walls, looking like miniature miners and carrying miniature mining tools, they banded together and walked towards him. These were the Coblynau.

The Coblynau are a race of goblins which can be found in every mine in Wales. Well when I say found, I mean that they are always there but very seldom seen. They weren't a very attractive race, never growing above eighteen inches tall with very hairy faces and huge mole covered noses that would often reach down as far as their buck teeth. It would be fair to say that they would be unlikely contestants in a beauty pageant but could probably have a fair shout at Crufts. They spent their time secretly working quite frantically in the mines but mysteriously never seemed to produce anything. Being very mischievous they liked nothing more than playing little tricks on both dwarves and people, often hiding tools or untying bootlaces, even switching the contents of lunch boxes, then enjoying the chaos when a dwarf, who had been labouring hard all morning, sat down, somewhat perplexed, to a ham, lettuce and tomato sandwich while next to him a man was scratching his head, wondering if his wife had gone mad by packing him a raw fish.

Despite all the pranks the Coblynau were held in high regard by the miners for you could hear them tap to guide them to a particularly rich seam. Or more importantly they would hammer loudly to warn of an impending cave-in. It was because of this behaviour, close cousins of the Coblynau who colonised the tin mines of Cornwall were dubbed "Knockers".

"Hi all, I hope you are all well" said the Fat Wizard to the vertically challenged assembly.

"Fine, FW, fine" said Jed, a particularly hairy Coblynau, whose beard reached as far as his belt, "s'pect your here about the goings on, we don't often see you round here."

"True, I don't get to wander around abandoned mines as much as I'd like to" smiled the Fat Wizard, "what goings on?"

"Strange people" said Jed "not proper miners mind you, hardly a pickaxe and shovel between em, but they have been drilling and using explosives, without nary a thought for us. Holes all over the place and no warning when they blast. We've been running from mine to mine to keep away from the buggers. No respect, that's the trouble, wouldn't have happened in the old days."

"Any idea what they're looking for?" asked the Fat Wizard.

"None whatsoever. If I didn't know better I'd think they were looking for wives, they keep going on about, reading meet hers, well they won't meet any women here!" said Jed confidently.

"No, I don't suppose they will" said the Fat Wizard stroking his beard again, "Look Jed do you think you could get a message to me if they come back?"

"No problem, we've got tunnels and shafts all over Pant y Gussett. One of them is in your back garden not far from your kiln, though obviously we can't use it when your Rebe's got her lot in full flame. Made that mistake once. Took a week to grow this back" said Jed now stroking his own beard ruefully.

"Thank you" said the Fat Wizard, "now if you don't mind handing my phone back, I'd better be on my way"

"Sorry FW, old habits and all that, we'll be in touch." said Jed apologetically.

Checking for any "missed calls" on his phone, despite knowing that even his magical prowess could not enhance reception in a mine shaft, the Fat Wizard headed home. He couldn't help but be slightly concerned about Downwinds' ability to get back to the village on his own, in his fragile state.

☐

10. PUT THAT TOAD OUT.

Back in Pant y Gussett the Fat Wizard was relieved to see Downwind Jones safely back at work in his role as senior street hygiene technician and equine waste removal specialist, a title that Downwind, Dug and Dai had devised during a long winter session one night, at the Cross. Despite being a peculiar shade of green and taking two steps to the left for every one forward, not unlike a crab attempting the fox-trot, you could not help but to admire his dedication to the job.

Upon seeing the dishevelled and sweat-stained appearance of her beloved spouse as he entered the shop, Mrs FW immediately barked, "you, upstairs now, I'm going to run you a hot bath, and while you soak you can tell me what you've been up to. Rebe.."

"Yes, I'll look after the shop, just take care of him, he looks awful" said Rebe sounding really concerned.

"Thanks both, a hot bath sounds good" he said, "maybe Pilates or that hack-key-do, their all talking about" he mused to himself, feeling guilty about how concerned they were over how out of condition he was.

Reclined in a tub full of hot water overflowing with bubbles, not of his own making I hasten to add, he had the constitution of an ox, the Fat Wizard recounted the tale of his morning ventures to his dutiful wife as she sat on the edge of the bath massaging his aching feet. A luxury only enjoyed by those who had shared and appreciated a long and healthy marriage.

"So what's next?" enquired Mrs FW.

"Not exactly sure but I've got a feeling that Brian will have some interesting news for me soon".
And as if on cue, as what happens in all the best films and books, the Fat Wizard's phone rang.

"Hello Brian, please tell me you've found out who that car belongs to" said the Fat Wizard blowing bubbles as he spoke.

"Hi FW, yes I have. It's registered to a company called Power Electricity Energy and Oil Field Finders LTD". replied Brian.
"PEEOFF! never heard of them" exclaimed the Fat Wizard as he dropped his loofah.

"No need to be rude" chuckled Brian but then in a more serious voice continued, "actually I have, they have their fingers in a lot of pies, so to speak, but the mainstay of their business is to explore and find new sites for fossil fuels to supply to power companies and recently they have started to specialise in fracking."

"Fracking, what's that?" said the Fat Wizard finally retrieving the loofah that had seemed to take on a life of its own having propelled itself around the bath three times before he managed to trap it under his left buttock.

"I don't know exactly but basically it's a system that pumps water and chemicals under high pressure underground to release any gas trapped there".

"Sounds a bit like what Downwind does to himself every Saturday night in the Cross" quipped the Fat Wizard.

"True" said Brian "but seriously FW these people are out to make money and little things like the environment do not rate highly on their list of concerns when it comes to making a profit. The reason I was so long in getting back to you is that I thought I'd do a bit more digging into who runs the company."

"And?" said the Fat Wizard getting worried over the grave tone in Brian's voice.

"Well it's owned by two partners, a Mr Adam Sweetman and a Mr Ritchie Brimstone and from what I can find out, they're very much "Old School", totally ruthless. My contacts tell me that if they want something, they get it, no matter what! Please, my old friend if they have got business in Pant y Gussett I beg you to stay out of their way. They are seriously dangerous people, and I don't want anything to happen to you".

"Thanks for your concern Brian, and the information. But you know me I'll always stay away from trouble if I can avoid it".

"It's the "If I can avoid it" bit that worries me. Take care, give my love to Jean and the girls and call me if you need any help".
"Will do, and thanks again." said the Fat Wizard with a thoughtful sigh as he slowly let himself sink under the hot water, quickly realising he hadn't actually taken his hat off yet.

"Right" said Mrs FW "I'll go and lay out a clean set of robes, socks and hat on the bed for you, and then you can tell me what Brian said over a fresh mug of tea, and by the look of you I'll make it extra sweet".

"But I'm trying to watch my weight" said the Fat Wizard, then quickly added with a smile, "but I'm sure that can wait until tomorrow".

"Just as well" said Mrs FW, "I'm doing a proper spread for tea. Kayls phoned to say she had a gig in Llanelli tonight so she's going to stop and have something to eat with us on her way through, and she's bringing her new partner to meet us; Ellie, and it sounds serious so be on your best behaviour!"

"Ellie uh, will she ever make up her mind? Hey what do you mean best behaviour, I'm always the perfect gentleman" said the Fat Wizard.

"Oh really" she replied, "have you forgotten how you went to great pains to explain to her last boyfriend how easy it would be for you to turn him into a toad!"

"Well that was a boy and besides I didn't like the way he kept pawing her in front of me. I'd never be so rude to a girl, honest" said the Fat Wizard with an almost sincere smile.

"Kayls is more than capable of looking after herself so don't interfere. Besides this Ellie sounds lovely and she teaches Latin in school you know".

"Latin eh?" mused the Fat Wizard suddenly interested, "I've got a couple of old texts that I could do with some help translating".

"Now you leave her be" warned Mrs FW "give the poor girl a chance to get to know us before you have her working on your dusty old books".

"Yes dear" sighed the Fat Wizard, "but I must admit I like the sound of this one already".

A few hours later, freshly talced and in a clean set of robes with his beard nicely combed (at the insistence of Mrs FW) the Fat Wizard went downstairs to answer a loud knock at the door. Kayls had forgotten her keys again. "Oof" he cried as Kayls gave him one of her customary and enthusiastic hugs.

"Hi Dad, how are you?" she said

"Well I was fine before the broken ribs" laughed the Fat Wizard returning the hug just as affectionately, "and who do we have here?"

"This is Ellie dad. Now be nice, this one's a keeper"

"Hello Ellie" said the Fat Wizard, to the slightly intimidated slim blond girl struggling to carry Kayls' guitar as she offered her hand out.

"Hello Mr err Wizard, I'm sorry I don't know what to call you," she said awkwardly.

"FW will do, that's what everyone else calls me, well to my face anyway." smiled the Fat Wizard ignoring the outstretched hand and giving her a gentle hug. I see she's made you her roadie for the night," noticing the guitar.

"Every gig so far", sighed Ellie, visibly relaxing after the warm welcome.

"Well go and take her upstairs Kayls. I'm afraid your mother's gone a bit over the top with the food again, and whatever you leave I'll probably end up having for breakfast tomorrow. I'll join you in a minute."

As they went upstairs the Fat Wizard stepped down from the step to the street. For while he was hugging Ellie, he had noticed a small boy hiding behind a cart that had been parked outside the shop. As he got closer, he could see three rough looking kids, probably in their very early teens, on the other side of the street standing beside a tree near Dai the Dwarfs place. They had that universal appearance of kids that were up to no good.

As he approached the cart he recognised the crouching and out of breath boy as Pog, who regularly called at the shop on errands for his mother.

Pog lived alone with his mother in one of the wooden shacks roughly halfway between the village and the car park. His father had been an engineer who had spent the weekdays working at some large firm in one of the big cities in England somewhere. When Pog was still a baby his father had tragically died during an accident at work, but no one really knew what happened as his mother, a lovely but very independent woman would never talk about it. Despite the hardship she raised Pog well and he grew into a polite and friendly boy who worked hard helping to tend the bees that produced enough honey to bring in just enough extra revenue to add to her husband's meagre pension for them to survive.

With his dark tousled hair, that resisted all attempts at combing, his woollen short sleeve vests and shorts that would comically flap around his painfully skinny legs, and white socks permanently worn loose around the ankles, Pog looked like the cover of one of those fifties comics where typically the father would be smoking his pipe and reading the paper while also watching his boy on the floor playing with a train set; and in the background mother, in a pinny of course, calling them both into the kitchen for dinner.

Pog was also well liked among the older villagers, with his ready smile and eagerness to help anyone struggling with tasks like lawn mowing, shopping and the like. He had even run a few errands for the Fat Wizard and would never take payment for his troubles, but would sometimes accept little gifts for his mother, like a bar of scented soap or a lavender infused candle.

Bending down the Fat Wizard tapped Pog on the shoulder and enquired,

"What seems to be the trouble, young man?"

"Bloo.... I mean oh hi FW, I nearly jumped out my skin then" exclaimed Pog standing up and keeping one eye on the kids who had now spotted him, who were now putting on a very unconvincing act of being a group of lads just shooting the breeze.

"Those kids bothering you?" asked the Fat Wizard softly.
"'Fraid so, they're always bullying me" sobbed Pog sounding more than a little frightened.

"Are they indeed" said the Fat Wizard with a hint of menace in his voice, "would you like me to turn them all into toads" he added.
"Oh no" exclaimed Pog, "they're not bad kids really, just get bored or something, I just wish they would leave me alone!"

"Good answer" said the Fat Wizard proud of the boy's attitude. Then in full view of the bullies who were now watching them intently, started to whisper in Pog's ear, "now here's what I want you to do".

Placing a small stick that he found on the ground into Pog's hand, the Fat Wizard said, "keep nodding while I'm talking to you and when I say, now, I want you to point the stick at that bucket on the back of this cart and say, loud enough, so the boys can hear you…

YOU STANDING IN FRONT OF ME ON THE ROAD, NOW I'LL TURN YOU INTO A TOAD!, got it."

"Got it" Pog said a little confused.

"Now!" commanded the Fat Wizard,

With his hand shaking slightly Pog aimed the stick at the bucket and with his voice a lot higher pitched than he intended, recited,

"YOU STANDING IN FRONT OF ME ON THE ROAD, NOW I'LL TURN YOU INTO A TOAD!"

There instantly followed a blinding flash of light glaring through a cloud of black smoke from the back of the cart, and as the smoke cleared the bucket had vanished, and in its place sat a large, slightly confused looking, brown toad.

"Cor Blimey" shouted Pog as he watched the three hooligans scream and run down the street as fast as their legs could carry them. "Did I really do that?"

"No, not really" laughed the Fat Wizard tucking his wand back into his sock, "but they don't know that. Now run along, I don't think you'll have any more trouble from them for a while."

"Shouldn't think so, thank you so much FW" said Pog,

considerably happier than he was a few minutes ago"

"Happy to help, just let me know if they start bothering you again and we'll come up with something even more spectacular".

And as he turned back to the house ready for the family meal the Fat Wizard picked up the toad and thought to himself, "Hmm, I think I owe someone a bucket".

"Get that toad off the table!", demanded a cross Mrs FW, "we're trying to eat here".

"Sorry dear" said the Fat Wizard putting the toad on an empty chair, "I'll put him out in the garden when we've finished, and turning to Kayls said, "So where's the gig tonight? Some posh club I suppose".

"I wish" she replied, "it's just a little pub in the centre of Llanelli. They don't pay of course but there's usually a good crowd".

"Perhaps I could get you another spot at the Cross, said the Fat Wizard.

"No thanks!" said Kayls horrified "The last time I played there, the dwarves got drunk and started fighting amongst themselves, the gnomes all covered their ears and when Downwind and his cronies started singing along all my guitar strings suddenly snapped!"

"But you did get paid, didn't you"? Said the Fat Wizard.

"I hardly think a voucher for half a stout, redeemable any Monday morning before twelve o'clock was really worth my while" said Kayls indignantly.

"Fair enough" said the Fat Wizard and turned to Ellie who seemed to be getting on really well with Rebe and was delighting Mrs FW by valiantly eating all the food put in front of her, "and what do you think of Pant y Gussett so far?" he enquired.

"It seems really nice," she replied hesitantly "but sorry, did you say you reared dragons Rebe, and Kayls what do you mean dwarves and gnomes?"

"Oh-oh" said the Fat Wizard trying to chew a particularly hot, boiled potato, "Kayls didn't you warn her about this place?"

"Was going to but I didn't think she'd believe me, so I thought I would let her find out for herself. I did tell her you were a wizard but she just assumed you had a stage act".

"A stage act" snorted the Fat Wizard, then softened his voice as he noticed Ellie staring down at the table and tightly gripping Kayls' hand. "Sorry Ellie, you weren't to know but let me assure you, Pant y Gussett is a, well, very multicultural society filled with wonderful people and wonderful creatures and you will be safe here, particularly as you are now a member of the Fat Wizard's family.
But I got to ask how come you didn't notice Eric when you crossed the bridge?"

"Eric?" quizzed Ellie.
"That was me dad" said Kayls. "While Ellie was locking the car, I ran ahead and threw Eric a banana and told him to hide. He'd do anything for me ever since I used to play rock music to him under the bridge. The acoustics are fantastic there!"

"Eric?" quizzed Ellie, again.

"Don't worry, I'll introduce you to him on the way back to the car. That reminds me it's time for us to go. Thanks for a great spread mam, love you all" and with that Kayls got up to leave.

Ellie stopped her in her tracks and turned to the family and said,

"Thank you very much for having me. I'm sorry I was a bit quiet but, well you know it was a lot to take in. I would love to come again, that's if you will have me of course, and explore this amazing place properly".

"You are welcome anytime" chorused the Fat Wizard and Mrs FW.

"And next time stay over and we can have a game of "Basements and Lizards" I haven't played that since Kalys moved out" said Rebe.

"Would love to", giggled Ellie as Kayls started dragging her down the stairs mumbling something about not having time to set up or something.

After waving them off from the window the Fat Wizard retired to his comfy chair, lit his clay pipe, much to the disgust of wife and daughter who both started coughing, a mite theatrically in his mind, and pondered over the day's events and thanking his lucky stars that, so far, there had been no more tremors. Poor Ellie had been frightened enough.

Full from his large meal and with his pipe burnt out, he felt his eyelids getting heavy and just as he was entering that wonderful euphoric state you experience before dropping off, he was rudely startled awake by a loud, shrill voice demanding,

"And don't forget to take that bloody toad out!".

11. A BAD DAY AT THE OFFICE.

Berkeley Square, Mayfair, not just a place where nightingales sang and home to a much sought after property title in a famous board game, it also boasts some of the most prestigious offices in the whole of London. Here, in the boardroom of the most elite of these buildings, we find ourselves in the company of Mr Adam Sweetman and Mr Ritchie Brimstone.

The palatial boardroom, situated on the top floor, as all good boardrooms are, was painted in a subdued shade of grey whilst the expansive carpet was such a sea of pale grey that most visitors would check their shoes, paranoid about walking any stains into it. The only furnishings, other than a projector and screen at one end, was a gigantic black table surrounded by a set of twelve matching, straight backed chairs, all finished to such a high gloss to give a smoky, mirror like effect. In the centre of the table was a large chrome charger upon which sat an array of decanters, all filled with spirits of differing shades of amber, several bottles of tonic water, a carafe of freshly squeezed orange juice and a dozen Waterford crystal glasses. At the far end of the table sat two computers, two writing blotters and a shiny black telephone cum intercom. Behind one these computers sat a very disgruntled Mr Sweetman, tapping a pen annoyingly on the table,

"He'd better get here soon" he snapped to Mr Brimstone, who was standing with his back to him as he looked out of the floor to ceiling windows that took over one complete wall, offering a panoramic view of the gardens below and the city beyond.

"Patience, Adam" he said without turning around "he'll be here as soon as he can, trust me, he won't want to keep us waiting".

"Still..." and stabbing a button on the intercom, barked, "Miss Jones, any sign of Charles yet?"

Miss Jones of course is an honorary title bestowed to many ethereal voices on the other end of an intercom.

"He's just coming up to the door now Mr Sweetman, shall I send him right up?" said Miss Jones from the floor below, where her desk was strategically placed between several offices, the lifts and commanded a view that extended the length of the reception room right up to the main door.

"No, let him stew in reception for a while, I'll call you back when we're ready".

Brimstone grinned to himself when he overheard his partner. He loved these little executive tricks that keep the subordinates down. Tricks like offering to light someone's cigarette but holding the lighter so low that the victim almost has to bow, and making sure that his office chair was always the highest so that whoever he was talking to had to look up to him, whether they wanted to or not.

As he watched, a flock of pigeons swooped past the window and landed on the immaculately tended lawn below. Their characteristic head bobbing and swagger reminded him of the disco dancers of the early seventies. 1974 in fact, he himself remembered using a similar movement while dancing to "Devil Gate Drive", a huge hit for seventies sexy rocker, "Suzi Quatro". It was also the year that he met Alan Sweetman.

They both went to the same boys' school. It was a very select school, so select you could only gain attendance under the recommendation of a magistrate.

At first, they were the greatest of enemies, both determined to gain the reputation as "Top Dog" of the institution in order to extort either money or tobacco from their unfortunate captive companions. It was common for these poor wretches to pay protection money to Sweetman only to get beaten up by Brimstone, then pay Brimstone for his help only to then get beaten up by Sweetman. This led to many violent altercations between the pair. Sweetman, being the heavier set of the two looked like the obvious favourite, but Brimstones' sheer savagery and streetwise fighting skills meant that they were actually very evenly matched.

Unfortunately for them neither of them was a match for their custodians, who after every brawl would "invite" them to spend a night or two in separate isolation rooms.

It was during these times of freedom from such brutal intimidation that other would be "Kings of the Hill" would rise up to fill the power void, only to be put back firmly in their place as one or the other of them was released back into the general population.

After a particularly lengthy spell of isolation, following a really nasty bout where they savagely raised the ante by introducing a kitchen knife and a hammer into the proceedings, did a singularly unpleasant individual, nicknamed "Spud" who was rumoured to be a distant cousin of the infamous "Kray" twins, set up his own army, complete with generals and sergeants.

This outfit proved to be a difficult nut to crack so, at first begrudgingly, they decided to join forces and together, they met Spud in the shower block and showed him the error of his ways using a large bar of soap and a not so safety, safety razor and managed to quickly regain control. This unholy union was the start of a lifelong partnership.

Working together they managed to forge an iron grip on all of the underground "commerce" within the institution. Pretty soon they had branched out into even greater forms of revenue, enlisting parolees and inmates who had served their sentences to smuggle in saleable goods such as chocolate, alcohol, electrical items; such as radios, shavers and the like and of course inevitably, drugs. This last product had been the centre of much debate between them and not for any moral reasons. The pair of them were far too canny to partake in any mind weakening substance, apart from the occasional drinking binge when celebrating a particularly profitable transaction. Far from it, the chance to profit from the misery of others was a bonus in their eyes. The only reason that they were initially reluctant towards peddling narcotics was the fact that they knew that of all their shady business endeavours, being caught dealing drugs would mean a much longer sentence, and as they were getting older, a chance of being promoted to proper jail time.

Not that jail held any particular fears for them but they had plans, big plans. With the contacts and money, they had now amassed they needed to be free, free to build the Empire they had been secretly plotting over the last twelve months.

Brimstone was rudely snapped back from his trip down memory lane by the click of the intercom button.

"Send Charles up please Miss Jones" said Sweetman, in a lofty superior voice as he turned to Brimstone and said, "I think he's stewed long enough."

"Certainly Mr Sweetman." replied Miss Jones in that slightly off hand way that suggested that it was her idea and he had merely beaten her to it.

Seconds later and there was a feeble knock on the boardroom door that somehow managed to sound almost apologetic. The poor creature behind the door was left with the awful dilemma suffered by many executives in the corporate world summoned to a boardroom of, "did they hear me? Should I knock again? what if they think I'm being rude by knocking again?" Ageing dramatically while pondering his next course of action, Charles was almost relieved to hear the word "Enter" shouted loudly from within. Charles poked his head around the door, giving the impression that his body was really reluctant to follow.

"Charles my good man, do come in" said Mr Sweetman with the sort of grin you could imagine a snake would give when encountering a mouse, "have a seat, make yourself comfortable".

With Sweetman engrossed in his computer screen without indicating which particular seat to use, poor Charles now found himself facing a new dilemma, "Do I sit far away, or will he think I'm trying to hide something? Do I sit close to him, or will he think I'm being too forward? Knowing what was going through Charles' mind Sweetman decided that Charles had almost suffered enough and pointed to a chair near the corner on his left. Brimstone, with his hands clasped behind his back, was still staring out of the window offering no indication that he was in any way aware of Charles's arrival.

Charles Bickford sat there quietly. He was used to fading into the background. Even at school he was the shy studious type that no-one seemed to know existed. Even the bullies didn't pick on him, he just wasn't interesting enough to catch their attention. An average boy, he left school and went to college where he achieved average results. Leaving college, he went on to university, not away to university but a local one where he didn't live in but commuted daily back and fore from home. He did alright at uni, nothing special, you know, average.

Through his student years he had the company of a small group of friends, joined the chess club and the drama society. Went out occasionally, though never on one of those debauched, end up with a traffic cone on your head and covered in your own vomit, sort of nights that students are so famous for, but rather a visit to a pub selling real ale where he, and his mates discussed the possibility of forming a debating society. It was at one of these social gatherings that he met his future wife Catherine, a quiet girl studying philosophy. She had short mousey brown hair, a figure that though not fat was bordering on chunky and always wore blue jeans, sneakers and woollen jumpers. She wasn't particularly attractive but certainly couldn't be called ugly either; she was, well, average.

Just scraping a degree in engineering, Charles was fortunate enough to land an apprenticeship with a firm in London, "Power Electricity Energy and Oil Field Finders LTD" this meant finally moving away from his hometown of Bristol and relocating to the capital. This proved to be quite a culture shock for the young Charles and lonely, managed to persuade Catherine to forgo the final year of her studies to become his wife and join him in this huge metropolis.

The first few years were hard, especially after the birth of their first child, Andrew, but became easier as a few years later Charles became fully qualified and started earning reasonable money. They were then blessed with a daughter, Andrea and life settled into a comfortable routine that suited Charles perfectly.

As the children grew Charles began to notice a distinct note of discord in his idyllic domestic situation. Catherine had started to snap at him whenever he asked questions over their family accounts. She started to go out with friends two or three times a week, leaving him to babysit which he didn't mind. It was reasonable enough that his darling wife had a life of her own. What he didn't like was the snarled "mind your own business" short replies to such reasonable questions like "are you going anywhere nice?" or "who are you going with?". Some nights she didn't return until morning, but he quickly learnt not to query her on it.

Whether it was some deep-seated animosity towards Charles, blaming him for her unfinished education or something entirely different, he couldn't work out, but her behaviour toward him got worse year on year.

They still lived together as a seemingly functional family unit, though the chances of a third child were definitely off the table, if you know what I mean. But this once shy sweetheart had become a domineering harridan even choosing what clothes he wore, hence the cheap suit, plain brown shoes and tan raincoat that was now his trademark uniform. With the children always siding with their mother and feeling like a stranger in his own home, Catherine had managed to turn Mr average into something much less.

After what seemed like an eternity, Sweetman finally looked up from his computer screen and turned to Charles and with a voice that shook with barely contained rage, demanded...

"What the hell is going on with the Pant y Gussett project!

Could you explain to Mr Brimstone and I why, despite sinking a small fortune into it, you still haven't started the fracking operation yet?".

"Sorry Sir, err I mean Mr Sweetman Sir" stuttered Charles using a handkerchief to wipe the perspiration from his brow before it ran clear tracks down his face, "Er it's like this, well I mean er, the place is cursed"

"What do you mean cursed" snapped Sweetman, clearly about to lose it.

"Well things keep happening, in the mines", "as well as the quarry" he added.

"What things?" enquired Brimstone softly, finally turning away from the windows and for the first time showing an interest in the proceedings. "We visited the site the other day and I didn't notice any, things, did you Mr Sweetman?"

"No I did not Mr Brimstone, other than the lack of any progress".

Using their surnames when addressing each other in front of subordinates was another little "device" they employed to intimidate employees.

"Well there's all sorts of weird noises and banging, don't half put the wind up the boys"

"It's an abandoned mine for crying out loud, there are always weird noises" laughed Sweetman in an exasperated tone.

"There's also the stuff that goes missing" exclaimed Charles, desperately trying to find a dry spot on his now sweat soaked kerchief, "I've lost three pens, one of them a graduation gift from my dad mind you, two notebooks, an iPad and a mobile phone while I was there, gone from right in front of me! Dan the drill operator reckons the laces from his boots disappeared while he was still wearing them, parts from some of the machines vanish, while we're using them and replacing the bits takes time."

"Must we remind you Charles" said Brimstone coldly, "that this project has been ongoing, at great expense I may add, for a long time, and after the untimely demise of your predecessor, a Mr Lewis if I recall correctly", at this point Sweetman quickly glanced up at Brimstone with an alarmed look as Brimstone continued, "due to a mysterious accident several years ago, we took a chance and promoted you, an inexperienced newcomer to the position of chief engineer to our firm and placed you in charge of this job. Is it really unreasonable of us, despite the foibles of this particular village, to expect some results?"

"No, of course not Sir, er I mean Mr Brimstone Sir" and unlikely as it sounds Charles noticed that even his arse was starting to sweat and added, "I'll get on it right away, honest Sir, er I mean gentlemen" and found himself positively bowing as he walked backwards clumsily towards the door.

"That was fun!" proclaimed Sweetman after Charles had finally escaped, anyone else we can call in?" He laughed to a smiling Brimstone.

Feeling the whole gamut of emotions, ranging from fear to shame, Charles headed for the tube home with his head hung low, knowing that the cold welcome that awaited him from his once loving wife and his now brainwashed children, was going to be the highest point of his day. As the train pulled into the station, he actually asked himself, "board it, or jump in front of it!"

Resignedly, he just went home.

☐

12. FRACKING PROTESTERS.

The last few days in Pant y Gussett had proven quite uneventful, well uneventful for Pant y Gussett anyway, no more tremors or loud bangs except, of course the ones coming from the Fat Wizard's workshop where he was experimenting with a new formula for a metallic hair dye. He reasoned that once perfected, he could make a small fortune supplying some of Kayls' more adventurous, musical friends. If, that is he could find a solution to the rather unpleasant side effect of rusty dandruff.

The unseasonably warm sunny weather had given way to some very heavy showers and an accompanying biting wind which had kept him pretty much indoors. A fat man with voluminous robes, large hat and curly beard tended to absorb more than his fair share of water, so any further exploration of the outlying parts of the village were put on hold. A soggy wizard was not a happy wizard.

He was still getting reports through the grapevine, not an actual grapevine of course because, as everyone knows, talking grapevines are consummate liars and simply can't be trusted, about more strange unmarked vans appearing in the car park and increasing activity in the quarry as well as some of the mines.

True to his word, Jed had started to send his associates with daily updates about visitors to the mine, Poor Rebe fair jumped out of her skin the first time one of the Coblynau called. She had been cleaning dragon poop from the run by the kiln, when she suddenly heard a rough voice, emanating from a hole behind a particularly glorious stand of petunias whisper, "Pssst, I got a message for your Da".

Now don't for one minute think that a bit of bad weather meant that the Fat Wizard was being idle in his promise to the villagers to get to the bottom of the cause of recent events. Far from it, in his spare time he had been busy researching all that he could about "fracking" on the world wide web.

Now I understand that you younger readers presume that I'm referring to some sort of computer database. Well you'd be wrong. The Fat Wizard had been consulting real webs, the same as you'd find in your garden at home.

What a lot of people don't realise is that spiders are very

intelligent and helpful creatures. After all they have been trying to protect us from disease carrying flies and biting insects for generations, often with no more than a swiftly wielded newspaper as a reward. Apart from catching pests, these webs are all interconnected and contain a vast amount of knowledge that the spiders share with each other. They are happy to freely share this knowledge with anyone who cares to learn how to read them.

The more the Fat Wizard learnt about fracking the more concerned he was getting. Yes, there were plenty of supporters for fracking claiming it to be the answer to all of the of the UK's growing energy needs. There were many citations from professionals, with so many letters after their names you would think they were playing "Scrabble", who declared fracking to be clean, sustainable and cost effective. The Fat Wizard couldn't help but notice that the majority of those in favour of fracking seemed to have connections, not always obviously so, with either Government departments or large power companies. Further research uncovered a smaller, but growing daily, body of people, many of whom had equally legitimate qualifications urging caution, saying that this new method for extracting fossil fuels was in its infancy and needed a great deal more research into its long-term effects.

The more vociferous protestors were pointing to events across the world in countries that had been fracking for a while. These reports ranged from tremors, subsidence, sinkholes and even earthquakes, events that the supporters of fracking quickly claimed were just anecdotal or were areas of general geographical instability where such occurrences happened all the time. Some were even bolder and went on to claim that such incidences were no more than a fabrication from the "greens" who had a, so far, undiscovered and possibly sinister, hidden agenda. Documented evidence of domestic water supplies igniting spontaneously as it poured from the taps in unsuspecting households in the USA were on the whole ignored.

The Fat Wizard was a fiercely intelligent man who prided himself on his ability to see things from all sides, but he was struggling to comprehend how a government, famed throughout the world for its ability to strangle innovation and enterprise in a sea of red tape, seemed hell bent on relaxing the bureaucracy surrounding such a new, unproven and possibly disastrous industry by issuing exploratory licenses to virtually every applicant.

Saturday morning was traditionally quite a busy day in the shop. Always hoping to finish early both the Fat Wizard and his better half manned the premises while Rebe, after her dragon rearing chores of course, could be found in the workshop mixing potions and learning new spells. She was after all her father's apprentice among her other duties.

With the door chimes sounding like a drunken campanologist, this Saturday morning was proving to be one of the busiest in a while.

"Morning FW, Mrs FW", said Griff in his deep masculine voice, "have you got any more of that wonderful burn ointment of yours?"

"Jean Griff, my name is Jean, "sighed Mrs FW "yes of course, one jar or two?"

She couldn't stay mad at Griff for long. Apart from being an expert blacksmith Griff was always happy to lend a hand with filing any overgrown claws on Rebe's baby dragons.

"Just the one this week Mrs... I mean Jean darling, perhaps I'm finally getting good at this blacksmithing lark" he beamed, showing his impossibly white toothy smile.

"Oh you", she replied with a slight uncontrolled giggle.

The Fat Wizard, overhearing the exchange, smiled inwardly to himself. He knew how much a little bit of harmless flirting made his wife feel good, though deep down he admitted to himself, a little bit of innocent attention wouldn't do his ego any harm either.

As Griff paid for his wares his brother entered the shop. He acknowledged Griff with a courteous nod of the head then turning to Mrs FW enquired,

"Mrs FW have you managed to make those special thimbles I commissioned?".

"Jean, Dai my name is Jean, and yes I have them here, ready for you."

"Thank you, Mrs FW" he said not even trying and then turning to the Fat Wizard said, smiling,

"And how are you today FW?"

"Fine thank you Dai", he replied instantly regretting his

earlier feelings of not having enough attention. The Fat Wizard was not the slightest bit homophobic but quite frankly, Dai gave him the creeps. He was actually glad of the interruption of Goodwitch Evans from next door as she flounced into the shop.

"Good morning all" she said with a humourless smile, looking over her glasses to each of them in turn. It had always amazed the Fat Wizard that someone so short managed to look down on everyone she met.

"Morning to you" they all chorused, followed by Griff and Dai the cloth mumbling something like "goodness is that the time? and "must dash" as they hastily beat a retreat from the shop. The Fat Wizard was racking his brains to think of a plausible excuse to join them when she continued,

"Now Jean", Mrs FW coldly looked up, of all the people she wished would use her actual name, Goodwich Evans was not one of them, "you know I don't like to make a fuss", at this the Fat Wizard had to make a conscious effort not roll his eyes, and taking advantage of not being addressed personally, made a big show of busying himself among the shelves. "But we have talked before about the horrendous noise your dragons make at night, all that roaring and bellowing I hardly slept a wink last night".

"Miss Evans" snapped Mrs FW with her hand on her hips and drawing herself up to her full height of five foot four, which she somehow managed to do imposingly, "and I have explained to you before, that dragons sleep soundly the moment it gets dark, I have no idea what you think you heard but it was not our dragons".

"Well perhaps it's your husband working late at those infernal potions of his!" she moaned.

"My husband never works late, he would rather spend his spare time at home with his family", a rather cold but nonetheless effective barb from Mrs FW who knew full well of Goodwitch Evans's spinster status.

"Well really", she harrumphed, "If that's all you've got to say, then good day to you!" and flounced back out of the shop.

Turning to her husband Mrs FW shouted "you can come out now, she's gone"

"Err, actually I can't, I seem to have got myself wedged behind these large jars of donkey shampoo, (that would be shampoo for cleaning muddy donkeys not a shampoo made from them. There were absolutely no donkeys harmed in the writing of this book!).

"My hero!", sighed Mrs FW staring at the wide bottom of the love of her life, as he was stuck bent over a low shelf in a very undignified and non-wizard like position. She resisted the temptation of leaving him there to suffer for a while and with a sharp tug managed to extricate him. "Why do you think she has to keep coming over here to complain all the time?".

"Oh, don't take it personally my love" replied the Fat Wizard untangling cobwebs from his beard, "Mrs Crimble had her in the bakery yesterday complaining that her bread left too many crumbs on the plate when she toasted it. I think we should feel sorry for her, after all pickling seaweed is a very antisocial occupation. It's only when complaining does the poor woman get to speak to anyone. Besides aren't her pickling vats set quite deep in the ground? I wonder if there could be a connection with recent events?"

"You really do try to think the best of people don't you! ok I'll try and play nice, but you can deal with her next time, promise!".

"Yes dear" he sighed, secretly wondering if people would really object to him turning Miss Goodwitch Evans into a plant pot or something else useful.

Probably coincidental, but it seemed that the departure of Miss Evans from the shop opened a floodgate of customers. For the next hour or so there was a steady stream of locals calling for all manner of potions, spells and indeed crockery including another order for a set of un- patterned tableware from Mrs Dorcas Evans. The Fat Wizard was fully aware that her husband Bill had been to an impromptu poker session with Downwind, Dai the dwarf and Dug yesterday that had involved a drunken late night and the loss of a small fortune. Remembering her outburst last week, the Fat Wizard refrained from mentioning the reason for yet another replacement set but could not stop himself from asking, "and how are you off for bruise liniment and sticky plasters Mrs Evans?"

"Fine!", she snapped, "why?"

"Oh, no reason, just being a salesman" smiled the Fat Wizard desperately trying not to laugh, which became considerably easier as he noticed Mrs FW glaring at him from behind the counter.

As the shop slowly cleared the Fat Wizard noticed Mrs Lewis and her son Pog, obviously waiting for all the other customers to leave.

"Mrs Lewis, Pog," smiled the Fat Wizard, and looking at Pog smiled and asked, "everything alright now?"

"Cor I should say" chuckled Pog "every time them boys come near me now, all I have to do is pick up a stick and they run off crying, worse than they do when their mams tell them it's bath night!"

"Yes FW" said Mrs Lewis, "Pog told me what you did and I had to thank you in person," she said with a warm smile, "with everything that poor mite has been through it means a lot to know that someone else is looking out for him. Please can I pay you for your trouble?"

"I wouldn't dream of it, I hate bullies" said the Fat Wizard, "besides, well to tell you the truth, it was kind of fun to see them little buggers learning what it's like to be scared for a change. Make them into better men one day, I reckon."

"I hope so" she replied. Then grabbing Pog's hand she turned to leave but stopped at the door and turned to Mrs FW saying, "I wish all the men of this village were as good and decent as your husband", and left with a grateful tear rolling down her cheek.

Turning to her husband she exclaimed "My hero, again, but what the hell was that all about?"

"Nothing dearest, all in a day's work for your local neighbourhood Fat Wizard. Now how about closing up and having some lunch? All this hero business has made me quite hungry; I think I deserve a bacon butty with ketchup at least, don't you?"

"I agree and while you're there you can make me and Rebe one too, if you can take time out from your superhero schedule that is", she laughed as she quickly exited the shop leaving him to lock up as well as prepare lunch.

Meanwhile on the bridge by the Pant y Gussett car park, a soaking wet Eric went to scratch his head, instantly regretting using the same hand that he was holding his club in. He was used to weekends being quiet, but today there seemed to be an awful lot of shiny black vehicles using the car park yet no one was crossing the bridge to the village. So despite there being all these extra people, there he stood, alone in the rain, and very hungry.

Amongst all of these shiny black cars and vans was a very average looking, beige coloured Toyota three door hatchback. The man getting out of it was wearing a tan raincoat, quickly getting darker the wetter it got. Eric could hear him shouting to the occupants of the other vehicles, "Right you lot, let's get this stuff unloaded and up to the mine before someone notices we're here!" With his voice carrying the authority of a damp sponge none of the vehicle's occupants stirred, "Aw, c'mon lads please" he begged and finally the car park became a hive of activity.

13. A HOT COCK-TAIL.

Somewhere, from behind the garden a cock crowed heralding the dawn of a new Sunday morning. Most mornings the Fat Wizard appreciated his free early morning call but not on Sundays. As we all know he enjoyed a long leisurely lie-in of a Sunday but this particular day the cockerel was relentless, constantly rasping out "cock-a-doodle-do".

"Will he ever learn some other words?" grumbled the Fat Wizard to himself as he staggered out of bed and went to the window.

Looking around to check that his good lady wife was still gently snoring he clicked his fingers sending a small blue spark winging towards the tail feathers of the offending poultry as it sat on a fence post. "Hmm time really does fly", he chuckled to himself climbing back into bed and, snuggling back into the warm spot.

The indignant cockerel quickly retired to the hen house with a little trail of smoke following behind him. Noticing the quizzical look from the members of his harem he announced airily, "I don't want to talk about it, just fancied a lie in this morning, that's all, OK!", and settled down gingerly with his bottom gratefully enjoying the draft coming through the hatch.

Several hours later and a refreshed Fat Wizard had enjoyed a nice breakfast of bacon and eggs, with ketchup of course, he knew the importance of having your "five a day", had showered and was marvelling how his wife had, yet again remembered to lay out clean robes, hat and socks on the bed for him. Thinking about it he couldn't remember the last time he had actually seen her doing the laundry. Yet there it was clean, and smelling as fresh as a mountain breeze. As he pondered over whether she was holding out over him about some mystical abilities of her own, he decided that any creature that could give birth to another, must be inherently magical.

Freshly suited and booted, well robed and sandaled, the Fat Wizard pecked his beloved on the cheek and said, "see you later".

"Be back by one or…"

"I know" he replied, "be back by one, or Jasper will think it's his birthday, got it" he smiled as he headed down the stairs to the door.

The rain had eased, although the clouds threatened of more to come as the Fat Wizard hurried his way to the shop for his paper.

"Morning Dodds" greeted the Fat Wizard to Mr Dodds, who was currently weighing out some strawberry bon bons for an excited looking child who could barely contain its excitement, hopping from one foot to the other and licking its lips like a puppy around sausages.

"Mornin' FW", replied Dodds making a mental note to wipe the dribble off the counter once the child had gone. "Things seem to have quietened down around here. Do you think it's over, y'know the tremors and all?", he asked.

"I'm afraid not" the Fat Wizard replied, "I suspect things are going to get a lot worse before it's over, but I could be wrong. Hell! I hope I'm wrong".

As the young child whose agonising wait for his confectionary delight was finally over had ran out of the shop to find a quiet corner in which to enjoy this new dental assault, old man Dodds took the offered payment for the newspaper that the Fat Wizard was now holding, and said, "Never seen you wrong before. Now I'm worried"

"Don't be. Whatever happens I'm sure we will all deal with it." he said trying to sound confident as he left the shop and headed for the pub.

"Peace and good health to all here." boomed the Fat Wizard announcing his entry to the pub.

"Morning deary" smiled double D affectionately as she started pouring him a pint of his usual, "you take your seat and I'll bring your drink over"

"Thank you my dear, you really are too kind.", he smiled as he made his way over to his reserved Sunday morning cwtch.

Cwtch is one of those wonderful Welsh words which can have several meanings. A cwtch can be a cupboard, though more often means a hug or embrace, but it is also used to describe a comfy or cosy place such as the Fat Wizard's seat and table by the fireplace.

A quick look around the bar as he took his seat and he noticed the clientele was almost identical to the previous Sunday. Same people sitting in the same seats only lacking the business men in suits and their crew. "Pity", he thought to himself, "I wouldn't have minded introducing myself to them". With a tankard of the Cross' best foaming ale now in front of him, courtesy of the still smiling Double D, he lit his long-stemmed clay pipe and settled in to read his paper.

"Young Girl Ravaged in Her Sleep" was the featured headline. The report continued with an interview with the distressed victim. "I don't care if he is a prince, he's got no right sneaking up on a girl when she's asleep" said Miss S Beauty, 21, "especially when she's recovering from a spot of food poisoning. What is the world coming too!"

Suspecting there was more to that story than meets the eye the Fat Wizard moved on to the next article, "Strange Lights reported Around Breakin Wind, Could They Be UFO's", "Of course they are", he chuckled "all the flying objects around Pant y Gussett are unidentified, until you're introduced to them of course." Bored with the serious stuff, and with Double D bringing a fresh drink right on cue, the Fat Wizard turned to the puzzle page.

Unusually for him, he just couldn't concentrate and after ten minutes with his quill poised over the paper he hadn't managed to answer a single question. Looking over his glasses he scanned the bar to see what was bothering him. It was the gnomes. There was nothing unusual about the gnomes being in the bar on a Sunday morning. Once they had scaled the dizzying heights of the bar stools they were often to be found with their miniature jugs of ale, their smiling ruddy faces getting redder by the pint and talking animatedly amongst themselves. That's not to say that they weren't social. Far from it, they were polite to everyone, and welcomed anyone to join them, but they were also quite happy to just be with each other.

Today was different. Today they were sitting in a tight group with worried expressions on their faces and drinking faster than usual.

Gnomes are a lovely peaceful and almost spiritual race. In fact, the word gnome means Guarding Naturally Over Mother Earth. They are natural and enthusiastic gardeners and spend most of their time earning pocket money doing gardening work for the village locals. When not doing that, they tend to the greenery around Pant y Gussett, trimming bushes, planting wildflowers and generally keeping things in order. Their only real vice, apart from an occasional drink or two, is fishing. Not catching fish you understand, just the act of fishing, usually in a garden pond with no fish in it. This provides them with an excuse to just sit in a garden and wonder at the natural beauty that surrounds them.

"Hello lads, can I get you a refill", said the Fat Wizard as he approached their table, determined to find out what was troubling them.

"OH, hi FW", smiled Gerhart. He was the one with the big red nose on which sat a tiny wire framed pair of glasses. For some reason he always carried his fishing rod with him wherever he went. "Thank you, another drink would be most welcome, please join us."

"Thank you I think I will". "Another round for my friends here please miss Dee, if you would be so kind", he called, distracting Double Dee from Downwind Jones' rather ribald account of a Bishop meeting an actress somewhere or other. It must have been an amusing story judging by the amount of ale suddenly emanating from Dugs' nostrils.

"Certainly dear, be right there" said Double Dee pretending to be far too innocent to understand the joke but giggling anyway.

Even with a fresh, and free, drink the atmosphere around the gnomes was really subdued.

"Ok lads, out with it, what's wrong?" asked the Fat Wizard, obviously concerned.

"Oh nothing, nothing's wrong", said Gerhart, "Yeah it's probably nothing", echoed Neville, the youngest of the group, clean shaven but ears big enough to shame an African elephant.

"Probably nothing?", said the Fat Wizard turning to face an embarrassed Neville who was wishing he hadn't said anything.

With all the gnomes now desperately trying to avoid eye contact with the Fat Wizard, Gerhart took a deep breath and explained, "Look, well it's the plants and trees you see". "And don't forget the flowers", interrupted Neville who quickly looked away, "and the flowers", sighed Gerhart, "They're worried, very worried".

"Worried you say" said the Fat Wizard, "what about? And for that matter since when have you been able to talk with the plants?"

"Talk to the plants, don't be silly of course we can't talk to plants", he laughed, then continued more seriously, "but we can feel em".

"Feel em, er I mean them, what do you mean feel them?" the Fat Wizard asked, confused.

"Well emotions sort of thing. We can tell if they're happy, sad, hungry or thirsty. That's why we're such good gardeners you see. We know what the plants want and at the moment they're worried, almost scared and we don't know why."

"I see" said the Fat Wizard stroking his beard, "that is

worrying. Let me get you another round". The Fat Wizard hadn't suddenly become a spendthrift, the gnome's jugs were very small. "I'm off to see if I can find out more".

"Thanks FW" they all chorused as they resumed staring into their beer, well lemonade for young Neville.

Leaving the gnomes behind the Fat Wizard walked over to a group of dwarfs standing in a corner on the opposite side of the bar. Like the gnomes, dwarfs are generally pretty friendly, to people that is, but between themselves, fights and arguments are rife, often leading to very bloody conclusions.

Not a lot is known about dwarfs. We know they live underground, somewhere, where their wives and children live a totally subterranean lifestyle. When boys come of age, they make one of two choices: to take up arms to go off and become a warrior, or take up the shovel and pick and become a miner. Apart from the obviously different hardware they carry, it would be impossible to tell the two divisions apart. All dwarfs grow their hair and beards long and usually plaited. Their clothes include knee high leather boots, pantaloons, a baggy blouse with a leather tunic over it, though the more muscular ones like to go shirtless, and big leather belts.

They never go anywhere without the tools of their trade. The warriors would always be sporting giant metal hammers or axes, even when eating and, as with this group, the miners go nowhere without their shovels, picks and candle lamps.

"Hi lads" greeted the Fat Wizard as he approached them.

He didn't offer to buy this lot a round, as with their fabled drinking capacity he knew he would be broke in no time, and trying to get more pocket-money from Mrs FW was more difficult than herding cats, "How's the mining business?"

"What mining business?" grumbled one of the dwarfs. The Fat Wizard wasn't sure but he thought his name may be Brock but as they all looked so alike he couldn't be sure. "Mines are all but played out now, we're all working at the quarry, breaking rocks".

"Breaking rocks!", exclaimed the Fat Wizard "but you're skilled miners why are you breaking rocks?"

"Well", said the same dwarf "we break rocks into gravel for drives and patios and such. Pays quite well I suppose. Besides, couldn't get back into the mines for what's left if we wanted to, they are all chained and boarded up."

"All of them, even the really old mines half way up?"

"All of them" replied the dwarf" sighing, "mind you there's plenty of things going on up there. Seen loads of people coming and going, with machines and lamps and all. The weird thing is that amongst all the noise they make, we've not once heard the sound of a pick or a shovel. Not natural that, is it lads?" he said to the others.

"No, it's not!" they cried in unison and then as if by some magic command, they all downed their drinks in one, then wiping the foam from their respective moustaches with the back of their hands, all looked up expectantly at the Fat Wizard.

"Bugger!" he thought to himself, they saw me treat the gnomes, "Same again lads?"

Drinking with dwarfs is not an activity that should not be undertaken by anyone other than professionals. For all his skills and abilities, this was well out of the Fat Wizard's league. It wasn't long before the floor seemed a little shaky and the furniture was bumping into him every time he moved, "Time to head home" he announced to no-one in particular, "what time is it anyway?". "Nearly one o'clock" cried a voice from the distance.

"One o'clock, bugger" he slurred, "I'd better run. Jasper won't leave me anything" and he hastened out of the pub. "At least I can run faster without all my money to weigh me down", he mused philosophically as he dashed down the street.

As the Fat Wizard walked into the dining room, reeking of beer, he was greeted by the dulcet tones of his good lady yelling "You cut that close. If the potatoes hadn't taken so long you'd have had it. Now go wash up I'm serving".

"Yes dear" he replied noticing Jasper sitting in front of him with his tail wagging frantically in greeting, yet wearing an expression of utter disappointment on his face.

The rest of Sunday seemed fairly predictable, The Fat Wizard snoring in his comfy chair, a film playing unwatched on the television, Mrs FW, sewing in the kitchen and Rebe in her room reading, well you know what, until that is, the early evening. It was about six o'clock' when the Fat Wizard found himself awakening to the world shaking around him "EARTHQUAKE!" he shrieked, slowly regaining consciousness.

"No no dear, that was just me trying to wake you. There was a tremor but you slept through it" said Mrs FW calmly.

"Tremor? No earthquake?" said the Fat Wizard trying desperately to get his faculties together, already feeling the onset of one of those piercing headaches that all those who have overdone a lunchtime session have experienced.

"Now you're not fit to do anything today. I just thought you should know about it. Cup of tea?".

With a fresh mug of tea helping to clear the cloudiness in his head, the Fat Wizard pondered over what the gnomes and the dwarfs had told him. This coupled with the information coming from behind the petunias, courtesy of Jed, he had to conclude that whatever was occurring up by the mines was certainly escalating.

"Sorry pet" he said to Mrs FW, "you'll have to man the shop again tomorrow. I'm off to pay my respects to some miners, if it's not raining that is".

14. GREAT BALLS OF FIRE.

Monday morning and the Fat Wizard was awakened by a slightly muted, cock-a-doodle-doo, from a cockerel sitting nervously on a nearby fence post. He was fervently looking around in a very paranoid fashion lest anything happen to upset his dignity again.

It was a cloudy and chilly morning but it was at least dry, so the Fat Wizard headed on down to his breakfast of tea, egg, bacon, beans, mushrooms, fried tomatoes and toast, unbuttered of course, as he had started his diet, to ready himself for his day's adventure.

Leaving the family to open the shop he decided to get an early start. With most of Pant y Gussett not up yet, he enjoyed a quiet walk through the village and on to the car park. It was so early that as he crossed the bridge, he could hear Eric snoring loudly from somewhere under his feet. Smiling to himself the Fat Wizard entered the car park, where to his astonishment alongside the handful of cars that belonged to the villagers there was parked a veritable fleet of vehicles, cars, vans and even a lorry. Most were black and shiny, though there were some other colours among them, notably a very average looking small Japanese thing in beige.

"Hmmm" he thought to himself once again stroking his beard. "There were only a few of them last week, this looks serious." But with no people in sight he carried on out of the other side of the car park in the direction of Brakin' Wind.

With increasing concern, and not a small amount of annoyance, the Fat Wizard was upset to see that some of his favourite paths had been vandalised by the tyre tracks of what he presumed were quad bikes and trailers. The paths weren't really wide enough for anything else but there were what looked like caterpillar tracks that had flattened a great deal of the hedgerow. Another sign of increased human activity and one that for some reason he found even worse than the damage done by machines, was litter. Everywhere he looked there were empty drink cans, plastic bottles and carrier bags. He knew that the plants could grow back but the harm caused by litter was forever.

Charles Bickford stood on a large boulder at the entrance to one of the mines, a fair way up the side of Brakin' wind. He loved it here. The peace and quiet. As he looked over the fields and woodland surrounding him he felt a sense of calm, of wellbeing. As he watched curly wisps of smoke lazily spiralling up from several chimneys that he could just make out through the gaps in the trees he romanticised about the families living within these quaint wooden cottages. Mother in a gingham dress and white apron, baking bread in the oven, the kids having finished all of their chores sitting on the arms of a big comfy armchair leaning against their father, their faces a picture of wonder while he reads them a story about pirates and the dog snoozing quietly by the fireplace.

Looking beyond the greenery he could just make out the sea and a hazy outline of a boat. A fishing boat he imagined, a small brave little boat crewed by a band of tough men, tough men who trusted and relied upon each other for their very lives as they battled the elements to bring food to a grateful and admiring port.

He was rudely snapped out of his musings as a loud and husky voice yelled,

"OI! Charlie boy, toss that rope down will ya".

"My name is Charles" said Charles, "I would remind you that I am in charge of this operation and the magic word is please!"

"I don't care if the magic word is abricabloody dabra, chuck that rope down…. please".

Charlie threw the rope down to the anonymous hard hat below. He knew very few of the men's names. He didn't know how many worked directly under him or who worked for a subcontractor. The only thing he knew for sure was that none of them treated him with any respect whatsoever.

"How on earth did I end up here?", he thought introspectively. "One minute I'm a junior engineer designing rides for children's playgrounds or helping install new sewers in Croydon, the next my old boss dies and I'm put in charge of a top-secret project that's apparently been going on for years".

Charles missed his old boss Mr Lewis. Mr Lewis had always treated him kindly. He would talk to Charles for hours about his baby son, his loving wife and the wooden log chalet that they owned in Pant y Gussett. Charles would sit and listen for hours about this idyllic lifestyle, secretly wishing his own home life could be more like his.

Looking back over the trees Charles wondered whether one of the cabins below was actually once Mr Lewis' home. These last eight years or so, since the accident and his sudden promotion, had not been good ones. Becoming chief engineer had involved instant responsibility in all the projects he had been involved in. No longer following Mr Lewis's instructions but actually ordering others to follow his instead, something he still wasn't comfortable with, and obviously a weakness as demonstrated by the attitude of his subordinates. This lack of respect from the people under him was more than matched by the people over him. Between work and home, he felt that each day he died a little.

It took some time before Messer's Brimstone and Sweetman trusted him enough to put him in charge of the Pant y Gussett project, and even then information was drip fed to him over quite a few months. He was well aware of the controversy surrounding such projects. By the time he had been given control of this one he had been involved in similar schemes in other parts of the country and had seen first-hand the resentment demonstrated by the local populace. Deep down it was starting to bother him that Mr Lewis was part of the original plans for the Pant y Gussett scheme, especially after telling Charles about the wonder and beauty of the place.

Rounding a slight bend at the slopes of Brakin Wind the Fat Wizard encountered a small group of men. All were wearing hard hats and high vis jackets. They were wearing other clothes as well of course but they were quite nondescript and not really worthy of mention. Around them was an assortment of large machines with an industrial generator being the only one the Fat Wizard could identify.

"Hello gentlemen" the Fat Wizard shouted. He had to shout to be heard above the noise of the aforementioned generator.

He was ignored.

"HELLO GENTLEMEN", he repeated adding a touch of magic to his voice. Well a touch of magic powerful enough to knock the hard hat off the head of the nearest man.

As you know the Fat Wizard hated bad manners and certainly wouldn't tolerate being ignored.

As the man retrieved his hat from the ground and scratched his head. Confused as to why it fell off, he looked up and grumbled "Heard you the first time, what do you want?".

"I want you to tell me what is going on here, that's what I want!", snapped the Fat Wizard in a tone that carried enough menace for the rest of the group to turn away and pretend to be busy doing something urgent, while grateful that they weren't the ones facing this large lunatic in blue robes.

Obviously feeling intimidated despite outnumbering the Fat Wizard by at least five to one, the man said politely, "Sorry you'll have to speak to the gaffer"

"Gaffer?"

"Yes gaffer, Mr Bickford the project manager. That's him up there by that mine entrance" the man said, pointing to a figure up the hill.

"I see", said the Fat Wizard "and would you be so kind as to call him down, please?", this request was spoken in a soft friendly manner and yet it was quite clear that this was in fact an order, an order that should really be obeyed, immediately.

"Yes certainly, right away", the man said fumbling at his belt for his walkie talkie", "Charlie, you there, Charlie, Charlie", with no answer and no movement from the figure on the hill, the workman, with a rising sense of panic, put his fingers to his lips and whistled loudly while gesticulating frantically for Charles to come down.

Finally, with movement from the hill the man turned to the Fat Wizard and said, "He'll be down now, please excuse me I really have to get on", and with an indecent amount of haste he returned to the others as they indiscreetly hid behind a large trailer.

A few minutes later and a man, looking faintly ludicrous in a raincoat with a baggy high vis vest over it and a two sizes too big hard hat, approached the Fat Wizard. With a large smile and his hand extended in welcome he said,

"Sorry to take so long. Can't seem to find my walkie talkie. I had it in my hand a minute ago, only put it down for a second, anyway, how can I help you?"

Smiling inwardly, sensing the handiwork of the Coblynau, the Fat Wizard shook the offered hand "Mr Bickford I presume"

"Yes, and you are?"

"Just call me FW, everyone else does",

"Mr FW? Okay and how can I help you?"

"Just FW will be fine. I was wondering if you would be so kind as to tell me what is going on here?",

"Ah!" said Charles, "I'm afraid I'm not at liberty to discuss it with anyone".

"That's OK" said the Fat Wizard, "I'm not an anyone, I am an elder of the village"

"Nevertheless, I am under strict instructions from my company not to discuss this project with anyone, even village elders" said Charles surprising himself with his confident tone.

Inside he was shaking like a leaf. His sixth sense was warning him that there was great danger in this FW character. Besides something was nagging in the back of his mind that he had heard of this man somewhere.

The Fat Wizard knew full well that he was capable of putting the fear of God into this man and force him to tell him what he knew, but he was also aware that this poor man was no more than a pawn in a larger game and probably didn't deserve such harsh treatment.

"Well if you aren't able to tell me about this project, you can at least tell me who can", said the Fat Wizard firmly.

"Certainly" said Charles fishing about in his pocket, "Dam I had a wallet somewhere. Where the hell has that gone? Never mind, I've got a loose one in my other pocket" and he handed the Fat Wizard a business card",

P.E.E.O.F.F.

Managing Directors

133

Mr R Brimstone and Mr A Sweetman

"The contact details are on the back", he added.

"Looks like Brian was right" thought the Fat Wizard. "Thank you for that Mr Bickford, I suspect we will meet again, soon".

"I will look forward to it Mr, er I mean FW, have a good day", said Charles warmly, while for some reason thinking he had just had a narrow escape. As he turned away to carry on about his business, he found himself turning back to the Fat Wizard and saying, "Please be careful if you do decide to talk to them FW, they can be...unpleasant".

"I will, and thank you for your concern. Good day Mr Bickford"

"Shame he's mixed up with this lot. There's a good man in there somewhere", thought the Fat Wizard to himself as he decided to take a more circuitous route home to ascertain the damage being done around the fields and woods.

Although there was plenty of evidence of "outside" activity he was pleased to see that the damage to the countryside was minimal and as he wandered deep in thought as to his next move, he was surprised to hear the screams of a very familiar voice. Rebe. As he ran panic stricken through a small piece of woodland and into a clearing, he could make out his eldest daughter with an armful of dragon eggs. She was hurling small firebolts from her free hand in the direction of another group of high vis hard hats using shovels as cover as they tried to attack her. Too stupid to realise just how much danger they were in they were screaming obscenities at her and were still trying to attack.

"Gentlemen" shouted the Fat Wizard in barely contained fury as he drew his wand from his sock, "My daughter may have strong morals that prevent her from doing serious harm to another human being, however, I DO NOT! Apologise to her immediately and be on your way or face being turned into slugs under a torrent of salt for eternity!" and just for emphasis he fired a massive bolt of lightning from his wand directly over their heads, stopping them in their tracks.

The now white-faced workers, realising just how much trouble they were in, dropped their tools, looked down at their feet and started mumbling things like, "Sorry, didn't mean anything by it", "we were just messing about" and of course the old standard, "he started it".

"Whatever!" said the Fat Wizard. "By my reckoning you were just about to push her to the point of no return and she has a far greater imagination than I have. I would consider yourselves lucky that I came along when I did. May I strongly recommend that you make sure that neither of us see you in Pant y Gussett again".

"We're going", "sorry again", "I wanted to be a dancer anyway" and the comment that made the Fat Wizard and Rebe laugh out loud, "My bum hurts!" this from a forlorn looking man with a cloud of blue smoke rising from his trousers, the result of a direct hit from one of Rebe's firebolts.

After the men had skulked away back to the car park, the Fat Wizard turned to Rebe and said "what the hell are you doing here and what the hell happened?"

"Well" said Rebe, composing herself and checking that the eggs were sound. "Just after you left this morning, Downwind came into the shop and said that Griff had mentioned that Dai the dwarf had heard…. Well the upshot is that there was reportedly an abandoned dragon nest near the mine and some blokes were going to take them home as trophies,"

"So you went to get there before them" said the Fat Wizard.

"Er no" said Rebe with a strange grin on her face.

"What they got there first?"

"Well er yes, they had the eggs when I got here", said Rebe smiling mischievously.

"So how did you get them off them?" asked the Fat Wizard getting impatient.

"Well I sort of made them think their man bits had fallen off" giggled Rebe "and while they were trying to pick them up, I grabbed the eggs. Unfortunately, the spell didn't last long enough and for some reason they got very angry, and then you arrived".

"OK" said the Fat Wizard, "Man bits falling off. Well you are my apprentice but firebolts, I've never taught you how to throw firebolts!'".

"Dad! I spend all of most of my life with dragons, don't you think that some of that would rub off on me".

"I suppose it must, I suppose it must, hey" he said as he put his arm proudly around his daughters' shoulder, "do you think the eggs would be okay if we took a very long route home and called in on the fairies? I would love a chat with Queen Megan before I decide to do something that might be quite stupid".

"You, do something stupid!" laughed Rebe "that would be a first"

"Sarcasm?"

"Yes, sarcasm Dad. The eggs will be fine, they're not heavy. Let's go".

The Fat Wizard, with Rebe alongside him, retraced his steps back toward the mines, which they had to pass to get to the home of Queen Megan and the fairies. As they walked through all the machinery, cables and pipes, so out of place amongst all this greenery, they couldn't help but notice how the various workmen they encountered were deeply engrossed in whatever task they were employed in. So much so that they were too busy to even look up at this father and daughter walking so freely among their worksite.

"Do you think those other men passed this way on their way out of Pant y Gussett", laughed Rebe.

"Certainly looks that way", smiled the Fat Wizard, noticing

that Mr Bickford was nowhere to be seen. They carried on past the mine and on past the little crossroads in the path where a right turn would take them back to the car park. They carried on straight through towards Queen Megan's domain. The Fat Wizard knew the general area where the fairies lived but the exact location was secret, even to him. They had been walking for a good half an hour or so and just before they approached some dense woodland a familiar dark cloud descended from high above them and stopped right in front of the Fat Wizards face. The cloud turned out to be a squadron of the "RAF" with a beaming Captain Riser in front.

"Good day to you FW, Rebe" he said grinning at her, "we were watching your little encounter with those idiots from high above, just in case you needed our help, but when we saw FW arrive we thought we had better get out of there in case we got caught in the crossfire".

"Very wise, but I think they have learnt their lesson" smiled the Fat Wizard. But thanks for looking out for Rebe, anyway. Riser" he continued, "do you think it might be possible for me to have an audience with Queen Megan?"

"More than possible" Riser smiled, "when I told her you were here, she said she wanted to see you! She'll be along in a minute".

And as the words left his lips, there approached another cloud from the distance, but this time the Fat Wizard could make out a solid shape in the centre of it. As they got closer he could see it was another squadron of fairies. Only unlike Risers' men who were dressed in an obviously military fashion, these were resplendent in ornate metallic tunics with ceremonial swords and decorated leather scabbards. Their helmets, again metallic, sported horns, their muscular bare legs ended in calf length leather boots covered in metal spikes. Eight of the largest of their number, with their wings flapping frantically, supported a large platform made of woven willow twigs which was beautifully decorated with the blossoms of many wild flowers. On the centre of this platform was an intricately carved wooden throne on which sat Queen Megan.

Megan was old, ancient old, with long silver-grey hair and a face heavily lined with the experience of generations. Yet in spite of her obviously advancing years her eyes were bright blue, piercingly bright blue, that gave tell to the fierce intelligence behind them. She wore what at first glance seemed to be plain flowing, silken white robes. But every time she moved the gown changed into different shades of blue, pink, yellow and green, she really was magnificent. Despite being a powerful queen, she wore no crown, preferring instead a simple garland of forget-me-nots and daisy flowers around her brow. On closer inspection the Fat Wizard thought he could make out a small figure hiding behind the folds of the gown beneath the throne.

"Hail FW, and of course you too Rebe" she said as Riser and his men bowed, not an easy thing to do whilst in flight, and moved over to allow her and her honour guard direct access to the Fat Wizard.

"Hail to you Queen Megan" said the Fat Wizard, as he and Rebe both bowed and curtsied respectively and respectfully.

"I have someone here who would like to say hello" said Megan, "I believe you have already met" and she pulled aside her gown to reveal a tiny little girl fairy. "This is Elspeth my great, great, great, great, yes I think that's enough greats, granddaughter".

"Elspeth, how lovely to see you again" beamed the Fat Wizard, "I trust you are fully recovered from your horrible ordeal".

"Yes thank you" said Elspeth shyly, as she offered the Fat Wizard a really pretty bluebell.

"As soon as she heard I was coming to meet you" said Megan "she insisted that she came along and she picked that flower especially for you.

"You did? Thank you Elspeth, it's a really pretty flower. I shall treasure it always" said the Fat Wizard genuinely touched, as he took the bloom and made a big show of smelling it before tucking it safely into a pouch on his belt.

Again, she reached out and grabbed his beard, kissed him on the cheek and said "Thank you for saving me", then kissed him again. "That one's from my mam" she said blushing.

"My pleasure" said the Fat Wizard and just as his heart was about to burst with the sentiment of it all, Queen Megan commanded, quite regally he thought,

"Captain Riser!"

"Your Majesty" he replied as he and his men snapped to attention.

"Be so kind as to take Elspeth home for me. It's time FW and I had a serious conversation".

"At once your Majesty". Extricating Elspeth from the Fat Wizard's beard, Riser winked and whispered, see you around, before flying off to the mysterious location of the fairies' home trees.

Alone, apart from Rebe and a few dozen of Megan's honour guard of course, the Fat Wizard brought the queen up to date on everything that he had learned so far.

"I must confess" said Megan, "I have been aware for some years of some minor "outside" activity in the mines, but they didn't seem to be doing anything important. I did send some spies in from time to time to keep an eye on things but the Coblynau were having so much fun with the visitors that I didn't really feel concerned. Now that they are having a real effect on Pant y Gussett and with what you have told me about "fracking, wasn't it, I think this might be getting very serious indeed. To be honest I have had several reports of patrols becoming sick after flying through what they described as "bad air". What do you recommend should be the next course of action?"

"Well" said the Fat Wizard, "I'm not comfortable about it but I think I should go to the source and have a chat with Messrs Brimstone and Sweetman".

"I agree" said the queen obviously concerned, "but remember my powers do not extend beyond the village, you will be alone out there".

"I know", he said "but knowing I have your support, whatever follows me back here, will be enough".

"You have my support and my blessing but take care out there, you may be a powerful wizard but from what I hear the "outside" can be a cold and dangerous place, even without these characters you've described. Possibly even beyond your great talents" she said sounding genuinely concerned.

"I'm going with you!" said Rebe determinedly.

"Not this time" said the Fat Wizard firmly, "and I'd be grateful if you didn't tell your mother about this conversation. No need to get her worried. Besides I'm just going for a friendly chat, what could go wrong?".

"Having said a respectful goodbye to Queen Megan the two of them walked quietly home, Rebe worried sick about the danger to her father. The Fat Wizard worried sick about how he was going to get permission from his wife to take the trip.

Crossing over the bridge from the car park, Charles Bickford tossed Eric a packet of mints, you know the ones with the non-fattening centres, alright the ones with a hole in the middle. He normally carried a couple of packets with him but for some strange reason this was the only packet he had left. He always felt more confident talking to people knowing his breath was minty fresh.

He watched as Eric caught the payment and waited while

the giant mumbled something in that deep baritone voice of his that might have been a thank you and turned to retreat back under the bridge. He'd met Eric the week before when his bosses insisted that he joined them, Miss Jones and a couple of the "boys" for a drink in the local. So he knew the protocol but didn't think he would ever get used to these encounters.

He was on his way to pick up some supplies, supplies such as pasties, crisps and fizzy drinks for his crew. Apparently, it was his turn though he couldn't recall anyone else doing it in the past. He knew that a man in his position should not really be doing such menial tasks at the behest of his lessers but to be honest he welcomed the excuse to get away from them, and the job, for a while.

As he approached the crossroads, with the funeral parlour's workshop on his left, he could see the pub ahead of him on the other side of the road. Just then he was overtaken by a scruffy looking small boy carrying a stick,

"Excuse me sonny" said Charles half expecting a vulgar reply, the sort that questioned his parentage. After all that is what he had grown accustomed to in London.

"Yes Mr?", said the lad with a disarming smile.

Slightly taken aback by the display of good manners Charles went on to say, "I'm a stranger round here I don't suppose you could direct me to a shop selling snacks and pop, could you?".

"It's the soupermarket you want. Sell everything they do. That's where I'm going now. I promised me mam to help her carry the shopping, I'll take you if you like".

"Thank you, that would be most kind", said Charles totally overawed by the good manners and helpfulness of the boy, while at the same time feeling slightly upset when he remembered that far off time when he had thought that his own progeny would turn out so well.

"Let me introduce myself, my name is Charles Bickford", said Charles offering out his hand, "but you can call me Charles, and who are you may I ask?"

"Pog", said Pog, "and you can call me Pog" he said giggling, pleased as punch to be treated like an adult. "Now come on I don't want to be late and leave me mam carrying them heavy bags".

As they walked the short distance to the soupermarket Charles found himself amazed at this small boy's knowledge and enthusiasm over the place he lived in. In the ten minutes or so that he had known him, Pog had introduced him to several of the villagers and had told him the history of every building they had passed. Sadly, his own kids would only talk to him about the latest video game and how they had to have it or be ridiculed by their friends. Oh, he had tried to introduce them to the joys of reading a book or constructing models. He even tried paying for piano lessons but apparently if it didn't have a joystick and buttons with basic geometric shapes, then it was "boring", and "what did he know anyway". They had even adopted the same dismissive tone of voice that his wife reserved for him. That probably hurt him the most.

"There she is!", said Pog as he pointed to a woman bent

over the "reduced while stocks last" bin, "Mam, meet my friend Charles".

"Oh, hello", said Pog's mam standing up with one hand desperately trying to control a trolley that evidently had a mind of its own. "Charles, was it?".

Charles just stood there his jaw agape. Never before had he encountered anyone with such kindness and wholesomeness in their eyes. She was not the professional model type with a size zero figure, nor was she a pop princess overdone with glamour and make up. She was simply a vision, an angel.

Charles's jaw was now moving up and down like a beached guppy, his eyes like saucers and his voice suddenly rising so high as to make him eligible to apply as a soprano in the Llanelli and District under twelves school choir, as he shrilly mumbled "Hhh hello", Mrs?".

"Please call me Melanie" said Pog's mam, "any friend of Pog's is a friend of mine"

"A voice like a piece of chocolate wrapped in silk", thought Charles to himself " sweet and soft" as he became very self-conscious of a bead of sweat threatening to migrate from his brow to run the length of his nose and drip onto the floor in front of the most beautiful woman he had ever met.

"Right" said Melanie to Pog, "let's go pay for all this and then you can grab the heavier bags, if you don't mind?"

"Course I don't mind silly, that's what I came here for",

said the ever smiling Pog.

Charles couldn't take his eyes off Melanie as she paid for her shopping. Though when he noticed that part of her payment consisted of the exchange of a dozen jars of honey, some little part of his brain started to feel uncomfortable. Though for the life of him, he couldn't work out why.

Loaded up with bags, Melanie and Pog nodded at Charles and with a polite "Nice to meet you" and they headed for the door.

Desperate not to let what could be the nicest people he had ever met walk out of his life so soon, Charles found himself dashing up to them saying,

"Please let me help you home with those bags, they look so heavy".

"Well thank you Charles but it is a fair way, and besides" she said looking him up and down "haven't you got shopping of your own to do yet?"

A veritable waterfall of emotions crashed over Charles all at the same time. Never before had he had the confidence to approach a beautiful woman like he just had, and when Melanie called him Charles, a name he had never before enjoyed, it seemed almost regal, a name for a man of importance, when she said it, it made him feel..., well feel like a man.

He also felt like a plonker, furiously scratching around the recesses of his brain for an excuse to explain why he hadn't done his own shopping yet. He settled for the rather feeble;

"Oh it was nothing important, I'll come back for that stuff later", while wondering how much trouble he was going to be in with his impatient, rebellious, hungry and thirsty workforce.

As they walked out of the village back towards Melanie and Pog's house, Charles was in heaven. He couldn't remember the last time he was so comfortable in a woman's company, anybody's company for that matter. They chatted about nothing in particular, giggled about things that weren't really funny and laughed out loud when Pog ran off to catch a passing rabbit. Pog knew he couldn't catch it, the rabbit knew it couldn't be caught, but they both played the game anyway.

Enraptured by the wonderful company and the stunning scenery, Charles was disappointed when Melanie walked up to the gates of a wooden cabin and said "Right that's us, thank you very much for your help Charles"

"My pleasure" said Charles handing over the bags he had carried, still standing by the gate awkwardly, trying to find an excuse not to let this moment end.

A reprieve arrived when in her melodic sing song voice Melanie asked "would you like to come in for a cup of tea, it's the least we can do".

"I would love to" said a very relieved Charles.

Melanie's home was beautiful, almost as Charles had

imagined these cabins to be when he was standing by the mine entrance looking over Pant y Gussett. The cabin had a large living room simply decorated with a floral covered three-piece suite, a log fire in a large fireplace, pretty patterned curtains at every window and a couple of tables all sporting vases with fresh cut flowers. Everything was immaculate and the whole room smelled of love, if that's possible, but Charles had no other way to describe how it felt to be there.

While Melanie and Pog went into the adjoining kitchen to put away the shopping and put the kettle on, Charles walked over to the large wooden mantelpiece to inspect the ornaments and pictures there. The first things he noticed were some prize certificates for her award-winning honey. Next to them were the usual sort of thing you'd expect to find on a mantelpiece such as a small wooden bowl with keys, rubber bands and a small hairbrush in it, and then some family photographs in simple wooden frames. The first one was what Charles presumed to be Pog on the day he was born, a baby in a crib. The next was a photo of Melanie as a teenager. Charles felt his knees tremble slightly as he thought about the beautiful young girl in the photo, and what an absolute stunner she would become as a woman. Moving on to the final picture at the end, Charles had to look twice. His blood ran cold and he started to feel physically sick. Life had played another sick joke on him, just when he felt that there might be a chance to climb out of the dank pit of despair in which he had lived most of his life, now this! Shaking badly, he dropped the picture he was holding to the floor. Looking down at the miraculously intact photo, he could clearly see the image of a family in the middle of domestic bliss. There was Melanie, beaming from ear to ear while cradling her new born son Pog in her arms and around her, the long strong arm and smiling face of a proud new father, his former boss;

Mr Lewis. Feeling like a guilty usurper in the home of someone he respected and admired, Charles yelled a quick;

"Sorry gotta go, just remembered something urgent!" and fled from the cabin back to the mines, praying that he would stop crying before the men saw him.

Back home in the shop the Fat Wizard and Rebe recounted the details of the day's drama to Mrs FW, omitting for the moment any talk of a possible trip to London.

"My hero!", said Mrs FW slightly less sarcastically than usual. "Rebe since when have you been able to shoot firebolts?" an odd but somehow typical reaction from a mother of an apprentice wizard's daughter who had just learned her daughter had been attacked. Then turning to her husband asked "so what's your next move?"

"Not sure yet, I'll have to think about" he said feeling guilty. He never lied to his wife. Not tell her stuff maybe. What husband doesn't? But he knew full well what he planned to do but needed time to think about how to tell her.

Once Rebe and her mother had left him alone to tend the shop while they went about their business, Rebe seeing to the baby dragons and his good lady seeing what she could rustle up for dinner, the Fat Wizard reached into a pouch on his belt to get his magical mobile phone. Actually, it was a pretty average mobile phone but with his rudimentary grasp of technology he considered all mobile phones as magical. Finding Brian's number, which unusually for him he had remembered to add to his address list, he pressed the dial button.

"Hi FW" came an instant jolly reply followed by a slightly more serious, "everything alright?".

"Yes, well sort of" he replied. "Look I've managed to confirm that those Brimstone and Sweetman characters you warned me about are definitely up to something in Pant y Gussett involving fracking".

"Oh dear" sighed Brian, "I fear you have a lot of trouble coming your way. I don't suppose I can convince you to stay out of it, can I?".

"Afraid not. From what I've learned these jokers threaten the safety of family, friends and indeed Pant y Gussett itself. That makes me firmly involved.".

"What do you intend to do?", asked Brian sounding genuinely concerned.

"Well, obviously I'm going to have to meet them and see if I can persuade them to leave us alone. I'm sure that once I've explained how much harm they are doing to the village they'll move on to somewhere else".

"FW" said Brian, "you are one of the most intelligent and powerful men that I know, but even you could not comprehend how evil these money grabbing bastards can be. I have managed to find out that they have already invested tens of thousands into the Pant y Gussett project and have even, if the rumours are to be believed, already dispatched one employee who threatened to stand in their way".

"What do you mean dispatched?", asked the Fat Wizard.

"You know damn well what I mean!", said Brian despairingly.

"I suppose I do", sighed the Fat Wizard, "still I have to try. I have their number and I'm going to arrange a meeting as soon as possible".

"I wish I could help but quite frankly Brimstone and Sweetman scare the crap out of me. I'm a numbers man and numbers aren't going to protect you from these two. Please take care, there's always a home for you Jean and the kids with me if you want it but that's all I can really offer. Keep in touch.", and with a tone of sad finality, Brian hung up.

Still with the phone in his hand, the Fat Wizard went into another pouch and retrieved the business card Charles had given him earlier and entered the number on the back of the card. Exactly three rings later an efficient Miss Jones said,

"Power, Electricity, Energy Oil and Fuel Finders LTD, how can I help you?".

"Oh hello", said the Fat Wizard in the most formal voice he could manage, "I'd like to make an appointment to see

Mr Brimstone and Mr Sweetman, please".

"You and a lot of other people. I'm afraid they are really busy at the moment" said Miss Jones quite kindly, "may I ask what it is regarding?".

"Pant y Gussett"

"Pant y Gussett, you say, and you are?"

"FW, just FW, that is how I am known"

"I see" said Miss Jones sounding intrigued, "hold the line please and I'll see when they are free".

For nearly five minutes the Fat Wizard was subjected to some ungodly caterwauling the like of which he had not heard since Downwind Jones ran his cart over the foot of Goodwitch Evans. Finally silence and then a very enthusiastic Miss jones came back on the line with, "Friday two o'clock at their Mayfair offices any good?".

"Friday two o'clock, Mayfair will be fine, see you then", said the Fat Wizard with just a slight feeling of trepidation which he quickly dismissed. He was glad of the distraction of the shop bell as it rang announcing the arrival of some potential customers. It turned out the customer was one of the hard hats from the mine.

"Hello", he said sheepishly. "Look I heard what happened to your daughter up at the mine. I just wanted you to know it was nothing to do with me. I could never behave like that, I swear".

"I'll have no swearing in my shop" said the Fat Wizard in a

very serious voice.

"No, no that's not what I meant, I mean…."

"Calm down" said the Fat Wizard smiling, "I was only teasing you and I appreciate that you weren't involved. I am not the sort to tar you all with the same brush".

"Oh good" said the man obviously relieved, "I saw you both as you walked past the mine, your daughter, alright is she?"

"Yes thank you, quite alright".

"And the eggs, they alright too?"

"Yes the eggs are fine, why?" asked the Fat Wizard suspiciously.

"Oh, I didn't mean anything by it. It's just that I'm an animal lover myself. I keep reptiles, rescue them when I can. People think I'm a bit odd but I just find them fascinating, and now I find out that dragons are real and your daughter raises them".

"Is that why you're here?"

"Uh no, not really. It's just that me and some of the boys think we might be coming down with a bug or something. Quite a few of them have a bad cough and their eyes keep watering and I've got a hell of, sorry, I mean I seem to have a really sore throat and when we saw you and heard of your shop I kinda volunteered to see if you had anything that might help sort of thing".

"And it hasn't occurred to you that this "bug" might have something to do with what you're doing in the mine", said the Fat Wizard.

"To be honest" the young lad replied, "I don't really know what we're doing up there. I'm just a spark, sorry I mean electrician, I just wire things up and help with the machines when they break down, which happens a lot by the way. Parts keep going missing, a real mystery it is, my gaffer Charles is pulling his hair out over it".

Looking the lad over the Fat Wizard estimated his age to be around the late twenties and quite tall, at around six feet. He had a shock of curly black hair only now visible as he took off his hard hat and fidgeted with it as he talked. He had a dark complexion and noticeably shiny white teeth. He had the physique of a man well used to hard work yet his working clothes were quite clean and smart, the signs of a man who took pride in his work in the Fat Wizard's opinion. His sixth sense also told him that this was a decent person.

"Sorry", said the Fat Wizard "I didn't catch your name",

"Jack, Jack Elias, pleased to meet you" said Jack formerly offering his hand.

"Hello Jack and you can call me FW" and shaking his hand, continued, "You from around here Jack?"

"Actually, I grew up in Pembroke but my parents emigrated to Carmarthen when I was twelve. Wanted to bring me and my sister up in a big city they always claim" he said laughing.

"Carmarthen eh" said the Fat Wizard smiling. "One of my ancestors is still well remembered there. Anyway, about this "bug". I can sell you some medicine to relieve the symptoms you describe but I suggest you and your colleagues look a little deeper into what is going on in the mines. I suspect there may be a more serious cause than just a bug".

"What do you mean?", said Jack.

"It's just a feeling" said the Fat Wizard, "besides it's not for me to tell you and your colleagues how to live your lives. Tell me, have you met your employers, Brimstone and Sweetman?

"No not directly, I'm self-employed and was hired by Charles. He's the only one from the company I've met. He seems like a nice guy but the other men don't treat him very well. Don't know why he puts up with it"

"Hmm, got his own business as well" thought the Fat Wizard to himself as he put together a small hamper of potions and medicines. "You married Jack?" he asked.

"Good grief no. Every time I meet a girl, they run screaming as soon as they see my reptile collection!".

"Sorry to hear that" said the Fat Wizard, positively grinning as he handed Jack the bag of medicines. "There are instructions and dosages on each bottle, exceed them at your peril, and remember what I said about your working conditions. Now", he smiled conspiratorially "I suspect you would like me to see if I can arrange for my daughter Rebe to take you around the dragon pens one day, am I right?

"Rebe, what a wonderful name" said Jack dreamily. Then suddenly remembering who he was talking too, "That would be wonderful, to see the dragon pens I mean, do you think she really would?"

"She is very hard headed and wilful, I can but ask. Call in again one day next week and I'll see what I can do. Besides I would like to know if the medicine helps you and your men anyway".

"Hard headed and wilful, firebolts too, she is magnificent" said Jack who quickly realised he might have said too much, and feeling slightly embarrassed, paid for his goods, slammed on his hard hat and yelled "Thanks Mr FW see you next week!" and raced out of the door.

"It's just FW, oh never mind" he said as Jack disappeared up the street at a jaunty pace. Now he thought, apart from getting his wife's permission for a potentially hazardous trip to London, he also had to find a way to introduce Rebe to Jack which, if she suspected for one second was a setup, could prove to be far more dangerous than anything Brimstone and Sweetman could throw at him.

15. NOT EVEN A RUMOUR OF A TUMOUR.

The next few days passed without too much in the way of incidents. There had been a tremor or two but these were weaker than the previous ones. The Fat Wizard was still getting reports of activity up around the mines, mainly from behind the petunias where Jed and his boys told him that they were having a high old time relocating items from these naive and careless workmen. Apparently, they had collected so much stuff they were considering opening another shaft to hide it all in. When the Fat Wizard asked Jed what were they going to do with it all, he seemed a bit confused,

"Do with it?" Jed had said, "we've done what we wanted to do with it, we've got it!"

"But aren't you going use the things or sell some of it?" the Fat Wizard asked,

"Oh no!" exclaimed Jed horrified, "that would be wrong, we just "keep it. It's like all the little tricks we play on them, we don't want to do anything to hurt them it's just funny to watch".

Jed then went on to relate some of his recent pranks such as sticking nettle leaves to the toilet paper in the portaloos, putting ants into their hard hats whenever they took them off, and his particular favourite, dropping old broken wooden beams and a few rocks from the ceiling behind the men every time they explored a new shaft. Funnily enough he noticed that this particular prank usually resulted in even more fun with the stinging loo paper.

The Fat Wizard was very fond of the Coblynau but he knew he'd never understand them.

His most pressing problem was, how on earth he was going to get his wife to let him go to London. Not prepared to actually lie to her and in the absence of any devious scheme where a half-truth might get him where he wanted, he decided to resort to what he was most comfortable with, the truth.

He spent his Thursday morning manning the shop and deliberating how to tell Jean what he intended to do. He played out several scenarios in his head, one of which, out of sheer desperation, involved flowers and chocolates, but he knew all too well she wouldn't fall for any of them and it would be dangerous for him to insult her intelligence with any such nonsense. So when she brought him a mid-morning cup of tea he braced himself and took the direct route.

"Darling" he said as affectionately as he could, "you know the other day you asked me what my next move was?"

"Yes dear", she said casually looking out of the shop window.

"Well it's like this. I've managed to get an appointment with Brimstone and Sweetman for tomorrow afternoon, and well er, it's in Mayfair so I'll have to go to London", he said, readying himself for both a verbal and possibly a physical reply.

"I know" said Mrs FW still looking out the window and taking a sip of her tea.

"You know" stammered the Fat Wizard, "how do you know?".

"Well apart from it being the logical next step, we've been married a long time and I can tell when you're afraid of upsetting me. I can also tell when you're really worried about something. Are they as bad as Brian says?".

"Oh I'm sure they're not, they are just business people. I'm sure when I explain to them how their fracking could hurt Pant y Gussett, they'll move on to somewhere else. I'm certain" he said trying to convince himself as much as her.

"I won't lie to you" she said, turning away from the

window to cross the shop and embrace him, "I'm frightened, but I know nothing will stop you doing anything you can to protect this village, and us for that matter!, I've laid out a shirt and trousers on the bed. Now go and try them on and see if they still fit. I'm not having you travel to London in your robes. City folk won't take you seriously. Oh, and I found an old satchel you can put your wand and some sandwiches in".

Stroking an errant hair off her face and kissing her fondly on the cheek, The Fat Wizard said; "What on earth have I ever done to deserve a woman as wonderful as you?"

"I really don't know" she replied, laughing, while a tear started to form in her eye, "lucky I guess!".

"Yes, you're right, I am lucky and I'm a bona fide wizard, what could go wrong", he quipped with a confidence that he didn't really feel.

The emotionally charged moment ended abruptly when Ed Dee entered the shop, obviously in some distress,

"Here FW, got any more of that special ointment", he said as he shuffled around in an awkward gait, "the old condition has flared up, bloody wooden bench seat".

"I'll make some up for you now" said the Fat Wizard, "While you're here I need to book a lift to Llanelli train station tomorrow morning, you free?".

"Llanelli! you say, well I don't normally take Clara and the cart that far, but anything for you, FW anything, provided you got that cream of course. If you know what I mean" he said with a wink.

"I know what you mean" said the Fat Wizard trying not to laugh at the poor man's misfortune, "I'll do it now".

Later on that afternoon the Fat Wizard squeezed on his old outfit that Jean had laid out for him. He was always amazed at how clothes managed to shrink when left in a wardrobe, even leather belts.

Satisfied that he could probably survive in them for a day he dug out his old shoes and an overcoat that he hadn't worn since his wedding day and admired himself in the mirror. Ok maybe not admire, but felt he looked official enough for his upcoming appointment.

"Dad" said Rebe as she entered the bedroom, "please let me come with you. You know I could back you up if things get serious, I'm really worried for you".

"Thank you love" said the Fat Wizard, "but it's just a meeting with some businessmen, there's really nothing to worry about. Besides if I need firebolts I am more than capable of making them myself, though not as good as yours", he smiled proudly.

"Please don't joke Dad, I've got a really bad feeling about this"

"Don't worry pet, I'll be fine. Did I mention about the young fellah I'd like you to meet?" he said trying to change the topic.

"No. and matchmaking at a time like this, really?" she sighed.

"No, it's nothing like that" he lied, "it's just that he has a keen interest in reptiles and would love to hear about your work with the dragons. Honest, will you meet him?".

"Loves reptiles does he? We'll see. But are you sure I can't come with you?".

Not this time, I'm only going for a chat. It'll be fine really, I promise".

"I hope so" said Rebe, leaving the Fat Wizard to worry about what he was actually getting into. So much concern for his wellbeing was starting to play on his nerves.

As promised, Ed was outside the shop bright and early next morning, "Mornin FW", he said, helping him up onto the carriage.

"Mornin' Ed", he replied as he got comfortable, well as comfortable as you can get on a wooden bench on a cart converted into a taxi. He waved back to his wife and daughter as they stood in the doorway of the shop. They were both smiling but he could clearly see the concern on their faces as Ed urged Clara on.

The village was really quiet at this unearthly hour of the morning so the trip started uneventfully but this changed dramatically as they hit the main Swansea to Llanelli road. Motorists, on such an early commute were unaccustomed to the delay being caused by a horse and cart and were impatiently trying to overtake at every opportunity. Many were beeping their horns or shouted angrily through their car windows. Ed being an ex-Llanelli taxi driver and Clara having been raised in Pant y Gussett took it all in their stride. They both had endured far more distractions than a few angry motorists could provide. Once they reached Llanelli things got quieter. Slow moving traffic was the norm in the town centre and the people they passed hardly even looked up at them. Llanelli was no Pant y Gussett but it had enjoyed its own fair share of weirdness over the years. So, a horse and cart sporting a large "Dees Taxi Hire" sign was hardly breaking news.

At the train station the Fat Wizard blessed Rebe for sorting out all the return tickets on the internet the night before and printing out a list of instructions on what to do. He boarded the train.

As a young man he had travelled quite extensively, but once he had married and opened his shop he hardly ever left the village and of the few times that he did, for holidays, magical conferences and the like, he always had either family or other wizards with him. Being on his own he felt very conspicuous, almost like everyone was staring at him. At one point he convinced himself that all the other passengers had somehow become aware of how much his trousers were beginning to chafe.

After the relatively short trip from Llanelli to Swansea station, the Fat Wizard managed to negotiate his way through the platforms to finally board the Swansea to London Paddington train, knowing that he had three and a half hours or so to ponder over what he was going to say at the offices of Sweetman and Brimstone.

As he entered the carriage he was delighted to immediately find an empty quartet of seats all sharing a table. He managed to squeeze himself in to the window seat facing the length of the carriage. The table had a Formica top which he found reminiscent of the picnic table his parents would take with them on family days out. Unfortunately, due to the fixed seats this one threatened to cut off the circulation to his midriff so while the carriage was still relatively empty, and making sure that no one was looking, he opened his satchel and putting his hand on his wand, whispered an incantation which reduced the width of the table by a good six inches allowing him to breathe in comfort.

The next ten minutes saw a surge of people getting on the train filling it to near capacity. An elderly couple joined the Fat Wizard in the seats opposite. They were of an age where good manners had been instilled in them both. They asked if the seats were taken before sitting in them and offered a warm "hello, lovely morning isn't it".

As they got settled a young man in a black "hoodie" proclaiming some band's love for Satan on the chest and "UK TOUR DATES" on the back, sat next to him. The Fat Wizard could not help but stare at his black denim jeans that seemed to have more slashes in them than actual material.

"I wonder if he's poverty stricken or had a violent altercation with a lawn mower" he mused to himself.

"What you staring at grandad!", said the boy aggressively.

As he stared at the Fat Wizard, the Fat Wizard could see the pale, pockmarked face and pinched expression of a would-be thug, that he imagined a lot of people would naturally like to smack.

"Actually", he replied coldly, "I have yet to enjoy the blessing of grandchildren and as to what I am staring at I fear the descriptive vocabulary for your appearance would be far beyond your comprehension".

"Uh" said the lad.

"Precisely!" said the Fat Wizard, who turned to the couple opposite that seemed alarmed at the minor exchange, and said, "please be at ease there is nothing to fear here".

The young lad knew that he had been insulted but had enough sense to realise that this strange, fat old man was not someone to mess with, so with a mumbled "Whatever" fumbled under his hood for a pair of earphones and played with his mobile phone while listening to something he considered to be music.

The train pulled out of the station and for the next few miles the Fat Wizard enjoyed the various "snapshots" of Wales' industrial heritage that can't really be appreciated by road. That is, of course, until you reach Port Talbot where the giant steelworks remind you, like a smack across the face with an old kipper, and just as smelly, that Wales is still a world contender in innovation and manufacturing. Only a few miles further on and the scenery reverts to panoramic views of sea and greenery.

As the Fat Wizard and indeed the elderly couple opposite relaxed into the journey they were becoming increasingly aware of an irritating background noise that overrode the rhythmic sound of the wheels on the track. A tinny sound of drums, bass and what could only be described as the sound a walrus would make while undergoing genital mutilation, all coming from beneath the obnoxious youngster's hood. Things got considerably worse as the lad tried to sing along, out of key and emphasising some of the more "colourful" words of the track.

Annoying as the Fat Wizard found it, he could see that it was really starting to offend the poor old dear opposite, who was desperately trying to prevent her increasingly looking frail husband from intervening.

Giving the couple his best "Don't worry" smile the Fat Wizard again reached into his satchel for his wand and whispered another incantation.

Instantly the lad started stabbing buttons on his phone, his face a picture of confusion and disgust. He looked accusingly at the people around the table.

The elderly couple tried to avoid eye contact, though in all fairness the husband did display some defiance. The Fat Wizard just smirked.

The boy resorted to smacking his phone on the table but apparently to no avail. Eventually he tore the headphones off his head and thumped them down onto the table shouting "Bloody thing" where to the couples' delight, all that could be heard was the easy listening strains of Mantovani.

The mood around the table improved as the obnoxious youth disembarked at Bristol still furiously shouting expletives at his phone. As the train pulled away the old man opposite leant forward and with a beaming smile said,

"I don't know how you did, it but I'm sure you had something to do with putting a stop to that awful racket, thank you.

"I'm sure I don't know what you mean", replied the Fat Wizard with a wink, "my name is FW, just FW are you going to London too?"

"Yes we are, FW. My name is Dennis and this lovely young lady is my wife Peg".

Like him, his lovely young wife couldn't have been a day under seventy. But where she looked spry and fit, Dennis had the sallow countenance of a man struggling with great pain.

"So" smiled the Fat Wizard, "are you on one of these sightseeing weekends I've heard so much about?"

"No afraid not" said Peg her voice breaking a little, as if she was on the edge of crying, "Dennis has got an appointment with a specialist about his headaches".

"Hush woman", said Dennis gently, "we don't want to bore the poor man with our problems".

"Headaches, what sort of headaches?" enquired the Fat Wizard leaning forward, obviously concerned.

"He's been having them for months and they're getting worse", said Peg, now on the verge of tears. "The doctors have done all the tests they can and can't find what's causing them. They recommended we see a specialist but they didn't sound very confident".

Sitting back in his seat and stroking his beard, the Fat Wizard looked Dennis straight in the eyes and said,

"Dennis, I know we have only just met but I want you to look at me closely and answer me this, do you trust me?

Dennis stared at the Fat Wizard for a few moments and replied,

"Yes, I don't why but I do, I trust you completely".

"Peg do you feel the same?" said the Fat wizard taking her hand.

"Yes I do", she said with a faint smile.

"Good, first of all I am not making any promises you understand but there is a slim chance that I might be able to help. Secondly a train carriage is hardly the right place for what I propose so I beg you to be discreet and not attract any attention to us. Lastly, and this is the most important thing, in a minute I will be pulling out a... er...stick from my bag and Dennis I want you to hold the end of it with both hands. Whatever happens you must promise not to let go. Letting go of it while in the middle of the procedure could harm us both, do you understand?"

Dennis nodded in agreement.

"Now Peg, do you understand whatever happens you must not interfere?".

"I won't, I promise".

"Right", said the Fat Wizard getting the wand from his

bag," hold this and just relax".

Dennis held the other end of the wand and just as he was starting to feel a bit silly about the whole thing he felt the wand getting warm. A moment or two later and he started to feel pins and needles shooting up his arms, then a jolt as he felt as if someone else had joined him deep inside himself. He fleetingly wondered if this was what it was like to be possessed, like in those horror films he secretly watched when Peg was out.

The Fat Wizard closed his eyes in concentration and pushed his will forward through the wand, "Contact" he smiled to himself as visions of a little boy being born filled his head. Quickly the visions moved on, the infant became a schoolboy, the schoolboy became a teenager, the teenager a graduate, then a young man in uniform, "oh so you were a fireman" mused the Fat Wizard, still the visions continued, a wedding, "Peg was quite a stunner" he noticed as rapid images of a young Dennis pulling people out of burning buildings flashed past him, then a party, no a retirement party and then he was firmly in Dennis's head.

Not in Dennis's brain as such, after all the Fat Wizard was not a doctor and wouldn't really know his way round anatomically, but using magic he could navigate his way round a psychic representation of a brain. As he walked through the inner pathways of Dennis's head he could see the still images of all the major events of the life that just passed before him. As he turned a corner he could see an image of Dennis at a christening looking as he looked today, albeit with a bit more vitality, and there right in front of him a large black pulsating blob. This throbbing mass was starting to send out tendrils to intercept the spaces left to be filled in Dennis's mind.

"Gotcha!", said the Fat Wizard drawing on strength from his body, "let's see how you like this!", he said as he directed a stream of flame into the offending tumour. Seconds later all sign of the mass was gone, nothing but a little wisp of smoke to tell of its existence at all.

The Fat Wizard gently retreated from Dennis and flowed back into his own head, where quite frankly his body had missed him.

Gently pulling the dazed Dennis's hands off the wand, he replaced it back into his bag and retrieved the sandwiches Mrs FW had prepared for the trip.

"AAAAh" he said, "I don't know about you but I'm starving after that. Let's see what we got. My Mrs always makes far more than I can manage. Ham and pickle anyone?".

Peg took the offered sandwich, stared dimly at it for a second then slowly looked up at the Fat Wizard and said,

"What just happened?"

"Something wonderful", Dennis interrupted, "my headache's completely gone, there's no pain".

"How?", asked Peg looking really confused.

"Yes", echoed Dennis to the Fat Wizard "How?".

"Oh you wouldn't believe me if I told you, but suffice it to say you are completely healed. May I suggest you enjoy your sandwich and plan a lovely little weekend break while you're in London. You can use the money you have saved by not needing to pay the specialist anymore".

"We will. Thank you so much FW, we owe you everything", said Peg unable to stop the tears of relief that were streaming down her face.

"Oh, there is a catch", said the Fat Wizard smiling.

"Oh, what's that?", said Dennis suddenly looking worried.

"If we meet on the train on the way home, the sandwiches are on you!".

The rest of the journey to London was spent in idle gossip and some snoozing, with Dennis and Peg able to enjoy each other's company again without the dark cloud that had been hanging over them for so long.

Exhausted after the morning's events, as the train pulled in to Paddington station the Fat Wizard decided against changing trains and all that hassle, so opted instead for a black cab.

16. ALL I REALLY WANTED WAS A CUP OF TEA.

Over in Mayfair, at about the same time as the Fat Wizard was enjoying his excursion into Dennis's mind, Mr Sweetman and Mr Brimstone were barking orders to Miss Jones about being in conference and on no account were they to be disturbed, as they stormed into Brimstones' office.

Closing the door behind them, Mr Sweetman turned to Mr Brimstone, who had already made himself comfortable behind the large oak desk at the end of the room and asked,

"Why so nervous Ritchie? it's not like you to get the jitters before a meeting".

"I know", replied Ritchie, "it's just that I've heard a lot of stories about this Fat Wizard bloke",

"As indeed I suspect he has heard about us", Sweetman interrupted, "and who do you think sounds the most frightening?", he smiled through tight lips.

"You're right of course Adam, but still, I think we should be careful with this one".

"And being careful is why we've arranged a surprise for him and invited some "guests to the meeting this afternoon, isn't it?", he said as he poured them both a small scotch from a well-stocked cabinet against the wall, "and let's use the boardroom again, our offices are a little bit too cosy".

"So, what are we going to say to him?", said Brimstone gently swirling the honey coloured ambrosia around the glass between sips.

"Nothing" said Sweetman, his smile becoming more reptilian by the second, "we'll let him have his five minutes in the sun so that he feels he has done something, and hopefully he'll leave".

"And if he doesn't?"

"Then we'll just have to persuade him that it would be in his "personal best interest" to go back to his wife and family and forget the whole thing".

"Personal best interest" mused Brimstone as he took another sip of scotch, "how often did we used to use that phrase back in the old days?". Whether it was the scotch or whether it was hearing that old phrase again, his mind wandered back to how their empire had started.

With their new found freedom from borstal they'd decided to rent a small office in London's east end and set up a small insurance company. It was a fairly unusual company in that it had specialised in personal safety insurance against physical attacks and muggings amongst local small business owners, and nothing else. "Personal best interest" was the most used selling point when interviewing new clients. Those who turned them down would, after a brief stay in hospital, often return to take out a policy. Over the next few years other "outfits" tried to muscle in on their business. These were all sorted out quite quickly, usually by the "crowbar and hammer" method as the boys liked to call it.

Some of these rivals opted to join Sweetman and Brimstones' company rather than relying on sickness benefit for the rest of their lives and so the business thrived. As their insurance business grew so they moved into larger offices in the more opulent south of London where they opened up into the more legitimate arm of the insurance game. This respectable front afforded the opportunity to expand into other enterprises such as building supplies and construction. Their ability to win contracts for large projects, despite not offering the cheapest tenders, was a matter of some concern but mysteriously no one had made a fuss about it. Occasionally some owners of rival companies might start to raise an objection in the right quarters but oddly enough they all took early retirement. The only thing that these men had in common is that they were all family men, a fact that did not go unnoticed among their peers.

With so many well-paying construction projects on the go, the boys decided to go into plant hire, earning even greater profits renting bulldozers, cranes and other heavy machinery to their own companies at inflated prices, the extra cost of which was later born by the customer under separate negotiations.

The plant hire was not without its problems. A rival plant company owner did start asking awkward questions and began making a nuisance of himself through the courts. His name was Emrys David Walters, a bear of a man who had worked his way up from being a simple labourer at a small building firm in Wrexham to owning his own nationwide plant hire company. He was a hard drinking, hardworking and hard fighting man's man, so much so that his employees nicknamed him "Dai Hard". The problem for Mr Sweetman and Mr Brimstone was that he was a single man with no kids or other family to speak of. However, fortune did smile on the lads after managing to pick up "Dai Hards" company for a song after he went missing, having last been seen inspecting the concrete foundations of a large hotel in Reading that he was constructing.

"Dai, is certainly hard now" Brimstone smiled to himself as Sweetman jolted him from his trip down memory lane with,

"Another scotch?"

"No thanks, I think I'd better keep a clear head for this afternoon",

"Fair enough, early lunch then? I've heard of a new Italian that's just opened" said Sweetman clapping his hands together in anticipation.

"I could go for some pasta" said Brimstone rising from his chair, "besides it's your turn to pay", and following Sweetman out of the office he couldn't help but shake the feeling that his partner should be taking this afternoon's meeting a bit more seriously.

Having arrived in Mayfair a lot earlier than he expected to, the Fat Wizard spent some time wandering around and admiring the architecture. Eventually he came across one of the famous coffee places, "Costbucks" or something, that he'd so often heard about on television and thought that a nice cup of coffee while sitting in the nearby park, which he had already checked was only a short walk to his appointment, would be a pleasant way of wasting an hour or two.

He joined the queue of people waiting to be served at the counter and then looked at the list of options available. He looked again. "What language is this?" he thought to himself. As far as he was concerned there should only be four options, black, black with sugar, white and white with sugar, yet before him was a menu with a whole host of terms he didn't understand and not once did it mention milky coffee with sugar. When it was his turn to approach the rather beleaguered, but pretty and somehow smiling girl serving behind the counter he found himself sheepishly asking,

"I just wanted a milky coffee please?"

"A latte?" she replied.

"No not a lot" he replied, "one cup will do, thank you dear",

"One milky coffee it is then", she replied with a giggle.

The Fat Wizard took the coffee but decided against asking for sugar. He wasn't sure how but he felt he had already made a bit of a fool of himself and didn't want to compound it by finding out there was more than one type of sugar!

Grateful that it wasn't raining, he took his unsweetened beverage to the park and found a bench near a tree where he could watch the squirrels and the birds and relax before his meeting.

Not wanting to be late, and certainly not wanting to be too early, the Fat Wizard managed to time his entrance into the offices of P.E.E.O.F.F. LTD at a perfect five to two. Walking the length of the reception he approached the stern but attractive looking woman at the main desk. He instantly recognised her as the woman he had seen in the pub in Pant y Gussett with what he now presumed were Mr Sweetman and Mr Brimstone.

"Hello" he said in a polite and friendly voice, "I have an appointment with Mr Sweetman and Mr Brimstone at two o'clock".

"And you are?" she enquired formally.

"FW, just FW".

"Ah yes Mr FW, they are expecting you, please follow me and I'll take you straight. up to the boardroom".

Once at the boardroom door Miss Jones knocked twice and without waiting for a reply, she opened the door and stood aside to allow the Fat Wizard to enter. No sooner was he through the door than he heard a clunk as Miss Jones immediately shut the door behind him and headed back to her desk

17. ALL THAT SHIVERS IS NOT COLD.

Dusting the shelves frantically trying to keep herself busy, Mrs FW glanced up at the clock on the wall of the shop and noticed it was nearly two o'clock. "He must be in with them by now" she thought to herself nervously, grateful of the distraction of the bell as two men entered the shop. It was not unusual to have "outsiders" visit the shop; indeed the shop could not survive on the business of the villagers alone so strangers were always welcome.

"Afternoon" she greeted them,

"Good afternoon" one of the men replied smiling, "just browsing.

"Feel free" she replied in a friendly voice, slightly concerned that these two weren't your normal tourists. Both men wore similar clothes, black jeans, black sweatshirts and black woollen caps covering their hair and most of their faces. She estimated that they were both in their late twenties, both were big not just tall but wide, and had a distinct aggressive attitude despite the smiles. The only thing that really set them apart was that one of them wore a thick gold chain bracelet on his left wrist. She decided to keep a close eye on them as they walked around the shop.

For a few minutes the men shadowed each other as they went around the shop intently reading all the labels on the potions and other products for sale, then they split up and one of them started looking at things on the counter, right in front of Mrs FW partially obscuring the view of the other man. He had gone over to the shop window seemingly interested in the pots, pans and other crockery displayed there.

"On your own luv?" asked the man in front of her, grinning widely,

"No, my husband's in the back room" she replied, with warning bells as loud as a cathedral's going off in her head.

"That's funny, I heard he was in London" he said, all pretence of a smile fading. "Why don't you call him?".

No sooner had the words left his mouth there was a large crash behind him. She moved to the end of the counter as the other man exclaimed, "Oops butterfingers", as he looked down at the mess on the floor that once was a very ornamental teapot. Smiling menacingly, he then proceeded to pick up a large decorative vase and started to juggle it from hand to hand. "Hope I'm more careful with this one", he said in a tone that suggested he wouldn't be.

"OI, PUT THAT DOWN!" shouted Mrs FW, furious.

"Or?", said the man in front of her, himself picking up a box of FW's specially made cough drops off the counter and tipping them over the floor.

"What do you mean OR, have you any idea who my husband is?"

"As it happens, we do", said the man in the window dropping the vase on the floor and picking up another. "Our employers thought it would be nice to arrange a little "surprise" for him for when he gets home. Just to show they're thinking of him sort of thing".

Incensed, Mrs FW flew out from behind the counter to stop the man smashing any more of her work.

Unfortunately, her way was blocked by the other one who stood right in front of her with his balled fists on his hips as if daring her to try and pass him. Instinctively Mrs FW kicked up with her right foot, right between the thug's legs with enough force to be the envy of any Welsh rugby player trying a conversion. The man exhaled heavily, his eyes crossed and he bent over double. As he did, she picked up a heavy pot from the counter and smashed it firmly over the back of his head. As he fell to the floor Mrs FW heard a mighty CRACK, and looked up to see the other man sprawled out on the floor and standing over him stood Downwind Jones with his shovel still raised.

"So what's all this then?" he asked, "I heard all the pots smashing from outside an' I thought I'd better see if you was alright".

"I am now, thank you Downwind, I owe you".

"So who are they and what did they want?" asked Downwind.

"They work for the men who run the mines. I think they were sent as a warning to FW not to interfere".

"OOH, he's gonna be pis… sorry, cross when he gets back, what do you want do with them?".

"We'll have to keep them here somehow. I think my husband is going to want to talk to them when he gets back".

"Cor I wouldn't like to be in their shoes",

"Nor would I! Look I've had an idea, could you keep an

eye on them for a minute while I get Rebe. She's in the dragon pens somewhere?",

"Sure thing Mrs FW",

"The names Jean, Downwind. Mind you after today you can call me anything you like" she giggled.

True to her word Mrs FW returned a few minutes later with Rebe in tow, obviously furious about the attack on her mother.

"Did they give you any trouble while I was gone?", she asked.

"One did start to come around", said Downwind, who pointing at a new dent in his shovel continued, "but no, no trouble at all", he grinned.

"Good" chuckled Mrs FW, "now do you mind giving me a hand? Rebe's had a good idea for them".

Sometime later the two thugs started to regain consciousness, one complaining of a headache, the other less concerned about the headache as much as the sickening pain in his nether regions. As their senses slowly started to return, they noticed that not only were they tied up but they were also sitting in a large wire cage, a bit like a dog run. Actually, it was a row of cages and they appeared to be in the middle one. They could just make out some dark shapes shuffling about in the cages each side of them.

"Ah gentlemen, you are awake", said Rebe sitting on a small wooden stool facing their enclosure. "Now before you say anything let me draw your attention to the occupants of the cages each side of you", she said quietly but obviously enjoying herself. "These are dragons that I hatched a few weeks ago and being so young they are really quite nervous and tend to flame at anything that startles them. May I suggest that for the sake of your safety you do not move around or make any noise. I fear that my father would be cross with me were anything happen to you before he has a chance to make your acquaintance and "discuss" the events in his shop earlier."

"Let me out!", growled one of the thugs, struggling to get to his feet instantly sitting back down as he noticed several reptilian heads whip round in his direction.

"Ooh, I'm afraid you'll have to be quieter than that", said Rebe glaring at the man whose face had now gone quite pale. "Please remember what I've told you, I've got to go now and I don't really want to have to scrape up your ashes when I get back. See you later......maybe", and with a malevolent grin Rebe left to check on her mother.

Back in the shop, Rebe found her mother frantically sweeping up all the debris off the floor,

"You OK mam?" she asked. "Don't worry about those two, they're not going anywhere in a hurry".

"I'm OK thanks love, but I'm really worried about your father now, and what he might do to those men when he gets his hands on them".

☐

18. ARE YOU CERTAIN?

The Fat Wizard stood by the door of the boardroom and quickly took in his surroundings. There at the end of the table in front of him sat two men, both had cropped hair and diamond studs in their ears. Judging by the broken noses and cauliflower ears he presumed they were not strangers to fighting. They were wearing expensive suits that did little to hide their barrel chests and prop forward shoulders and with the swallow tattoos just visible above the collar and the love and hate written on their fingers he knew they weren't exactly church going charity workers. In fact, he wouldn't have been surprised if they both had labels somewhere on them saying, "Goons R Us".

At the far end of the room sitting at the other end of the table, were the two suits he had seen in the pub that Sunday morning. They both stood up and one of them said,

"Mr FW, please come and join us. I'm Mr Sweetman", said the thicker set of the two, "and this is my partner Mr Brimstone. Do take a seat", he said without indicating which one.

"Please, just call me FW, I'm pleased to meet you", said the Fat Wizard walking confidently down the length of the room and pulling out a seat on the side of the table close to Mr Brimstone.

As he sat down, he noticed a man sitting in a chair away from the table next to the window. He was totally bald, clean shaven and was resting his chin on steepled fingers as if in prayer. He was wearing some sort of black satin tunic fastened by black bows up the front and so far, had not shown any acknowledgement of the Fat Wizard's arrival at all. Something about this man bothered the Fat Wizard. He could sense strong magic coming from this man, maybe stronger than his own.

"Now Mr, sorry just FW", said Sweetman as he and his partner sat back down, "how can we help you?"

"Well", said the Fat Wizard noticing that the introductions hadn't been extended as far as the goons or the mysterious figure opposite him. "I'm from a village called Pant y Gussett",

"Yes we know of it" interrupted Brimstone sounding bored, "and?".

"Well" continued the Fat Wizard feeling his hackles rising, "I gather you are preparing a "fracking" operation up at the old mines".

"Yes, what of it?" replied Brimstone his disinterested tone now changing to one of mild annoyance.

"I would like you to stop. There have already been some incidents such as tremors that have damaged properties in the village, and we have evidence of some pollution affecting the water table".

"And what exactly makes you think that has anything to do with us?", said Sweetman politely.

"It would seem more than a coincidence that these things start happening just as you start drilling and digging, don't you think?", said the Fat Wizard firmly, "and besides I've done a lot of research into this "fracking" and it is pretty clear that if you carry on, the situation will get considerably worse".

"Mere conjecture" tutted Brimstone, "where is your proof. You can't just go around making accusations about the so-called damage done by fracking without cold hard proof".

"By the time I could "prove" it, the damage could be immeasurable, do you realise that apart from the villagers there are many rare species of plants and animals that live in the area, not to mention the ancient races, some of which are not found anywhere else on the planet?" said the Fat Wizard trying desperately not to shout. "Who said you could work the mines anyway? You certainly didn't have the permission of the village elders of which I am one".

"Ah, now there you raise an interesting point", said Sweetman with a confident sneer, "Mr Brimstone would you be so kind as to pass the relevant documents to FW here for his perusal?" Brimstone dutifully opened a blue cardboard folder and took some official looking documents out of it and slid them unceremoniously across the desk to the Fat Wizard.

"Now as you can see," continued Sweetman," these are the legal title deeds to the mines, as ratified by the village elders many years ago. You see, we were able to track down the descendants of the original owner who had emigrated to the United States after the mines had become uneconomical. The original owner had thought the property to be worthless but nonetheless the deeds were passed down from generation to generation until, and at great expense I may add, we found the current heir. Fortunately for us, but not so much for him, he had fallen on hard times, unemployed and living in a trailer park near the Texas border he was delighted when we offered him an er... fair price for the deeds. Indeed, I believe he managed to purchase a second-hand pick-up truck with the money we paid him".

Sweetman stood and pointed at the documents and said, "So you see FW, we are well within our rights to work our own mines".

The Fat Wizard went through the documents with a fine-tooth comb but was dismayed to find that they appeared to be all in order. He was no legal expert but even he could tell good money had been spent on their preparation so proof of their ownership of the mine was pretty certainly airtight.

Sitting back in his chair he pondered for a moment then leant forward again "OK ". he said, "I get it you own the mines but there must be hundreds of licences, applications and planning requirements you would need before you were allowed to even survey the area let alone start operations there, surely?"

"I wondered when you were going to get to that," smiled Sweetman still standing but now crossing his arms and exchanging knowing winks with Brimstone. "You see, over the past few years we have spent a great deal of money employing a legal team to look into exactly what we need to get permission for fracking in Pant y Gussett and do you know what they found?", he paused to pour himself a glass of mineral water, an obvious ploy to increase the tension. "Nothing. No license, no applications and certainly no planning requirements and shall I tell you why?".

The Fat Wizard sat bolt upright in his chair taken aback by the confidence and arrogance being displayed in Sweetman's speech.

"It appears, he continued, "that the good people of Pant y Gussett, have declared themselves to be an independent state, a medieval sort of republic if you will, and as such do not pay any taxes to the Crown. Furthermore, none of the residents appear on the national census, you don't even appear on any official maps. As far as the UK government is concerned, you don't even exist, therefore you are not under any UK jurisdiction, which also means that you are not protected by any UK legislation. To put it bluntly FW, we can do whatever the hell we like and there is nothing you can do about it!".

Sweetman retook his seat and dismissively swivelled round to face away from the Fat Wizard, an obviously previously arranged cue for Brimstone to take over.

Brimstone sat upright in his chair and with a smug grin, looked straight at the Fat Wizard and said, "Now FW, we have gone to great pains to clarify our position and as you are up to date with the situation, I suggest you leave" and turning to the goons at the end of the table who had sat passively throughout the proceedings said, "Bertram, Earnest, would you be so good as to escort our "guest" off the premises please".

"HOLD", shouted the Fat Wizard, jumping to his feet and staring at Brimstone, while at the same time extending his left arm in the direction of the two hired "Gorillas". They both slammed back into their seats, sinews and muscles straining to no avail, as they tried to get back up out of their chairs.

"You may well be right that we don't come under the protection of UK law, but as for not being able to do anything about it, I assure you that we can, and we will, protect our village!".

"Please calm yourself FW", said the strange man from the corner, "this is hardly the place for parlour tricks. Be so kind as to let the poor men go. I will vouch for their behaviour, he said in a gentle soothing voice.

"And you are? demanded the Fat Wizard who did not appreciate his magic as being described as a "parlour trick".

"I am Surten"

"Certain of what exactly", said the Fat Wizard who judged that by the shape of the eyes and the hint of an accent, that this man was of oriental descent.

"My name is "SURTEN"" he corrected, with a slight look of exasperation that quickly faded into a self-assured smile. "As you may have guessed I am not from around here so I forgive you for not having heard of me, but you, you I have heard of, indeed you seem to enjoy quite a reputation in certain circles".

Surten rose to his feet gracefully, so gracefully in fact that the movement somehow didn't seem natural. He was tall and slim; his satin robes went from the floor right up to a high collar that stopped just under his chin. The Fat Wizard could sense great age in this man, yet his eyes were bright blue and his complexion was flawless almost like a porcelain doll's. The Fat Wizard knew that his appearance was magically enhanced and was slightly envious that it made his best anti-wrinkle creams look about as effective as one of those overpriced brands available from all good chemists. The only thing that let this youthful facade down was his hands Each finger was adorned with large silver rings all embellished with mystic symbols, worryingly symbols unfamiliar to the Fat Wizard. His hands were extremely wrinkled and had prominent blue veins and liver spots. His nails were long and filed to sharp points. These were the hands you would expect to see on an old crone, the sort that followed the darker side of the "craft".

"Now FW, if I may be so bold," he continued, "I suspect you have achieved all that you can from this meeting. May I suggest that you follow me downstairs for a walk around the park where we can continue this discussion in a civilized manner?".

Without waiting for an answer, Surten walked, well more like flowed, you couldn't see his legs moving beneath his robe, behind Sweetman and Brimstone both of whom sat back quietly in their chairs obviously happy for Surten to take the lead, then behind the Fat Wizard and headed for the door.

He held the door open and looked back expectantly at him, "Oh, and please?" he said, pointing at the two thugs. They were now swearing so badly as they strained against the chairs that they could shame a drunken carpenter after an errant hammer blow to the thumb.

Though still angry, the Fat Wizard found himself

compelled to follow Surten. He knew he had to find out more about this mysterious character and what his involvement in all this was. With a curt, "Gentlemen, we will meet again", to Sweetman and Brimstone, both of which ignored him, he went to leave the boardroom after Surten.

He paused momentarily at the door, and with a small hand gesture shouted, "RELEASE" at the two stricken men. Suddenly freed from their invisible shackles both men sprung up out of their seats, caught their knees on the edge of the table and both fell over, spouting in between groans, a fresh tirade of abuse against the Fat Wizard.

It was a silent walk to the park. Neither men exchanged a word until they found a quiet, tree lined path with no one else in ear shot. Unable to contain his curiosity any longer the Fat Wizard turned to his strange companion and asked,

"So what's your involvement with those two jokers then?".

"Ah, direct, I like that", said Surten. "I do some er… "consultancy work for them. They call me in when they encounter certain problems that they feel they can't handle. Perhaps you could think of me as a sort of a "trouble shooter" if you like".

"And what trouble have you been asked to shoot this time? if you don't mind me asking," said the Fat Wizard flippantly.

"Actually, they haven't given me many details yet, I only arrived a few minutes before you. All I have been told is that they wanted me to attend the meeting this afternoon and said they might have need of my "talents", nothing more".

"'Talents", meaning your magic, I presume."

"How very astute", smile Surten.

"Sarcasm?" wondered the Fat Wizard. "And what do they use your talents for exactly?".

"Oh. all manner of things, my work for them can be very varied, I think that's why I enjoy working for the likes of them. It's never dull. I hate tedium, don't you?".

"Tedium can be preferable, in my humble opinion. It depends what the alternatives are. Did they give you any indication as to what they need your special talents for in this case?`` asked the Fat Wizard.

Conversation was paused for a moment while they waited until an approaching mother and her young child walking hand in hand had passed by. There was a slight delay as right in front of them the mother stopped and, as mothers do all over the country, discreetly spat into a handkerchief to wipe away a choc ice "moustache" from the complaining toddler before moving on.

"The coast's now clear", Surten replied,

"Well, they didn't say much but they did mention needing some protection".

"From who? the Fat Wizard asked, the penny not dropping.

"From you my dear fellow, from you". Said Surten with a wide smile.

Confused, the Fat Wizard said, "So if they were so worried about me, why did they allow me to arrange a meeting with them?

"You still don't get it, do you? The meeting wasn't arranged for you to meet them. Far from it. The meeting was arranged so that I could meet you".

"I see", said the Fat Wizard finally getting the point, "and now you've met me are you going to take the job?".

"I don't know yet", said Surten sounding genuinely unsure. "I am going to have to think long and hard about this. The only thing that I am sure of is that if I do take this job my fee will be…. considerable".

"Trust me", said the Fat Wizard getting really annoyed about this veiled threat, "no amount of money will make crossing me worthwhile!".

"We shall see what we shall see", said Surten philosophically.

"We shall indeed. Meanwhile" said the Fat Wizard, "where the hell are you from? I cannot place your clothing or your accent".

"Dudley, North Yorkshire, and before you ask, my parents ran a Chinese take away there".

"Oh I see" replied the Fat Wizard stifling a chuckle, "so are you registered with the "Old Cows" … er I mean the

Council of Wizards?".

"I was, years ago but I chose a different path. I'm not one for rules and regulations. It's not so...profitable".

"So really you're not much more than a mercenary, a "wand" for hire so to speak".

"Nothing so crass FW. I consider myself a specialist, an expert in my field paid good money by large corporations for services rendered, no more no less".

"As I said, a mercenary". The Fat Wizard was enjoying the effects that his comments were having on his, so far, inscrutable companion. He knew that any weaknesses he could discover now may be invaluable if things turned ugly. "Well I really have enjoyed our little chat", he continued, "it has been quite illuminating. Unfortunately I have a long journey home ahead of me and I really should be going.

I sincerely hope that should we meet again it will be under more amiable circumstances, for your sake".

"A threat?" asked Surten.

"Interpret it as you will", smiled the Fat Wizard. "But I think you should know, I take any threat to the inhabitants of Pant y Gussett very seriously, and I also am happy to flout rules and regulations if I feel it justified. I also think that you should be aware that I am not alone, the villagers and our allies will unite against a common enemy and that is a force that could really ruin your day!".

"I must say, the passion with which you speak of this, Pant

y Gussett intrigues me. I most definitely will visit…. but under what circumstances still remains to be seen. Have a safe journey home my friend. Whatever happens I am sure our paths will cross again".

And with no further ado, Surten turned around and slowly headed back to the offices of P.E.E.O.F.F., leaving the Fat Wizard to exit the park and hail a cab back to the train station.

Walking back into the boardroom where an expectant Sweetman and Brimstone were still in conference, Surten walked over to his original seat, sat down and resumed his pose of resting his chin on his fingers and said quietly, "Gentlemen, you have a problem".

19. UNDERCOVER EH! GENTS?

Friday night was always a busy night in the Cross Inn and tonight was no exception. Downwind stood at the bar with Dai the Dwarf and Dug and regaled everyone with tales of his heroics earlier in the Fat Wizard's shop. As more and more people plied him for details, often accompanied by an offer of a "free pint", the more the story became embellished. Eventually the tale became a saga involving six men armed with knives and a detailed account of how he laid them all out single handedly saving Mrs FW's life.

"So where are they now", said Huw Puw, in his best official voice. "I think I had better put them in proper custody".

"Actually" said Downwind trying to find a way to save face, and keep the free drinks coming, "four of them managed to get away but I did manage to put two of them in one of Rebe's dragon pens. Besides where would you put them in "proper custody?"

"The elders did install a real jail cell in my office you know" said Huw indignantly.

"Ah yes" said Dug, knowing full well that the cell was only put in place to shut Huw up. "But that's where we store the tables, chairs, bunting and other decorations for village festivals, isn't it? Where could we put all that?".

"I'd leave them where they are". said Downwind, "They're

not going anywhere. Besides, I'm pretty sure FW will have some ideas what to do with them when he gets back, poor buggers".

"Hear hear", said Dai. "I almost feel sorry for them myself, almost" he laughed, ordering another round.

Meanwhile at the back of the pub, landlords Jack and Jason were looking confused and scratched their heads in puzzlement at the latest addition to the Cross. Ivor and Penny had approached them last week and asked if they could construct and install a pool table for free and just share the profits with them. They of course, happily agreed. They had given up their plans to make the pub more "sophisticated". Hell, nothing had worked so far, but they knew a good pool table could be a real money spinner. They had visions of it attracting new punters, perhaps even joining a local league to bring visitors from other pubs. This was going to be great!

However, they had not taken into account the fact that Ivor and Penny had hardly ever left Pant y Gussett let alone had much experience in other pubs and clubs, let alone bar games. So here they were completely dumbfounded, staring at a four-legged, six foot by four foot and three-foot-high wooden contraption containing a four-inch-deep recess across the top, filled with water and an array of different coloured balls floating in it.

"How about a quiz night?", sighed Jack.

"Look around, what do you think?" said Jason, dismayed.

"Aye fair enough, I see what you mean" replied Jack, who

went back to staring at his reflection in the waters of the "pool table".

"Hey, I've got it! said Jason suddenly, "what about speed dating nights, that'll bring the punters in!".

"Good idea", said Jack but no need to spill your drink over it!".

"I haven't got a drink.... oh bugger, the pool table's leaking!".

Back up in the mines things were quiet. Most of the men had finished for the day and had gone back to their respective bed and lodgings or hotels in Llanelli, depending on their pay grades. Except that is for young Jack Elias. Jack liked to make sure that all his tools were accounted for and tidied away before the weekend. He had been struggling to find his particularly expensive wire strippers which, like so many other things, had gone missing the day before. In desperation he decided to have a look in the gaffer's little prefabricated office that had been installed on some flat ground near one of the mine entrances. There he found Charles, his head in his hands staring at a closed box file.

"Oh, sorry to disturb you gaffer. I mean Charles, I was just looking for my wire strippers. Don't suppose you've seen them, have you?" he asked.

"Uh, no sorry", said Charles distractedly.

"Ok" said Jack, but as he turned to leave he looked back at Charles saying, "Why are you still here boss, there's nothing planned until Monday? You should go home and rest".

"Suppose so. It's just been a bit of a bad week, that's all, and I don't really feel like sitting in a small hotel room all weekend", said Charles.

Jack and the others had noticed that Charles had been acting a bit "odd" over the last couple of days. He hadn't made a major fuss when they found all the portaloos doors had been glued shut, nor had he reacted when the coffee machine had been filled with soil and the sugar had been replaced with salt. But seeing him looking this down worried him.

"Look", said Jack, "it's Friday night, why don't we walk down to the village and I'll let you buy me a pint. It's got to be better than sitting in here on your own".

Charles liked Jack. Apart from being a good electrician he also treated Charles with respect, unlike the rest of the workforce who seemed to argue with him at every turn.

"Go down to the village?" replied Charles, "I don't think I'd be very popular there. Thanks for the offer but I think I'd better give it a miss". He didn't tell Jack that he was afraid he might bump into Melanie and he really couldn't face her, not after walking out on her so suddenly without an explanation.

"Oh come on, I've met some of the locals and they seem really nice, "odd" but nice". Jack handed Charles his coat that had been hanging on a hook on the back of the office door, "I won't take no for an answer".

"Ok you're on" said Charles taking the coat. "But you're buying the second round" he said a bit more cheerfully. "Perhaps some company might do me some good at that", he thought.

A chilly breeze had sprung up as they made their way to the village, stopping to pay Eric with a packet of cheese and onion crisps on the way past of course, and they were delighted to see the welcoming lights and the sound of laughter coming from the Cross.

As they took their first steps inside the entire bar became deathly silent. Everyone was like statues, frozen in their tracks, drinks halted halfway from their mouths. One of the goblins dropped their fishing rod and a drunken elf slipped on the edge of his tankard and fell in (don't worry, Huw Puw fished him out, there were no elves injured in the writing of this book).

"What'll it be, my lovelies?" said Double Dee from behind the bar, ever the professional.

"Er… two pints of your best bitter please", said Jack self-consciously, leading Charles up to the counter. "Have we disrupted something", he asked.

"Maybe you have," said Dai, pointedly keeping Downwind between himself and the two men, "you're with the company working the mines aren't you?".

"Yes" said Charles, "what of it?".

"Well you've got a bloody nerve showing your faces in here after this afternoon", said Downwind, puffing his chest out.

"Why what happened this afternoon?" asked Charles, intimidated by Downwind and the mood of the rest of the patrons.

"You know damn well what happened", said Downwind. "It was your company that sent those two, er...I mean that group of thugs to threaten Mrs FW".

"I swear we don't know anything about it" said Jack sincerely, "Is Rebe, I mean are Mrs FW and her daughter alright?".

"Quite alright, thanks to me", said Downwind scanning the room to see where his next free pint was most likely to come from, "but good job I was there".

"I promise you all, Jack and I haven't left the mine all day, and we certainly wouldn't countenance violence against anyone, certainly not against women. Are you sure they were from the company?".

"Said so themselves, said it was a warning to FW not to interfere in your mines", said Downwind, loving being the centre of attention for a change.

"Where are they now?" asked Jack. "Have you called the police?".

"We don't have police, we have Huw. Besides I think you'll find they're sitting very quietly and behaving themselves until FW gets home", laughed Downwind quickly joined by the rest of the pub.

"What will he do to them", asked Charles nervously.

"I don't know" said Huw joining the conversation, "but knowing FW it'll be...imaginative".

"Right then!", shouted Double Dee, "I'm sure you all agree that these two gentlemen had no part in this afternoon's events. What say you let them buy a round for the pub and let them have their drinks in peace".

"Splendid idea" replied Downwind, quick to pass Double Dee his empty tankard before the bar got overwhelmed.

"Certainly "said Charles, thinking that this was going to be the most expensive "quiet drink" he'd ever had.

After paying his considerable bar bill, he noticed that most of the customers had suddenly gone from pints to large whiskeys, he and Jack found a quiet table to discuss what they had just heard.

The Fat Wizard had managed to find his way back into Paddington station and safely boarded his train. He was a bit concerned about the expense of using taxis instead of the buses and tube that he had originally planned for as a cheaper alternative to get back and fore from the train to Mayfair, but he was sure Jean would forgive him, considering everything.

As he settled down in his seat, he fished out his mobile phone to let the family know he was on his way. He hit the roof when Mrs FW related the details of the attack to him.

"Are you alright dear?" he asked going out of his mind with worry.

"I'm fine" she said, "though I am a bit shaken, but I don't know if it's because of those two monsters or whether it's finding out that Downwind is a hero!" she laughed. "So how did it go with you?" she asked.

FW quickly brought her up to speed about what Sweetman and Brimstone had said and then went on to tell her about Surten.

"So what do you think this Surten will do?", she asked.

"I'm not sure, he's certainly no angel but I don't believe he will be happy about thugs threatening helpless women",

"Oi, who are you calling helpless?".

"Sorry dear", he replied. "Nonetheless I suspect he would consider such behaviour as beneath contempt.

The Fat Wizard snoozed all the way back to Swansea where he got off the train and reasoned, "in for a penny in for a pound" and took another taxi back to Pant Gussett. As he left the car park he gave Eric a plastic cup full of jellied eels, as much out of curiosity as payment, that he had bought from a street vendor outside Paddington station. Eric ate the eels, cup and all, smacked his lips, belched in gratitude and ambled back down under the bridge. "Is there nothing he won't eat?" he thought to himself.

As he prepared for the long walk home, the Fat Wizard was delighted to see Ed pulling up in his horse drawn taxi,

"Thought you'd be getting in about now. I'm guessing you'd prefer a lift before it gets darker, you must be knackered.... Er I mean really tired by now!", said a smiling Ed.

"Thank you, Ed," he said, "but I think my day isn't quite over yet".

After a welcoming hug off Jean and Rebe he quickly, and gratefully, changed back into his comfortable robes, then sat down to a steaming hot mug of tea with extra sugars, Jean had really missed him, followed by a huge meal of steak and kidney pie and chips. After dinner he retired to his favourite chair and enjoyed a pipe full of tobacco. Feeling a bit calmer than he did before, he then ambled out over to the dragon pens.

The two men were both sitting in their cage, sweat pouring down their faces as the Fat Wizard approached them.

"Now gentlemen", he said, "what am I to do with you?".

Alongside the car park in Pant y Gussett is a small lake. Now you won't find much in the way of wildlife living on this stretch of water as it is inhabited by a particularly unsociable water sprite who has the terrible tendency to throw muddy stones and sticks from the bottom of the lake at anyone or anything passing by. The lake was imaginatively known by the locals as the "duck" pond.

At one end of the lake there are some open fields and tree lined spaces used by villagers and indeed some outsiders, as a "dogging" spot. Not "dogging" as with its seedy modern connotations, but dogging as a favoured place for people to let their pampered pooches run free.

The more observant visitor might notice the sudden addition of two new trees, both thicker and darker than the others and oddly, one sporting a thick gold bracelet hanging from a high branch. Both trees were positioned such as to attract the immediate attention of visiting male dogs determined to advertise their presence to others.

If it's at all possible, both these trees looked quite sad.

"Hmm, only a six month spell, I must be getting soft in my old age!", thought the Fat Wizard as he retired for bed.

Worn out after all the travelling the day before, the Fat Wizard was a few minutes late opening the shop the following morning. He was surprised to find that outside waiting for the door to be unlocked were a very sheepish looking Charles and Jack.

"Mind if we come in?", said Charles nervously.

"It is a shop and it is open", said the Fat Wizard, curtly.

"Thank you we will, look", Charles continued following the Fat Wizard to the counter, "we only found out about what happened here yesterday when we went to the pub last night, and we both needed for you to know that we had nothing to do with it".

"That's right", said Jack, "if we'd known what was planned we would have warned you, honest! We're both furious about it!".

"Thank you, gentlemen, I appreciate that", said the Fat Wizard softening his tone.

"Obviously", said Charles, "we will both be tendering our resignations from the company first thing Monday morning.

Rebe came down from upstairs, "I made you a cup of strong coffee Dad" she said, "you looked like you needed one".

"Thank you dear, let me introduce you to Charles and Jack, Jack is the young reptile keeper I told you about".

"From the mining company?", she said with her eyes narrowing and her fists balling.

"Yes dear, but they had nothing to do with yesterday's incident", he said quickly. "Far from it they are as upset as we are.

"Well Ok then. Hello, pleased to meet you", she said politely.

"P….p… pleased to meet you", said Jack a little too hastily, interrupting Charles' attempt to respond.

"Actually dear, would you be so kind as to fetch another two coffees for these gentlemen?", said the Fat Wizard, stroking his beard. "Milk and sugar? I thought we might have a little chat. Oh and Jack, if you have time afterwards perhaps Rebe might introduce you to her dragons.

"Why not, I've got a spare shovel", she grinned.

Armed with fresh coffee, the Fat Wizard took Charles and Jack into his workshop leaving Rebe to man the shop for a while.

Sitting on some rickety old stools around the workbench he clapped his hands together and said,

"Right then, you have both told me that you intend to resign from Sweetman and Brimstone first thing Monday, correct?",

"Most certainly", said Charles.

"Too right, added Jack, firmly.

"And would it be fair to say such resignations are likely to cause you some financial hardship, at least temporarily?".

"Well yes I suppose so", said Charles.

"So, may I suggest that you stay on with them, at least for a little while, while you line up other employment. And perhaps while you're still there you could act as my eyes and ears sort of thing, let me know what they're going to do next".

"Happily,", said Charles looking at Jack, "I've never liked those buggers anyway".

"Count me in", added Jack, I don't know them personally but after what they tried to do I'm happy to do my part".

"Excellent", said the Fat Wizard, "but be careful. I don't want you taking any risks, we've seen what they're capable of".

"I can already tell you", said Charles, "the survey work is almost complete, they will be starting the fracking in the next couple of weeks".

"Will they now", said the Fat Wizard stroking his beard again. He was about to say more when Rebe came in and said,

"Right Jack. I can't leave it any longer, the dragons won't clean themselves out you know" as she passed Jack a pair of asbestos coated gloves. "Put them on, you're going to need them", she laughed.

After Jack had followed Rebe, somewhat eagerly to the dragon pens, Charles followed the Fat Wizard back into the shop.

"What's the matter? said the Fat Wizard noting Charles' increasingly worried expression. "Having second thoughts?".

"...Er no, not at all, it's just that something else has just occurred to me".

"Well spit it out, perhaps I can help".

"It's just that... well... I", Charles stopped for a moment as if gathering his thoughts before continuing, "Did you know Evan Lewis?".

"Evan Lewis", repeated the Fat Wizard, "Melanie's late husband, yes I knew him. Not well but he always struck me as a decent sort, why?".

"Did you know that he used to work for Sweetman and Brimstone? In fact it was his job I was given after he died".

"No I did not know that, mind you villagers seldom talk about life "outside" so nothing odd about that. Why?

What are you getting at?".

"Well it's probably nothing but there were rumours that it was Mr Lewis who brought attention to the mines here in Pant y Gussett to Sweetman and Brimstone. Some people have said that it was his intention to survey the mines to see if there was any prospect of finding new seams of precious metals to reinvigorate the local economy. They say that Sweetman and Brimstone commissioned an exploratory survey and that found that the land was an excellent site for fracking. Apparently when Mr Lewis found out that they were going to invest in fracking and not mining he went berserk and threatened all sorts.

"So what exactly are you saying?", said the Fat Wizard.

"Well I have always known that my employers are not the nicest of people but I just presumed that to be successful you had to be hard and ruthless. After the stunt they pulled on you yesterday I am beginning to wonder just how bad they may be. You see it was the day after he had threatened them that he had the "accident"".

"I see", said the Fat Wizard. "Having met them I fear you could be right. Let's keep this to ourselves for now, but I'll certainly look into it".

"OK", said Charles turning to leave, "but how can I ever face Melanie and that wonderful lad of hers ever again?".

The Fat Wizard raised an eyebrow. He hadn't known that they had ever met and he sensed there was more to it. "Try not to worry" he said, "things have a way of working out for the best. By the way, and just out of curiosity, I see you're not wearing your wedding ring".

"Oh, it's just another thing that has gone missing. Trust me it's the least of my worries".

"Indeed" thought the Fat Wizard.

The shop was particularly quiet for a Saturday. In fact he had only one genuine customer, young Peter the farmhand. He had dashed in excitedly grinning from ear to ear.

"Have you got some more of that wonderful soap and toothpaste?" he asked.

"I take it worked and you managed to get a date with your young lady friend", said the Fat Wizard.

"I should say, had a fantastic night, if you know what I mean" then leaning forward he whispered conspiratorially. "Had an even better night with her sister last night and I got a date with Griff's daughter tomorrow".

"I see" said the Fat Wizard, "and shall I add some bruise liniment and some dentures to your order?".

"Sorry what… I mean why?", said Peter confused.

"Because I know all the fathers involved. If they find out what you're doing with their daughters, you're going to need all the help you can get!".

"Oh", replied Peter who thought for a second then continued, "What the hell, it's worth the risk", he said paying for the items before he bounced merrily out of the shop.

As he was locking up the shop a very animated Jack and Rebe came back in from the pens.

"That was amazing", he said to the Fat Wizard, excitedly, "Rebe is fantastic with them and she has said I can tag along this afternoon and help with releasing some of the maturing ones".

"Has she now", said the Fat Wizard smiling "Well you can't go lumbering young dragons all the way up those hills on an empty stomach. Rebe, go and ask your mother to set another place for lunch, I'm sure she won't mind. She's doing one of those famous hot pot inventions of hers and there's is always plenty spare".

"Thank you FW, if you're sure you don't mind, that sounds lovely". said Jack sounding like an excited puppy, "I haven't had a home cooked meal in weeks. By the way, Rebe showed me the pens that she locked those two thugs in. Dare I ask what became of them?".

The Fat Wizard smiled and said rather cryptically, "Let's just say that they have "branched" out into other forms of employment whilst they consider the error of their ways".

20. SPEED DATING?

It was later on in the afternoon, while having a little nap with Jasper curled up on his lap, that the Fat Wizard became aware of a strange buzzing noise. Tired as he was it took him a minute to realize someone was calling his mobile.

"FW" came a friendly voice, "how are you?".

"Oh it's you, Brian", said the Fat Wizard slowly regaining his senses. "I'm fine, and you?" he said, while Jasper grunted at having been disturbed.

"I'm doing well, thank you. I gather you caused a bit of a disturbance with our "friends" in London, yesterday".

"Not really a disturbance, just a little difference of opinion".

"What? Freezing two muscle bound goons to a chair? I think that counts as a disturbance".

"How on earth do you know about that, I haven't told anyone not even Jean. I didn't want to worry her, not after the day she had".

"Yes" said Brian, "I heard about that too, are Jean and Rebe alright?".

"Fortunately yes, have you been spying on us?"

"Nothing so dramatic", laughed Brian. "It appears we have a mutual acquaintance".

"Who?" asked the Fat Wizard mystified.

"A gentleman by the name of Surten".

"You're friends with Surten", exclaimed the Fat Wizard angrily.

"Good heavens no", said Brian. "Actually he's a client of mine. I look after his books which I don't mind telling you is not easy for a man in his particular line of work".

"So if he's just a client, how did the conversation about yesterday's meeting come up?", said the Fat Wizard who, in deference to their long standing friendship, tried not to sound suspicious.

"Actually, he rang me. It seems you made quite an impression on him. It appears he did a bit of digging into your background after you left and somehow found out about our friendship. He called me for some advice".

"And what did you tell him?".

"Only the truth. I told him you were the most powerful

wizard I'd ever met and if he valued his health, oh and keeping me as his accountant, he should stay out of it!".

"And his reply?".

"Well to be honest I think after meeting you he'd already made up his mind not to take the job, and when Sweetman and Brimstone tried to persuade him to change his mind by explaining about the little "surprise" they had arranged for your return home, he was furious. Apparently he does have some morals but unfortunately they are negotiable, so when Sweetman and Brimstone waved a cheque with a figure akin to a telephone number on it, he thought he'd talk to me before making a final decision".

"And did he give you his final decision?", asked the Fat Wizard impatiently.

"Yes he did. He said for me to tell you that you can expect a visit from him one day, but only as a tourist! He's taken a bit of a shine to you and hopes you will give him a tour of Pant y Gussett. He said he'd even buy you a pint. He also wanted me to assure you he had nothing to do with the thugs sent to your shop and sends his regards to your wife and family".

"And do you believe him?"

"Yes I do. He might be a lot of things but I've never known him to lie".

"That's a relief", said the Fat Wizard. "His involvement could have complicated things".

"It's not all good news I'm afraid, I know I said that I

didn't want to get involved but I have been making some quiet, enquiries into the legal side of their intention to start fracking, and it appears that Sweetman and Brimstone were right. Pant y Gussett is outside of any government legislation, therefore it seems they can do whatever they want".

"Thank you for trying, but I think the village will have something to say about them being able to do "whatever they want"", Said the Fat Wizard.

"I wish I could do more", said Brian. "Take care and keep me posted".

"Will do" said the Fat Wizard sitting back stroking Jasper's ears which were in the way of his beard and promptly fell back asleep.

At about the same time, Jack and Rebe had managed to push the large handcart with two large metal barred cages on it, high up Brakin Wind towards her favourite release site. Jack had been relieved to find that Rebe had taken them to the other side of the hills from the mines. He couldn't face seeing them today. On the way Rebe had shown him the many rare plants and herbs that grew in this area as well as introducing him to some gnomes they'd encountered on the path.

He was fascinated to learn that the gnomes had been clearing stones and twigs from a small area of ground to give some wildflowers a chance to spread out.

"Hello Rebe, got some more ready for release have you? And how's your Da?" another asked as they approached.

"Hi Linden" smiled Rebe, "Dad's fine, thank you. I'm just letting Jack here see the dragons being released."

"Looks like hard work pushing that cart all the way up here" said Linden reaching for a big clay jug at his feet. "Care for a drink?"

"Oh, no thank you" replied Rebe. "We'd better get on, these youngsters are getting a bit over excited, better let them go before they burn my cart down."

"So how old are these two?" asked Jack, once they reached the release site.

"Just over a year" said Rebe. "You see dragons live for a very long time, hundreds of years actually, so they're very slow to grow up. Mature dragons are very nomadic and enjoy exploring hills and mountains worldwide. My research has found that elder dragons return home less than once a year, if that."

"I thought nearly all reptiles abandoned their eggs once laying them leaving them to make their own way. So how come you collect abandoned eggs and rear the young?" asked Jack eager to learn.

"Ah well, that's where it gets interesting" said Rebe as if addressing a class. "You see dragons are not typical reptiles, they do in fact have a complex social structure. The young are raised by the dragons who have not matured enough to fly off yet. They teach them to fly, hunt and when it's their turn, how to bring up other dragons. It's a fragile system but it has worked for centuries.

Occasionally a young mother will mate, I think for social status more than for the need to reproduce, actually I'm doing a paper on it, but is too immature to have learnt where to lay and how to incubate them."

"And that's where you come in?" smiled Jack.

"And that's where I come in" laughed Rebe. "I incubate the eggs and then teach the babies enough to be able to defend themselves while waiting to be adopted by the others."

"So how intelligent are they?" asked Jack, eager to learn all he could.

"Depends on how you define intelligence. They have managed to survive for countless generations. Their main enemy, man, no longer believe they even exist. They have learnt to avoid aeroplanes, radar and the millions of cameras that people carry round with them. I suspect that by the time they are mature enough to fly off they will have gained a good deal of knowledge and experience, but until then they are just like naughty teenagers. Now give me a hand we'd better get these cages open."

Free from the confines of their pens, the two young dragons immediately started to flap their wings managing to get a good few feet up in the air before tumbling back down to the ground with a thump. Watching them squealing happily and exhaling short bursts of flame, Jack was delighted to witness their total joy at their new found freedom.

It wasn't long before Jack noticed large shadows wheeling

overhead.

"Right" said Rebe. "The others are here, it's time we left them to get to know each other."

"Aw," said Jack reluctantly "I don't want this day to end, er…. I don't suppose I could   interest you in joining me for a drink in the local tonight?... I mean it's the least I can do after all that you've done for me this afternoon."

"What do you mean, after all I've done for you? You pushed the cart all the way up here and by the way you can push it all the way back as well" laughed Rebe. Then seeing the blush arrive on poor Jack's face, she decided to put him out of his misery.

"I would love to let you buy me a drink tonight. Now come on that cart ain't going to push itself."

And Rebe and Jack laughed and giggled together all the way back to the village.

Early that evening another shiny black car, an expensive limousine of some sort, pulled into the car park in Pant y Gussett. Out of the driver's side slid a graceful young woman. She was dressed casually in white trainers, skin tight blue denim jeans that she must have put on with the aid of a shoe horn, and a simple puff sleeved white cotton blouse. This woman was curvy, the sort of figure that zero sized models in the fashion industry should strive for instead of trying to imitate living clothes hangers.

Her long black hair cascaded down her back and as she walked her bum looked like two boy scouts fighting in a tent.

It was only her horn-rimmed glasses that betrayed her as being "Miss Jones" secretary at P.E.E.O.F.F.LTD.

"How on earth did I let myself get roped into this?" she thought as she recalled being called into the boardroom late yesterday afternoon as she prepared to leave to go home.

"Miss Jones" Mr Brimstone had said while Sweetman was in his customary position of staring out of the window. "As you know we have invested a great deal of time"

"And money" interrupted Sweetman without turning around.

"And money" continued Brimstone. "In our latest project in Pant y Gussett" he continued. "Now as you're also aware we had a representative from said village in here this afternoon. I don't mind telling you, it did not go well. In fact, I would go as far as to say it was disastrous. This Fat Wizard character has threatened us, despite the legality of our claim, with all sorts of vandalism and I'm afraid, even violence. Yet it is imperative that this project go smoothly."

"We don't have to tell such an attractive young lady as you the importance of good business. How else would we pay the wages?" said Sweetman rather, patronisingly thought Miss Jones.

"So Miss Jones" said Brimstone quickly noticing her slightly bristling at his partner's last comment, "Mr

Sweetman and I were discussing how best to deal with such a possible insurgence and we came to the conclusion that what we need is someone on the "inside" so to speak."

"What about Mr Bickford?" replied Miss Jones, not liking where this was heading.

"Ah Charles" said Sweetman finally turning away from the window. "He's a very good engineer."

"Oh a very good engineer." repeated Brimstone.

"But" continued Sweetman, "we wonder if he has the strength of character for this sort of thing".

"Indeed" said Brimstone back in the driver's seat. "You see we need someone who could "ingratiate" themselves with the locals, someone who they might consider friendly, someone who they might feel more at ease talking to and tell what "skulduggery" they might have planned. Then it occurred to us, who better for such a task than our very own Miss Jones, someone who was both beautiful and intelligent."

About to lose her rag and explode at the sexist way they were talking Sweetman followed with:

"We would of course offer an admirable recompense for such services!"

Miss Jones had stopped in her tracks. She may had been furious about the way her employers had suggested that she should almost 'prostitute' herself to gain information, but the cold hard truth was that she loved her flat in

Mayfair but the cost of living in such an area were crippling, especially on a single wage. She hated to admit it but the chance of earning some extra money was too good to ignore. Reluctantly, she found herself agreeing to do it.

Miss Jones left the car and headed for the bridge. She knew about Eric and the toll so had stopped at a sandwich bar in Loughor and bought a chicken and ham baguette to offer Eric as payment. The young girl serving in the shop that she had got talking to told her that quite often, when they delivered to the village, rather than pay Eric they had found a place to cross under the bridge while he waited up on it. They called such sandwich deliveries "Subways." Miss jones had told her not to worry, the sandwich was not for her and it was all claimed back on expenses anyway.

Eric was delighted with such a bounty and chomped away merrily as Miss Jones made her way to the Cross Inn.

Jack was totally dismayed as he held the door to the pub open for Rebe, to be greeted by gaudy signs all around the bar. Looking like they had been written by a child that had been given a new set of fluorescent pens for Christmas they all depicted crudely drawn hearts with phrases like "Speed dating tonight", "Meet your soulmate!" and "The road to love starts here!"

"I'm sorry" said Jack, "I had no idea, honest!"

"That's ok," said Rebe mischievously, let's give it a go, might be fun" as she brushed past him.

"Not what I consider fun" sighed Jack under his breath.

"What would you like to drink? he asked resignedly.

"Anything blue with a brolly in it" laughed Rebe, as she grabbed a form and pencil from the bar.

"A pint of best and something blue with a brolly in it" sighed Jack to Double D, thinking this wonderful day had taken a turn for the worse.

"Pint of best and a brew on the screech, coming right up" laughed Double Dee.

"Speed dating" Jack overheard one of the locals remark, "that's how I met the wife. I wasn't speedy enough I reckon" he said downing his drink dejectedly.

Jack paid for the drinks and while he waited for Rebe looked around the bar. He couldn't help but notice that there were considerably more men than there were women and indeed most of the women seemed to be married and with their husbands. All the small tables had been arranged in a circle, each with two chairs facing each other.

"Right" said Rebe holding a piece of A4 with the number 7 written on it. "This is for you. Apparently, all the women will be designated a table and all the men have been given a number to wear, and they get five minutes to talk to a lady at a table then a bell will ring and the men have to move on to the next table. Each pair will have to fill in a form about how well each date went and later on they'll announce any matches. Sounds simple doesn't it?" Still giggling she led Jack away from the bar saying; "C'mon let's get a seat while we wait for it to start.""

Jack followed Rebe, disgruntledly, as he surveyed the bar again, this time to suss out the competition. First thing he noticed were the three gentlemen standing alongside him at the bar. He had met them at exactly the same spot last night, Downwind, Dug and Dai he seemed to recall, but they looked different somehow. Then it occurred to him, they had all brushed their hair.

Standing behind them were a large group of dwarfs, all dressed in their usual mining attire but their tools had been polished to a mirror like finish. On the first table behind them were four greasy looking youths who had gone more than a bit over the top with the hair gel and, judging by the aroma, cheap aftershave. By the lecherous grins and raucous laughter emanating from them, they were obviously all sharing their opinions on how "lucky" they were going to be tonight.

There were some other men dotted around the pub already displaying their numbers by having them pinned to their chests, but most of them looked like they were approaching pensionable age, and all shared a rather 'desperate' look.

As Rebe lead him further into the pub he noticed a table packed with gnomes. They had taken the trouble to dress up in clean clothes and combed their beards tidily. One of them had even gone so far as to bring his Sunday best fishing rod with him.

Feeling better now that he had seen his potential rivals, Jack thought he should have a quick look at the ladies he was going to have to spend his five minute dates with. There was a table of young girls who were giggling nervously to each other as they glanced around at the potential suitors, but most of the single ladies, well as far as he could tell, were also approaching a 'certain' age. He also noticed that all the potential female participants were human, absolutely no representatives from the other races.

"Hmm, I wonder how that is going to work?" he mused.

"Hello, may we join you?" Jack heard Rebe say as she sat down at a table without waiting for an answer.

"Charles!" exclaimed Jack, "I didn't expect to see you here tonight. Didn't think this was your sort of thing."

"It's not" said Charles hardly looking up from his drink. "Just thought I'd have a quiet drink. I wouldn't have come if I'd realised this 'speed dating' thing was on."

"Oh come on, it's just a laugh," said Rebe. "Here let me get you a form." she offered.

"No thanks" said Charles sounding very unhappy, "Unfortunately I'm already married."

"Oh it's only a bit of fun, it's not like you're being unfaithful or anything" urged Rebe.

"Really, I don't…." Charles stopped mid-sentence as he recognised Pog's voice at the pub's entrance saying, insistently,

"C'mon Mam, you could do with having a laugh. Now go get yourself a drink, I'll be back at ten to walk you home".

Charles looked up to see Pog dragging his mother by the

hand to the bar.

"But Pog..." she said.

"No, I mean it Mother. You've been miserable as sin these last few days, now go and enjoy yourself. I'll pick you up later" and with that Pog raced out the door.

Whether it was the drink or whether it was seeing Melanie again, Charles found himself saying, "Actually Rebe, would you mind getting me a form. After all what harm could it do?"

"Glad to, it'll be fun, you'll see" said Rebe as she skipped off back to the bar.

For the next hour Rebe had been merrily teasing Jack with comments like "Well I'm spoilt for choice" and "Good job I like older men" followed by "Ooh, not much for you here" when the bar suddenly went quiet. There was a slight 'whooshing' sound when, in unison, all the men sucked their stomachs in and slicked back their hair, as Miss Jones entered the pub.

"Oh, that could be a problem" sighed Rebe.

"Miss Jones!" exclaimed Charles, what on earth is she doing here?

"You know her?" said Jack, enjoying Rebe's reaction.

"Yes, she's Sweetman and Brimstone's secretary but I've never seen her look so... "

"Sexy!" snapped Rebe.

"Well I was going to say so... casual, but yes you're right, sexy." replied Charles.

"She's got no idea who I am, and judging by the fact she is filling in one of the forms at the bar perhaps I can find out why she's here during our 'date'" said Jack, relishing the chance to pay Rebe back for her earlier teasing.

"Perhaps you can" snapped Rebe folding her arms.

"Hello everyone and welcome to the Cross Inn's first speed dating event" announced Double Dee, without needing a microphone. "If the ladies could take their appointed tables we shall begin in about ten minutes so charge your glasses while you can, you might need it" she added looking around the bar.

As far away from the festivities as they could get, Penny and Ivor were drinking heavily and commiserating with each other,

"And this is better than our 'pool' table? Crazy" said Ivor.

"I know, crazy…. Hey what about running a pop quiz?" said Penny excitedly.

"Don't be daft woman, there's only about six flavours, it would never work" replied Ivor getting back to his pint, dismissively.

As all the women settled themselves at their respective tables, the men started to form orderly queues in front of the women of their choice. Unsurprisingly the majority of hopefuls were jostling for position in front of Miss Jones. Much to Rebe's annoyance, one of them was Jack.

Next to Miss Jones, a small handful of men were queueing up to meet an overwhelmed looking Melanie. In the middle of that particular queue stood a very awkward looking Charles, who was staring down at his feet with absolutely no idea what he was going to say to her.

There was no one queuing up in front of Rebe. In all fairness she never expected anyone to, she was after all the Fat Wizard's daughter and no local would put themselves in the position of doing anything that might upset her father. She had only signed up for this to tease Jack but the joke had backfired when she saw him in the queue for Miss Jones.

She was pretty certain he was only trying to find out what Miss Jones was up to, nevertheless she had been taken by surprise by how much the thought of Jack and Miss Jones together bothered her.

The Bell rang and Ann Jones found herself confronted by a rather scruffy looking individual,

"Oh hello number four" she said, "My name is Ann jones,

"I'm a Jones too but people call me Downwind" he replied,

"Downwind... And why do people call you that?" replied Miss Jones politely, while surreptitiously pulling a small perfumed handkerchief from her sleeve to cover her nose.

"Dunno, they just always have."

There followed one of the longest five minutes of Miss Jones' life. Every attempt to gain inside information was curtailed by Downwinds' insistence on explaining every detail of the importance of being the chief sanitation engineer for the village. He even went on to infer that without his skilful endeavours, the entire village would grind to an unhygienic halt.

Her relief at the ringing of the bell was short lived as she looked up to see the next candidate, a shorter and stockier version of the one that had just left.

"Hello" he introduced himself. "I'm Douglas the gravedigger. Now I bet you didn't know just how important the job of 'senior, recently deceased, interment officer was?"

"No...no I didn't" sighed Miss Jones realising that this was going to be a very long night. Dug, like Downwind before him, rattled on at great length hardly leaving a single pause in which Miss Jones could ask a searching question or two. Blissfully the bell rang just as Dug was explaining that without him, 'the entire village would grind to an unhygienic halt'.

She was still looking down at the cards she had to fill in thinking, "What the hell do I say about those two?" when she heard her next date announced himself,

"Hello, I'm Dai...Dai the dwarf"

"Indeed you are" said Miss Jones again reaching for the scented handkerchief, her eyes watering.

"I have my own business" he said proudly.

"Oh yes, and what business is that?" she asked politely,

desperately trying not to breathe in through her nose.

"Actually, my company specialises in 'nocturnal domestic waste emissions, removal and disposal"

"Let me guess" interrupted Miss Jones, "If it wasn't for you 'the entire village would grind to an unhygienic halt'".

"Well…" Dai replied pompously, "I wouldn't go that far...but now that you mention it…."

Charles was on the verge of changing his mind when he suddenly found himself taking a seat opposite Melanie,

"Oh it's you" she said coldly, "Are you going to be here for the full five minutes or are you going to run out again?"

"P..P..Please, let me explain" stammered Charles still not knowing what he was going to say.

"Why not, you've about four and a half minutes left!"

"Look I really enjoyed that afternoon with you and Pog, I really did, it's just that… well I'm married…"

"I see" said Melanie. "So you thought I'd be a pleasant distraction, take advantage of a widow while working away from home did you? So what happened, a sudden burst of conscience?"

"What!, No not at all"

"Three minutes" snapped Melanie.

"What? Oh, it's nothing like that I promise. My marriage is

all but over anyway, my kids hate me, the dog wants nothing to do with me and I'm pretty certain the wife has already found someone else."

Melanie glared up at him, "If it's sympathy you're after you joined the wrong queue. One minute!"

"I'm sorry" was all Charles could manage as the bell rang and he was all but barged out of his chair by Downwind Jones, who clapping his hands eagerly, started to recount to Melanie how important he was to the hygiene of the village.

Rebe beckoned Charles over to the still vacant seat opposite her, "You Ok?" she asked.

"No not really" he said almost in tears.

"Well come on" she said sympathetically, "You've got five minutes to tell me all about it."

Jack was relieved to see Charles seated with Rebe. Although he desperately didn't want any rivals for her affection, he also didn't enjoy seeing her sitting there all on her own. He had no idea of the Fat Wizards unintentional influence on the local men or that Rebe knew this would happen and was just playing a joke on him.

So busy watching Rebe, he almost missed the bell that signalled his turn with Miss Jones.

"Uhm... hello I'm Jack" said Jack nervously.

"Hello Jack, I'm Ann" said Miss Jones, finally feeling it was safe enough to put her scented handkerchief back up her sleeve, "And what do you do?" she asked.

"I work up at the mines, I'm an electrician" said Jack wondering if he should have adopted some sort of alias.

"Oh I see" said Miss Jones thinking that maybe another employee of the company wouldn't be the best source of information but, as everyone else had proved to be a dead end, she carried on. "I work for Sweetman and Brimstone too, are you enjoying the job? I gather some people don't want us here" she probed.

"Oh I love my job" lied Jack, "what do you do in the company?" he asked.

"Just a secretary" she replied, "but I've heard so much about the place I just had to see it for myself. How well do you get on with everyone? I see Mr Bickford is making himself at home."

"It's a very homely place, lovely people." said Jack sincerely.

"Yes they are" said Miss Jones wondering why she kept looking at Downwind talking to Melanie. "Have you heard of anyone being against the fracking project?"

"All of them are!" said Jack

"But why? Think of the extra revenue it would bring to the village" said Miss jones genuinely curious.

"Revenue to who?" exclaimed Jack barely able to contain himself. "There would be little or no jobs for the locals and any profits would be swallowed up by Sweetman and

Brimstone. Not to mention the environmental damage. Do you have any idea of the amount of amazing plants and creatures that live here, all of them are at risk from the pollution of fracking...or so I've heard?" said Jack pulling himself together, instantly regretting his outburst.

"I... I didn't think about it like that" said Miss Jones confused, and also annoyed with herself for watching who Downwind was going to see next as the bell rang again.

"Well I think I've well and truly buggered that up" said Jack slipping into the chair Charles had just vacated to go to the bar.

"How do you mean?" asked Rebe, still reeling from Charles' confessional.

"It's just that instead of questioning her as to what she's doing here, I think I just gave her a speech about why we shouldn't be here."

"Ok" laughed Rebe, "perhaps you're not the best secret service agent in Wales, but I like you anyway."

"You do?"

"Yes I do" confirmed Rebe, "now let's see this night out and then the we'd better report to my dad."

Now generally, organisers of speed dating events take it quite seriously and genuinely try and use the collected data to match suitable partners. However, this was Pant y Gussett and Landlords Jack and Justin had decided to leave the final results to Double Dee, who had a notoriously wicked sense of humour. The resultant matches were:

Eileen, a six foot four tall, prize bull breeder and Dai the Dwarf.

Jane, a sweet sixteen florist's daughter and Dug the gravedigger.

Rebe, FW's daughter and a brave young man named Jack.

Sweet Melanie and a newcomer called Charles.

And after a lot more amusement from Double Dee, her ultimate wind up, Downwind Jones and Miss Jones.

As the matches were announced, and most of the single women raced out of the door, Miss Jones was surprised to find herself standing at the bar accepting an offer of a pint from Downwind Jones, a man who she would normally consider as beneath contempt.

Melanie had opted to ignore Double Dee's suggestion as Charles for a perfect match and waited outside the pub for her Pog to walk her home.

Charles ordered another drink.

"Hello Mr Bickford" said Miss Jones a bit squiffy, not used to real ale.

"Hello Miss Jones" replied Charles not bothering to look up from his pint. "What are you doing here?" he asked, clearly not interested.

"Ohh... hic please call me Ann" she replied. "Just wanted to get to know the village a bit better, you Ok?"

"I'm fine, thank you Miss…...I mean Ann and please call me Charles, just having a bit of a bad day, that's all."

"Nothing wrong at the mine is there?" she asked concerned. "Our bosses think you've been doing a marvellous job."

"Have they indeed? Well isn't that great, nice to know I can do something right." said Charles who had now been joined by Jack and Rebe. "A round of drinks for my friends at the bar please Miss" he said to Double Dee.

"Top man!" said Downwind slapping Charles quite heavily on the back. "Make mine a large un" he said to Double Dee, pointing to an obscure bottle of thick brown liquid on the top shelf.

Charles's mood improved as the evening went on and the drinks flowed. Downwind proved to be good company with his constant stream of ribald jokes and humorous anecdotes about the villagers. Even Dai and Dug entertained the group recounting the various strange predicaments that Downwind had managed to get himself into over the years. Downwind actually blushed when Dug recounted Downwinds' slightly exaggerated heroics of the day before.

"They did what!" Ann exclaimed mortified, "I had no idea I swear."

"Don't worry, we believe you." said Downwind.

"Still" replied Ann visibly upset. "A round of drinks for everyone, on me. I'll take great pleasure in claiming that back on expenses!" she laughed.

Ann noticed that she no longer felt the need to reach for her scented handkerchief, but whether this was because she had got used to the certain body odours present, or whether it was because her nostrils had burnt out, she wasn't really sure.

Well toward the end of the night they were joined at the bar by Huw Puw and Mr Cribbins who was dressed in his usual sombre attire. They had timed their late arrival to avoid the speed dating which they considered lewd and somewhat sordid. They were surprised to find a brave young man with Rebe, amazed to find Downwind with his arm around an attractive woman, who wasn't actually screaming for help, and totally dumbstruck to see Dai the Dwarf with his arm round the waist of Eileen, the bull breeder, desperately trying to reach up and whisper in her ear.

Despite these almost 'paranormal' events they joined in with the conversation at the bar and a really good night was had by all. Except that is, for Charles. Even surrounded by such gaiety and good company as he was, all he could think of was Melanie.

Landlords Jack and Justin looked around their pub,

"Did we just get it right at last?"

"Had to happen one day" said Jack smiling.

Apart from the small crowd at the bar there were still quite a few people left, even though it was late. One of the gnomes was showing off his fishing rod to a group of young ladies while a group of young lads looked on enviously. Some of the older single men and women had all gravitated around a large table discussing the subject as to how. "Things were harder in our day. This lot have it too easy in my opinion" while Ivor and Penny were still staring angrily at the spot where their 'pool table' had stood. At one point Justin had overheard Penny say,

"What about a jukebox?"

To which Ivor had replied drunkenly, "What the hell's a juke, when it's at home, and why would it need a box.?"

"Never mind" sighed Penny.

Justin caught Double Dee's eye and pointed to his wrist and nodded.

Double Dee braced herself for the reaction as she shouted the immortal words that for centuries have filled hearts with dread throughout the land;

"Ladies and Gentlemen, Last Orders Please!"

As Jack gently pulled Rebe away from the immediate onslaught approaching the bar he exclaimed,

"Blimey is that the time? I think I'd better order a taxi to meet me in the car park. I might have had one or two too many to drive, how about you Charles, Ann, do you want to share a cab with me?"

"Probably should" moped Charles,

"Ooh" said Miss Jones, definitely the worse for wear, "I think I'd better. I wouldn't want to scratch P.E.E.O.F.F's shiny company car now would I?"

"No pet, I suspect you shouldn't." said Downwind, "Any chance I could see you again?" he asked hopefully.

"I should think so" she giggled. "Are you likely to be here tomorrow night?"

"Oh, I don't know, on a Sunday night?" said Downwind,

The bar erupted into spontaneous laughter,

"But!" he said, glaring warningly at everyone, "If you're going to be here, I could make the effort."

Everyone around the bar composed themselves, after hearing about Downwinds' recent heroics they thought it best not push him too much.

"What about you Rebe?" asked Jack. "Do you want to join me here for a drink tomorrow?"

"Go out two nights in a row? I don't know…"

Jack looked crestfallen.

"But tell you what, come for lunch tomorrow and in the afternoon you can help me get the dragons ready to fire up the kilns for my mother. That's always…interesting" she laughed, "In the meantime, I think you'd better help Charles and Ann to the car park, I doubt if they'll make it on their own.

"It's a date," said Jack daring to lean in and kissing Rebe

on the cheek.

Blushing heavily, "It's a date" she replied surprising herself.

"Time gentlemen please!" announced Double Dee. "On behalf of the management I would like to thank you all for such a successful evening, and on a personal note" she continued, "Now bugger off the lot of you, I need my beauty sleep!".

As Jack, aided by Downwind escorted Charles and Ann to the car park he couldn't help but smile as he glanced back at Rebe who was being accompanied home by Eileen and a very happy Dai the dwarf who was hopping up and down like a rabid kangaroo desperately trying to put his arm around Eileen's shoulders.

21. THERE'S NO ACCOUNTING FOR TASTE.

As you all know by now, Sunday morning was almost a ritual for the Fat Wizard But this Sunday was different. Instead of his customary lie-in, he was up bright and early.

"Don't worry about doing a breakfast for me my love" he called to Jean, still in bed, "I'll pick something up from the bakery on my way."

"See that you do!" Jean replied wiping the sleep from her eyes. "I don't want you reading your paper on an empty stomach, especially when we have a dinner guest."

"Oh yes, young Jack" thought the Fat Wizard as he headed down to the door. "Nice young lad that one I hope she doesn't scare this one off."

The Fat Wizard marched purposely up the street relieved to find that despite the early hour the bakery was open.

"Good morning FW" said Mrs Crumble, "Don't normally see you this early on a Sunday, actually don't normally see you this early on any day."

"Oh, just errands to do, such is the life of a busy wizard you know. Would you have something nice I could eat while I'm walking?" he asked.

"As it happens these have just come out of the oven, it's my latest invention" Mrs Crumble said proudly. "It's a baked dough base covered with cheese and tomato with a thick black laverbread layer over it, cut into rectangles with dollops of mashed potato on top."

"Oh I see" said the Fat Wizard, "A sort of pizza that looks like a domino."

"Exactly" she said, "Pizza domino's that's what I'll call them, thanks FW."

"My pleasure" he said, "Always happy to be of service, I'll take two. I bet it's been a long time since Eric has had a warm breakfast."

"The Fat Wizard decided against eating his food as he walked, opting instead to keep the two 'pizzas' wrapped together to keep them warm until he got to the bridge by the car park.

Sitting on the lichen encrusted wall of the bridge, he gave Eric his share of the food.

"What do you think?" asked the Fat Wizard biting into his 'pizza', glad to find it was still warm.

"Iss good" replied Eric smiling and drooling at the same time, "Thankoo."

"Glad you like it" said the Fat Wizard, "Look, you know you're an important part of the village, don't you?"

"I know" said Eric chewing.

"And you know everyone loves you, don't you?"

"I know" he said again, licking his lips before taking another bite.

"It's just that…" said the Fat Wizard unsure how to word this in a way Eric would understand, "Well I think there is some trouble coming to Pant Gussett"

"I know" repeated Eric again.

"No…. I don't think you understand what I mean…"

"I know" said Eric with some emphasis, "Bad men want to hurt village, I know."

"How do you know?" asked the Fat Wizard confused.

"People think I stupid cos I ugly 'n don't talk good. They talk in front of me cos they think me stupid. I ain't stupid' I listen. Posh men know what they do is bad, they joke about it and throw sweets at me, I listen. when you need me I will help, I strong." said Eric stroking his club, "I strong."

"Indeed you are!" said the Fat Wizard, whose fondness for Eric had been added to by a newfound respect, and just a hint of sadness.

"Go now" said Eric, "Megan waiting for you."

"How did? let me guess you knew"

"I know" smiled Eric as he finished the last piece of his 'Pizza'. "Iss good."

The Fat Wizard continued on his journey, still bemused about how much he had underestimated Eric. He hadn't gone far before a familiar cloud descended from the sky and stopped in front of his face.

"Hi Riser" he said, "I gather you've been expecting me."

"Yes we have" he replied chuckling, his company of warrior fairies watching for his every command. "Please don't be upset about Eric, he has been a friend to all of us for many years."

"Oh, I'm not upset about Eric, I'm upset about how I didn't realise just how intelligent he is. I never thought I would judge anyone as superficially as I have done him. I feel guilty for not treating him as well as I should have."

Captain Riser puffed out his chest in indignation. "The entire village, and you in particular," he said, pointing directly at the Fat Wizard, "have always treated Eric with nothing but respect which is why he is so loyal to the village. He may well be one of the magic folk but he would lay down his life to keep the humans of the village safe. It is no fault of yours that he preferred to live the life of a perceived simpleton in order to enjoy the gifts of food he is so readily offered. Don't think of yourself as being fooled, merely understand that this is how he has chosen to live."

"Right enough" said the Fat Wizard as suddenly Riser's men split into two rows, heralding the arrival of Queen Megan and her imperial guard.

"Good morning FW" smiled Queen Megan.

"Good morning to you" replied the Fat Wizard with a bow.

"I gather you had an eventful trip to London and indeed

that your wife had an eventful time while you were gone, I do hope she has recovered from her ordeal."

"Indeed she has your majesty and thank you for asking" said the Fat Wizard not in the least bit surprised that Megan knew what was going on, she had eyes and ears everywhere. "I fear these men are every bit as bad as I'd heard."

"So it would seem. By the way I have noticed the addition of two new trees in the woods, I heartily approve, very...imaginative."

"Thank you M'lady but I suspect there will be a lot more and a lot worse to follow over the next few days. I was hoping to call a meeting of the elders to discuss the situation."

"An excellent idea" said Queen Megan, "But may I suggest that because of the gravity of the situation, you take charge of warning and rallying the villagers while I do the same with the magic folk. That way we can avoid the 'personality' clashes that would most certainly hamper proceedings."

The Fat Wizard knew what she meant. Although the magic folk and the humans got on well on a day to day basis, whenever there had been a crisis involving the whole village there was always some bickering as the leaders of each race sought to take control. He knew the magic folk would unite behind Queen Megan and he was fairly certain that the villagers would unite behind him. Between them they should be able to unite the entire village, he hoped.

"An excellent idea your Majesty but we'll need to keep each other informed every step of the way." said the Fat Wizard.

"Oh I agree," said the Queen smiling, "That is why I have arranged for the head of the Coblynau, Jed isn't it? To get his men to act as messengers between your garden and a small shaft that comes up near my Royal tree. Tend your petunias well FW I fear there will be much to report. Now go my friend, it's Sunday you have a newspaper waiting for you" and breaking into a wide grin, added, "But try not to …'read' too much, you need to keep a clear head."

"Indeed your majesty" replied the Fat Wizard slightly embarrassed by the Queen's good natured jibe, made worse by overhearing his good friend Captain Riser's unsuccessful attempt at stifling a chuckle.

As he headed back to the village, the Fat Wizard stopped to give Eric a bag of pear drops that he still had after his trip to London. He didn't stop to talk to him, other than to say hello this time, as he still felt a bit awkward about not realising how bright the Troll was. Moving on down the lane he saw Melanie, still in her dressing gown tending to the hanging baskets on the front of her log cabin.

"Morning Melanie" he said brightly, "How are you this fine day?"

"I'm well thank you" she said. "And you?"

"Splendid, thank you" said the Fat Wizard noticing that her eyes were puffy as if she had spent most of the night crying. "And that lad of yours?"

"I'm fine too" said Pog from behind the well at the end of the garden, struggling with a full watering can that he was obviously fetching for his mother. "Nice to see you Mr FW."

"Please just FW. Any more 'trouble?'" he asked.

"None at all" Pog laughed, tapping his back shorts pocket which had a large stick protruding from it.

"Good, good."

"Would you like a cup of tea?" asked Melanie. "I was just about to put the kettle on."

"I would love one." Actually all the Fat Wizard really wanted to do was to sit at his favourite table in the 'Cross' and enjoy an ale, or two, with his paper and relax. But he was curious to find out what had upset such a pleasant neighbour and more importantly see if there was anything he could do to help.

As he settled down inside and they waited for the water to boil, Melanie asked him if he would like a biscuit with the tea.

"Oh no thanks, I'm trying to watch my weight" he replied. The truth is the Fat Wizard would never normally turn down the offer of a biscuit but the 'Pizza Domino' was starting to weigh quite heavily on his lower regions and he was desperately trying not to burp. He hoped the tea might settle his stomach down a bit.

Melanie brought him his tea and sat in the chair opposite.

"I don't want to pry but are you sure you're Ok?" asked the Fat Wizard, concerned.

"Yes just a bit of a bad night, I'm alright, really."

"I heard you went to that speed dating night last night."

"How did you… oh of course your Rebe was there."

"She said that Charles was quite upset after you left"

"Was he indeed!" she snapped, "Oh sorry FW I didn't mean to be short with you."

"That's Ok, you're forgiven" said the Fat Wizard kindly. "But what happened? He seems like a very nice chap."

"Yes I thought so too," said Melanie tearing up. She found herself telling the Fat Wizard all about the wonderful afternoon her and Pog had spent with Charles, right up to the time that he had upped and walked out on them without a word.

"So you see when he approached me in the pub and told me he was married, well that was the final straw so I left."

"Not much of a marriage from what I can gather," said the Fat Wizard. "Did he go on to say anything else?"

"I didn't give him a chance, I just left."

"I see, …you really like him don't you?"

"He's the first man since Evan's accident that I've met that I've felt comfortable with, and he was so good with Pog, but now…"

"Yes he thinks the world of Pog. Look Melanie," said the Fat Wizard earnestly, "Things might not be as bad as they appear. I know it's none of my business but let me talk to Charles and see if I can help him to explain himself better. You might be surprised as to what he might have to say for himself."

At this point Pog walked in from the garden and overhearing the last part of the conversation said threateningly,

"If he upsets my Ma again I'll use my stick, you see if I don't!"

Pog was a bit miffed with their reaction at first, but seeing his mother and FW laughing so hard he couldn't help but join in.

"What about one of those 'Pyramid' selling schemes I've been reading about?" said Penny to Ivor, sitting at the same table they had occupied the previous night.

"Look around you daft cow," said Ivor angrily, "Could you see any of this lot moving to Egypt."

"Never mind" sighed Penny as the Fat Wizard announced his arrival, paper in hand.

"Peace be upon all here" he boomed.

"Mornin' dearie, you're running a bit late, I was getting worried. Table's ready take a seat I'll bring your drink over now." said Double Dee with a wink.

"Thank you my love" said the Fat Wizard. "But before I

take my seat I have an announcement to make, if you would be so kind".

"The floor is yours my love." said Double Dee with a curtsy.

"Ladies and Gentlemen!" said the Fat Wizard with a magically enhanced voice, not really necessary given the relatively small crowd in attendance. "I need to convene a meeting of the village elders to be held here at nine o'clock this evening, if that's alright with you gentlemen" he added looking at Justin and Jack.

"Fine by us" they said in unison from behind the bar, rubbing their hands together in glee, looking forward to the extra custom such a meeting would surely bring.

"Please make sure that all interested parties know" said the Fat Wizard making his way to his table where he lit his pipe, opened his paper and took a long drink from his tankard, brought to his table by the ever-professional Double Dee.

Everyone knew it had something to do with the 'happenings' at the mines but muted their speculations. They knew better than to disturb the Fat Wizard while he was reading his paper.

At this point I really should explain about the 'village elders'. Each of the magical races had their own appointed leaders, but for the humans, it was not as one might expect, an exalted group of eminently qualified scholars. It was more a collection of villagers, most of whom could definitely be considered as being elder, who lived in the village and held positions of respect, or at least were well known in the community.

Most prominent was of course the Fat Wizard himself. Alongside him was Mr Cribbins the undertaker, Goodwitch Evans of the pickling emporium, Dodds from the paper shop, Mrs Crumble the baker and of course Huw Puw who couldn't bear the thought of being left out of anything official.

Somehow, and nobody could ever work out how, Downwind Jones had managed to make himself a part of this important body. He always claimed to represent the common man, and let's be honest, they don't come more common than Downwind!

The Fat Wizard smiled as he looked at the huge bold headline emblazoned across the front page of his paper;

"LOCAL MAN DECLARED HERO"

And underneath, a huge photograph of a grinning Downwind Jones in the sort of pose you would normally expect from a prizewinning boxer in a publicity shot.

He almost laughed out loud as the article continued;

'Downwind Jones, local highways hygiene consultant, was declared a hero today when he single handedly foiled a large gang of armed robbers from raiding a local shop. Downwind, 34 of….'

"That'll keep him in free beer for the week" he thought to himself, turning the page.

'Man Eating Fish, Spotted in Pant y Gussett' was another headline that caught the Fat Wizard's attention, until he read on and found it was just a review of a new cafe that had recently opened in the village. With no more real news the Fat Wizard sat back and turned to his favourite 'puzzle' section but not before almost choking on his beer as he overheard Penny ask Ivor,

"What about a tombola?"

And Ivor's patronising reply,

"You are really grasping at straws now my love. You know full well that neither of us can play a musical instrument of any sort!"

The Fat Wizard returned home earlier than usual for a Sunday morning. He didn't want to drink too much now as he knew he was going back to the pub later. He was delighted to find Jack already there, being licked to death by Jasper who also hadn't expected him back so soon.

"Hello all, oof" he announced as Jasper jumped off Jack's lap, and in his excitement, head butted the Fat Wizard in a place that should never be head butted.

Quickly getting his breath back the Fat Wizard went on to say,

"Right, I've called a meeting of the elders for tonight at the 'Cross' to discuss the situation at the mines and I'd like all of you to be there, including you Jack. Oh and Charles if you can get a message to him."

"I'll phone him now" said Jack.

"Oh I'm sure it can wait until after we've eaten. Is that roast beef I can smell?" said the Fat Wizard licking his lips.

It had been a splendid afternoon. Mrs FW had outdone herself with a particularly lavish roast dinner which, much to her delight, Jack had managed to completely polish off. The Fat Wizard was pleased to see Jack and Rebe getting on so well. They had talked and laughed, mainly about dragons, all the way through the meal with Jack further ingratiating himself by insisting that he and Rebe did the washing up. Later on Rebe had lead a very excited Jack down to the dragon pens ready to get the baby dragons set for their first lesson in flaming while Mrs FW went to organise the pots she had ready for glaze firing set up in the kiln.

Now on his own the Fat Wizard reclined in his favourite chair in front of the television, with Jasper curled up on his lap, he lit his pipe. Feeling quite content he finished his after-dinner smoke and closed his eyes to enjoy his customary Sunday afternoon nap, but sleep wouldn't come. Instead he found himself worrying about the possible battle to come, and how he could keep everyone safe.

A couple of miles away on the outskirts of Llanelli in a room in a hotel, part of a famous chain that one of Britain's best loved actors and comedians would have you believe was a panacea for insomnia, sat Miss Jones.

Still in her dressing gown, she lay on the bed nursing the kind of hangover that makes you wish you had joined the temperance movement. She hadn't managed to face breakfast and was still struggling to keep down what passes for a cup of tea in these sorts of rooms.

With the curtains still drawn despite it being well into the afternoon she kept her head on the pillow while she tried to remember what had happened the previous night. She was fairly certain that the villagers hadn't given away any information that her employers might be interested in. In fact it was information that she had learned about her employers that worried her more. She knew that they were cold and ruthless but she had no idea of the level of violence they were prepared to stoop to. What made her feel worse was that as she getting to know some of them. She really liked them including that …. Man, Downwind Jones who, like a fungus, was starting to grow on her. She was embarrassed to admit to herself that she dreamed about him last night, smell and all.

"Maybe I'll find out more tonight" she thought, "If I live to make it?" She wasn't very happy about carrying on with her 'spying mission' but told herself, "Morals are fine, for those who can afford them! Oh and where the hell did I leave the car?"

Charles sat alone at his desk in the mining office. Back at his hotel he had tried ringing his wife Catherine only to have his son Andrew answer.

"Oh it's you Charles", both his kids had stopped calling him dad a year ago. "What do you want? I'm in the middle of a game!" he said rudely.

"Is your mother home?" asked Charles thinking about how well-mannered Pog was.

"No, she's gone for a meal with uncle Tony, said she probably won't be back until tomorrow. Damn she shot me, gotta go, only got one life left!" and he hung up.

That's when Charles decided that he couldn't stand being alone in his hotel room any longer and headed back to the mine until it was time for the meeting that Jack had rung him about.

He needed a drink; the kids didn't have an uncle Tony.

22. RALLYING THE TROOPS.

Eight thirty and the Cross Inn was packed, it seemed like the entire village was eager to find out what was going on, though admittedly some of them just didn't want to feel 'left out'.

Double Dee had arranged a row of tables in front of the fireplace for the elders and had taken all the tables and chairs from the middle of the bar and had stacked them in a back room, those who needed to sit could use the small tables and chairs against the walls.

The elders had already arrived and had taken their seats, Huw Puw had of course gotten there early to ensure a seat in the middle and had brought his own gavel specially polished for the occasion. Downwind waited at the bar talking to Dai and Dug but keeping one eye on the door eagerly awaiting the arrival of Miss Jones.

"Peace be on all here" boomed the Fat Wizard's voice as he entered the pub, wife, daughter and Jack in tow.

"Your drinks already on the table dear" said Double Dee. "Now take your seat while I serve Jean, Rebe and... Jack, wasn't it?"

"Thank you my dear" said the Fat Wizard looking around. "Charles not here?" he asked her.

"The sad looking one from the mines? Haven't seen him yet" she replied.

"Hmm disappointing" he said as he noticed Downwind breaking into a huge smile as an attractive young lady walked into the pub behind him. Even though she was wearing sunglasses he recognised her instantly.

"Miss Jones isn't it?" said the Fat Wizard.

"Yes?..." she said, distractedly as she returned Downwinds' smile.

"We met on Friday at…"

"Oh Mr FW isn't it?" she interrupted, "Sorry, didn't recognise you with those robes on."

"Hmm yes indeed. What may I ask brings you to our little village in the middle of nowhere?" he said suspiciously.

"Nothing in particular" she replied coyly. "Just heard some people talking about the village and I thought I'd come and see it for myself."

"And would those people be Mr Sweetman and Mr Brimstone by any chance?"

"Amongst others, yes. It sounded so quaint I just had to

see it for myself" she said sweetly. Just then Downwind walked up to them;

"It's alright FW, she's with me" he said passing her a cocktail.

The Fat Wizard couldn't make up his mind about what worried him most, the fact that she was here in the village, the fact that she seemed to be genuinely pleased to see Downwind or the fact that Downwind had apparently bought someone a drink with his own money!

"So what's going on, why are there so many people here?" she asked changing the subject.

"Us village elders," said Downwind trying to sound important, "are having a meeting to discuss what your employers are doing at the mines."

"Ooh" she said trying to sound impressed. "This could be useful," she said to herself. "I might actually get some information tonight... if I can only keep this drink down" she thought.

The Fat Wizard took his seat at the table and allowed Huw his five minutes of glory as he banged his gavel loudly on the table to call the meeting to order.

"FW, you have the chair!" he said pompously.

"Thank you Huw" said the Fat Wizard. "I have called this meeting tonight to explain the cause of recent unusual events in the village and to make you aware of the imminent dangers we face…"

He went on to talk in great detail about the exploratory drilling and digging and how it had been the cause of the recent tremors and other side effects that had affected the village.

The entire pub had gone silent, hanging on to his every word but when he mentioned 'fracking' he was bombarded with questions, it seems nobody had ever heard of it, in fact at the sound of the word Goodwitch Evans even commented,

"Well I don't hold with that sort of language!"

After calming everyone down the Fat Wizard went on to explain everything that he had spent hours researching about fracking. He broke it down into basic terms that even the slowest of the villagers could understand, but as soon as he reached the part about pollution and the possible damage to the environment, the entire pub went into uproar. It got so bad that Huw was banging his gavel like a drunken heavy metal drummer.

"ORDER, ORDER!" he shouted to no avail. It was only when his gavel snapped in two that the Fat Wizard intervened and using his magically enhanced voice shouted,

"QUIET!"

The pub went silent. "Thank you" he said. "Now as most of you are aware, I had a meeting in London with Mr Sweetman and Mr Brimstone who own the firm that have, quite legally, bought the mines......" With everyone now listening intently he went on to explain what had happened at the meeting.

"But surely" said Huw incredulously, "There must be some legislation...some licenses...."

"I'm afraid not, I have checked and it seems we are on our own."

"Then we'll just have to stop them ourselves!" roared Griff the blacksmith.

"Too right we will!" cried Dai and Dug in unison.

The whole pub erupted again, this time cheering in a patriotic fervour.

"Silence!" boomed the Fat Wizard again, "Before this gets any further you need to know the sort of people we're dealing with". He then went on to explain how the two goons Downwind had dealt with were there on the orders of P.E.E.O.F.F. Ltd.

"Only two of em?" said Dug looking at Downwind.

"Sssh man, let him talk" said an embarrassed looking Downwind who turned quickly to Miss Jones. "Another drink dear?"

"What I do know about Mr Sweetman and Mr Brimstone is that they can afford to hire a lot more muscle than just those two clowns. At this point he spied Melanie and Pog standing among the crowd and thought it prudent not to mention what might have been the fate of her late husband, just yet,

"...and don't forget, even if Surten doesn't join them they can certainly afford to employ other magical creatures, more maybe than even Queen Megan and our magic folk can handle."

This time the pub stayed silent apart from the elders whispering amongst themselves. Eventually Griff spoke out.

"Are you saying that you don't think we can beat these bast…., sorry, people" he corrected himself remembering where he was.

"Oh no, far from it" replied the Fat Wizard, "It's just that you need to realise how rough this could get, personally I think that together….."

With that the door to the pub barged open and a very dishevelled and red-faced Charles limped in.

"FW" he gasped, "I got here as quick as I could. P.E.E.O.F.F. have sent a security team up to the mine!"

The Fat Wizard raced over to him, noticing a worried looking Melanie was just behind him. "Charles catch your breath a minute" he said while turning to the bar and said "Quick someone get me a brandy!"

Downwind was about to automatically say, "Make mine a double" when he realised that FW wasn't calling a round. Double Dee poured a large one and took it over to the elders' table where the Fat Wizard had helped Charles to a seat.

"Now drink this and then tell us what happened."

Charles took a large swig and then coughed for a few minutes. This was the good stuff, not the supermarket brand his wife normally bought for the house. "Thank you" he said gratefully to Double Dee as he pulled himself together. "I was on my way here, for the meeting like you asked, when I heard all this commotion on the path to the mines. It was a bulldozer and it was clearing a path for caravans and mobile homes, dozens of them. When I stopped them and asked what they were doing they told me they were from "Strong Arm Security" and they had been employed to run security for the mines. I told them they couldn't just rip up the countryside and that they should stay at the car park. Then some big guy just laughed and threw me to the ground. He warned me to stay out of the way or there'll be 'trouble'.

"What did you do then?" asked the Fat Wizard as Charles finished his drink.

"I managed to get back to my office and look up who 'Strong Arm Security' are."

"Let me guess" said the Fat Wizard. "A Sweetman and Brimstone company?"

"Yes, and then they threw me out of my own office and told me that no-one is allowed on site out of hours, not even me. They knew who I was and still physically threw me out. You know what this means, don't you?"

"Yes I'm afraid I do" said the Fat Wizard. "It means they are ready to bring the machinery in to start the fracking. How long do you think we've got Charles?"

"Well said Charles scratching his head as he gave it some thought, "A lot of the infrastructure is already in place, so if they bring in the rest of the machinery over the next few days it'll take about a week to assemble and install it all. I'd guess about ten days and they'll be ready to start."

"Right" said the Fat Wizard turning to the elders. "You've heard what's at stake and I've explained what we're up against. What we need to do now is decide either to let it happen and hope it doesn't destroy our village or to unite and fight this threat together, whatever the cost."

The elders huddled together and for a few minutes debated animatedly while everyone in the 'Cross' watched them silently.

Huw stood up and banged the remaining part of his gavel on the table.

"Ladies and gentlemen" he said "We have come to a decision, but as this matter will affect everyone here we believe it only proper for you all to have your say. Unanimously the elders have voted to fight. What say you?"

In the time it takes to raise a glass into the air, the pub replied with a resounding "FIGHT!"

The Fat Wizard smiled as he looked around and saw the look of determination on the faces of the community that he loved so dear. His grin broadened even more when through all the noise and cheering he could see Mrs FW mouthing the words, "My Hero", spoilt only slightly by the overly dramatic fluttering of her eyelashes.

The Fat Wizard let the crowd shout and cheer, which increased in pitch every time someone offered such suggestions as "I'll set my bull on em!" and "Sod that I'll set my wife on em!" and his particular favourite from Dai the dwarf, "I got something we can spray on them, and it don't smell like perfume!"

After a while the crowd calmed down and started to look to the Fat Wizard. Eventually Griff asked loudly,

"So what's the plan FW?"

"I have a few ideas, but I think it would be prudent not to discuss them here and now." If Miss Jones, who was now recovering quite nicely from her hangover and seemed to be preparing to have another one tomorrow, noticed that the comment was directed at her, she didn't let it show.

"Over the next few days I will contact each of you with instructions. Downwind I hope that you Dug and Dai will act as messengers for me."

"Sure will" said Downwind with his arm around Miss Jones's shoulder again. Dug and Dai also nodded their agreement.

"Huw, I will need you to act as coordinator and help draw up the battleplans."

"I will indeed" he said puffing his chest out again, delighted to be asked to do something important.

Much to the Fat Wizard's surprise, Goodwitch Evans stood up and with her hands on her hips shouted,

"And don't go thinking you're gonna leave me out of this. I aint had a good scrap in ages!"

The pub erupted again.

23. MINE! YOU CAN KEEP IT.

Nine thirty the following morning Sweetman and Brimstone's direct line started ringing.

"Ah, Miss Jones what have you managed to find out for us?" said Sweetman immediately switching to speakerphone.

Miss Jones had spent the last hour agonising over whether or not to report any of what she had heard the night before. Nursing another hangover, she had thought about the incident at the Fat Wizard's shop and the fact that they had sent their security firm to intimidate the villagers, people that she couldn't help but find herself growing fond of. Eventually she had reasoned that P.E.E.O.F.F. Ltd were an internationally successful company and couldn't possibly do anything to break the law. Besides she did work for them and she considered herself to be a loyal person.

She felt it her duty to report on what had happened in the pub last night.

"I see" said Sweetman. "Thank you for that Miss Jones. Would you mind staying down there a bit longer. You're doing a marvellous job and you will certainly find us most 'grateful'"

"Most grateful!" echoed Brimstone.

"Happy to" she replied, feeling uncomfortable as she pictured Downwinds' face if he found out what she was doing. "Damn what is it about that man?" she thought to herself.

Brimstone looked at Sweetman as he disconnected the line. "Looks like Charles is becoming as soft as his predecessor" he said.

"Certainly looks that way" said Sweetman, who looked thoughtful for a second and then added, "Wouldn't it be unfortunate if, like his predecessor, he had a similar 'accident.'

Brimstone smiled, "Most unfortunate indeed, Big Ron again?"

"Why not, our head of 'Strong Arm Security' did a good job last time" smiled Sweetman. "And tell him it's a matter of some urgency, we can't afford any delays"

Big Ron was a thug. He had always been a thug, even

during his school days in Swansea, he was the one who took everyone's lunch money. He was the one that owned the school toilets so much so that those poor unfortunate pupils that couldn't afford to pay his toll, of money or fags, went on to get bladder infections or even worse have 'juvenile accidents' the stigma of which would stay with them for the rest of their lives.

At the age of fifteen he was over six-foot-tall with a barrel chest and hands like the buckets of a hydraulic digger.

By the time he had reached twenty, he had shaved his head and was covered in tattoos. Not the artistic 'inks' that many people proudly show off, but dark pictures that depict decapitation or mutilation. He looked like a fanatical hard right fascist, but to be fair he was neither a racist nor a homophobe. He hated everyone, equally.

His parents could do nothing with him. They tried to be loving and supportive but the older he got the more terrifying he became. It got so bad that they were so scared to live in the same house as him that they emigrated to Spain without telling him, and left him with the house.

It is often said that children from a broken home shouldn't be blamed for how they turn out, but in his case, the home was fine. He broke it!

It was during his illustrious career as a nightclub doorman that his particular style of 'eviction' was brought to the attention of Sweetman and Brimstone, when some of their employees were visiting a nightclub and were removed by Big Ron in a spectacularly violent fashion.

At first it was just the occasional odd job, collecting overdue payment and suggesting rivals ply their trade elsewhere. But as the Sweetman and Brimstone empire grew, they realised the benefit of keeping their hands as clean as possible, so started relying on Big Ron more and more. When they decided to open up their own 'legitimate' security business Big Ron was the obvious candidate to run it.

Later that morning the Fat Wizard had a long chat with the petunias, where Jed had assured the Fat Wizard that one of his men had been in the cellar of the pub last night, and had already reported back to Queen Megan about the villagers' readiness to fight. He also went on to explain that the Queen had had the same reaction from the magic folk and had already put Captain Riser and the RAF on full alert.

It was the reaction that the Fat Wizard had expected but nonetheless was relieved to be sure that he and the villagers were not alone.

The other thing that had been bothering him was the Charles and Melanie situation. It seemed clear to him that they should be together, but he also knew that common sense told him not to get involved. "What the hell!" he said to no one in particular. "I didn't become a great wizard by listening to common sense!" and off he went to see Melanie.

As the Fat Wizard walked up the 'High Street", well with a pickling emporium and a night soil company on it, what would you call it? he could see many of the villagers were preparing for conflict. A sign in the bakery window boasted 'rock cakes, a tasty snack and a handy weapon. Get them while stocks last'. As he walked past the bakery still chuckling to himself, he saw Downwind pushing his handcart down the street proudly pointing out the two bread knives he had gaffer taped to its axles, looking to all the world like an extremely budget Roman chariot.

"Be prepared I always say" he said to the Fat Wizard. "I'm on my way to fit some to Dai's carriage now."

As if that wasn't weird enough, he noticed that every villager he passed was carrying some kind of home-made weapon, ranging from crude bows and arrows to ruddy great clubs with six-inch nails driven through them.

"Well I don't know about P.E.E.O.F.F.'s men, but this lot are starting to scare the hell out of me!" thought the Fat Wizard to himself. But just when he'd thought he'd seen it all there were Ivor and Penny standing by a small cart loaded with thin sheets of steel and copper. Ivor was pounding the sheets with a large hammer over a small boulder while Penny cried out,

"Helmets, made to measure helmets, have your helmet made while you wait, only ten pounds!"

"Blimey, they didn't waste any time." thought the Fat Wizard actually impressed.

Beginning to wonder if this was getting out of hand, he turned right at the funeral parlour to find the pavement blocked by a delivery wagon parked just outside their workshop. There stood Mr Cribbins rubbing his hands in glee as he watched Wilf help the delivery driver unload a mountain of timber.

"Good morning FW" he said grinning from ear to ear. "Lovely day isn't it!"

"Maybe for some" grumbled Wilf under his breath struggling with another armful.

"What's all this for?" said the Fat Wizard afraid that he already knew the answer.

"Well opportunity doesn't knock very often in Pant y Gussett for people in my line of work and I can't afford to pass it up when it does!"

"No... no I suppose you can't, but let's hope this is all for nothing eh, no offense" he said grimly.

"What!" exclaimed Cribbins, ".... I mean of course, let's hope" he said the grin vanishing off his face, "Still best be ready, just in case." Feeling guilty under the Fat Wizard's glare he went into the workshop to help stack the timber.

By the time he got to Melanie's cabin he found himself in urgent need of a nice cup of tea. With no answer at the door he walked round the side to the back garden to find Melanie in full protective gear collecting honey from the hives.

"Good morning" he shouted from a safe distance

"Oh hi FW. Go on in the back doors open, make yourself at home. I'll just close this up and I'll be with you in a minute."

Sitting comfortably sipping his hot tea, the Fat Wizard made polite small talk. Eventually he took a big breath and said "Look Melanie I actually came to see you about Charles."

"What about Charles?" she replied quite sternly, but her expression displaying a mix of emotions.

The Fat Wizard went on to explain why Charles had suddenly walked out on her when he realised who her late husband was and the guilt he felt being with the wife of someone he had respected so much. He also told her what he had said to Rebe in the pub about his marriage being over and that he had finally decided to sue for divorce.

"Oh" said Melanie with tears in her eyes. "I didn't know, and I was so beastly to him…you see Evan never talked about his job. I didn't even know that he worked for the same company who are at the mines now. He only used to say that he had a good friend that he worked with but how he hated his employers. We only started the honey business to see if we could make enough money for him to leave his job so that he could be at home with me and Pog."

"I'm afraid that's not all." said the Fat Wizard leaning forward and taking Melanie's hands in his. "Charles suspects, and to be honest I agree with him, that what happened to your husband may not have been an accident at all."

"What…what are you saying?…"

Suddenly there was a huge bang coming from the direction

of the mines. This was quickly followed by a small tremor.

"What on earth?" exclaimed the Fat Wizard. "They can't have started; they haven't had the equipment delivered yet."

They both raced outside to see what was happening only to be confronted by a very excited Pog

"Mam…. Mam" he panted, "There's been an explosion at the mine. There's people running about all over the place. I heard a man shouting something about someone being hurt."

"I'd better get up there right away, they might need some help!" said the Fat Wizard "'I've got a bad feeling about this.

"We're coming too," said Melanie, "You might need all the help you can get."

As they reached the mine they were confronted by absolute chaos. There were men in hard hats and high viz jackets running around like headless chickens, all seemed to be barking orders at each other. As they looked up at one of the many mine entrances they could see that one of them had clouds of smoke and dust still pouring out.

"What happened?" asked the Fat Wizard to a group of security guards who were just standing around drinking tea.

"A big explosion would be my guess" said a giant of a man who grinned and winked at his colleagues.

"Was anybody hurt?" asked the Fat Wizard instantly detesting this tattooed brute.

"Hurt!" he replied, "Naah if anyone was in there they wouldn't have felt a thing" he laughed. "Here, why are you wearing a dress?"

"These are wizard's robes; I am a wizard!" he snapped.

"Really! Well go wave your wand at that lot" he sniggered pointing to the still smoking mine. "It's gonna take the boys weeks to clear that rubble"

Afraid of losing his temper with this shaven gorilla, the Fat Wizard, followed by Melanie and Pog, carried on walking up to the mine. As they approached the entrance they could see a familiar figure emerging from the cloud of dust. It was Jack.

"Jack!" shouted the Fat Wizard as he raced over to help Jack to some fresh air. "Are you injured?"

"No...no I'm fine, I wasn't in there when the explosion happened but it's really bad. The entire roof of the shaft has caved in, there's nothing left but rocks and rubble."

"As long as you're Ok" said the Fat Wizard.

"No you don't understand, Charles was in there. The head of security reported a strong smell of gas deep down in the shaft and Charles took a monitor down to check it out. He was in there when it exploded. Nothing could have survived that!" and breaking into tears he added quietly, "he's dead."

At the news Melanie burst into tears and clung on to Pog who, for his mother's sake, valiantly put on a brave face.

"I see" said the Fat Wizard visibly shaken. "Melanie, as your house is the nearest may I suggest we all head there and I'll make us all a cup of tea. I'll add some herbs I have with me to help with the shock."

Sobbing uncontrollably, Melanie nodded in agreement as the grieving quartet made their way solemnly back.

As they approached Melanie's place the Fat Wizard became aware of a single familiar figure dropping from the sky.

"Captain Riser," said the Fat Wizard. "Don't often see you on your own."

"Trying to keep a low-profile FW", he replied. "I have some good news for you, Charles is alive" he smiled. "We hope we weren't being too presumptuous but noticed you had Mrs Lewis with you and thought you might all stop at her place so we brought him here."

"Charles...alive...How!" spluttered Jack while Melanie looked up confused.

"Go on in, I'll let them explain. Besides I have to get back to my unit. See you later." And with that Riser flew up into the clouds and disappeared.

The group rushed eagerly into the cottage to find Charles, battered and bruised lying on the sofa with a blanket around him and drinking a cup of tea. On one arm of the sofa sat Jed while another of the Coblynau sat on the other by his feet.

"Charles you're alive!" shouted Melanie as she rushed over to hug him.

"OUCH!" winced Charles.

"Oh, sorry" said Melanie letting him go

"Don't be, and don't stop either." He smiled looking at the Fat Wizard for an explanation for all this affection.

The Fat Wizard just smiled and shrugged.

"How the hell did you survive that explosion?" asked Jack

"I wouldn't have if my two new best friends hadn't pulled me out in time.

"But how?" continued Jack. "That shaft was a dead end."

"There are no dead ends to a Coblynau" explained Jed. "We just pulled him through one of our shafts. Unfortunately, Charles didn't really fit so I'm afraid we pulled him through a bit forcibly like. That's how he got all the cuts and bruises."

"So why bring him here?" asked the Fat Wizard. "Why not just take him to the mine people, they've got medical staff haven't they?"

"I think I'd better let young Harold here explain that. He was the one on duty when it started."

"Hmm" said the Fat Wizard stroking his beard. "Jed why don't you and Harold join me in the kitchen, we can make everyone a cup of tea while Harold tells me exactly what happened."

Leaving Melanie, Pog and Jack to fuss over Charles, the Fat Wizard lead the Coblynau into the kitchen and keeping his voice low said,

"I get the feeling there's a lot more to this story, so Harold from the top if you please."

The Fat Wizard was pretty certain he was addressing the right one. Jed and Harold could have passed for twins, apart that is, from Harold looking a bit younger and had considerably less hair growing out of his nose.

Harold beamed with pride as started to relay his story. "It's like Jed said, it was my turn to watch that particular shaft, and a while ago I noticed two of the security guards wandering around down there and I thought to myself, this a strange place for security guards, so I kept a close eye on them. Duw, one of them was a big bugger, even by people standards, and ugly too. Ron, I think the other one called him but I didn't catch his name, but I did get his wallet." he smiled obviously pleased with himself.

"And what did they do?" asked the Fat Wizard impatiently.

"Ah well they were laughing about something, I heard the big one say something about 'Don't mess with the classics, it worked on that Lewis fellow and it'll work here'. Anyway, then I saw them plant a big charge, dynamite I think, on a timer. After they'd gone I was about to see if I could 'acquire' it when I heard someone coming down the shaft so I hid again. By the time I realised what was going on I managed to get Jed to help me pull this poor bugger out before the bloody thing went off."

"Aye" said Jed. "We managed to get him to a little shaft around the hills when we bumped into the RAF. We told Captain Riser about what happened and he suggested that we quietly brought Charles here without the mine people knowing."

"Well done, the two of you, you've done the right thing" said the Fat Wizard genuinely impressed. "Does Charles know about the explosives?"

"No" said Jed. "He took a bit of a beating being dragged through our tunnels. He'd only just come 'round when you arrived."

"Good, let's keep this to ourselves for now, pointless worrying everyone yet."

"You have our word as Coblynau." said Jed solemnly.

Nobody noticed Pog just the other side of the kitchen door, listening to every word.

The Fat Wizard brought the tray of fresh tea into the living room. "Right then tea's up" he smiled. "Melanie, under the circumstances would you mind putting young Charles here up for a few days?"

"I don't mind at all, if that's alright with you Pog?" she replied. Pog nodded in consent but seemed distracted.

"Good, that's sorted then. Jack would you mind walking back to the village with me once we've drunk our tea, there's something we need to discuss?"

"Certainly FW. I doubt if there will be any work for me this afternoon. That's if it's alright with the gaffer of course."

Charles managed a smile but injured, and still wrapped in Melanie's arms, he fell asleep.

Pog went to his room, tears of rage streaming down his face.

As they walked back to the village, the Fat Wizard told Jack what the Coblynau had told him.

"Surely not. Tried to kill him!" he said astonished "and they killed that Mr Lewis too? I can't believe it"

"I'm afraid it's all true Jack, they really are that evil. Look this is not your fight. I think you should resign immediately and get out of here, for your own sake."

"Quit now and leave Rebe… I mean all of you to this. I think not! I'm with you till the end, and that's final."

"Thank you Jack. I hope you don't live to regret it." said a humbled Fat Wizard. "Now let's hope the missus has left us something to eat, I'm starving".

Walking down the street to the Fat Wizard's shop, Jack was bemused by the number of villagers wearing ill-fitting, crudely hammered 'hats'.

"I'll explain later." laughed the Fat Wizard.

24. SOMETHING WICKED THIS WAY COMES.

"Thank you Ron, you can expect the normal bonus, in cash of course, at the end of the month." said Brimstone replacing the receiver.

"It's done?" asked Sweetman standing in his customary position looking out of the window in the boardroom.

"It's done, fair play Big Ron doesn't hang about." said Brimstone adding, "I sometimes worry that he's a bit too keen, enjoys it a bit too much for my liking."

"It's his enthusiasm for these little 'extras' that keep him so loyal, and cheap for that matter" laughed Sweetman. "What's the news on our little "surprise" We need to speed things up."

"The ship will be docking in Cardiff docks tomorrow morning, there will be a lorry waiting to deliver the 'package' to Pant y Gussett by late tomorrow afternoon."

"Good" said Sweetman approvingly. "Better still, tell them to park up at the motorway services overnight then they can join the rest of the convoy of men and equipment to arrive together on Wednesday. Any more from Miss Jones yet?"

"Give her a chance, she only rang this morning" chuckled Brimstone. "You getting impatient?"

Turning away from the window Sweetman snapped, "With the amount of time and money we have already invested in this damn project, too right I'm getting impatient."

Miss Jones had decided to spend the rest of the day shopping in Swansea. She thought that a bit of retail therapy might ease the uncomfortable feelings she was experiencing about spying for her employers. To add to her confusion, she found herself trying on outfits that she thought would impress Downwind Jones. "What on earth is the matter with me?" she thought to herself. "He's normally the sort of man I would cross the street to avoid." Nonetheless she opted for a very short skirt and low-cut top that she knew would send his blood pressure through the roof.

Back in his shop, the Fat Wizard had called a meeting with Dug, Dai and of course Downwind. Jack had volunteered to help Rebe with her chores.

"Right lads" he said. "I want you to spread the word. I suspect that after the 'accident' at the mine they might speed things up a bit. I want you to make sure that all the villagers are ready at a moment's notice. As soon as we get word that the equipment has arrived, we need to stop them before they get beyond the car park. That way we can destroy the bulk of their gear before the security guys can get there. Now hopefully they won't have Surten with them but I have no doubt there will be other 'surprises'. I have liaised with Queen Megan. We will take care of the humans, and her army of magic folk will deal with whatever else they throw at us.

These are vicious violent thugs but we outnumber them. If

we fight together, we will beat them, but make sure everyone knows to look out for each other. I want casualties kept to a minimum.

"Will do!" said his intrepid heroes, so caught up in the moment that they had to fight the urge to salute.

"Oh and Downwind, could you stay behind a minute we need to talk?"

There was something different about Downwind today and it took a few moments for the Fat Wizard to put his finger on it. Downwind was clean! He had clean clothes on, had had a bath and was even wearing aftershave, you know the cheap stuff that caught your breath and made your eyes water.

"Downwind" said the Fat Wizard in what he hoped was a diplomatic voice, "I couldn't help but notice that you seemed to have formed an... attachment to that Miss Jones from P.E.E.O.F.F. Am I right?"

"You mean Ann, cor she's a cracker ain't she?"

"Well...yes she probably is but...did you know that Charles was supposed to have been killed in that explosion earlier."

"I.... I'd heard a rumour that someone may have got hurt... but I had no idea... Charles... dead" said Downwind obviously upset. It seemed Charles had been becoming quite popular.

"No he's alright. The Coblynau managed to get him out in time, but it wasn't an accident."

"What are you saying?" asked Downwind confused.

"It seems" said the Fat Wizard quietly, "that P.E.E.O.F.F. tried to kill him off, presumably because he had warned us about the security team that had arrived at the mine."

"But… how did they know… wait a minute what are you suggesting?"

"Miss Jones was in the pub last night. She was there when Charles came in and warned us."

"B….but Ann wouldn't do that, she wouldn't."

"Sorry Downwind" said the Fat Wizard gently, "I know you're keen on her but you must admit it's a bit strange her turning up here on her own and to be honest how often have beautiful young women taken such an immediate interest in you?"

"I thought it was too good to be true, I just hoped my luck had finally turned" said Downwind crestfallen. "Is this why she wanted to meet me down the pub again tonight?"

"Possibly" said the Fat Wizard, hating to be the bearer of such hurtful news". I suggest you still meet her but try not to let her overhear any of our plans or let her know that Charles survived. Maybe you could even get some information out of her about what her bosses have got planned next?"

"Okay FW, I'll try" said Downwind as he walked out of the shop, his head hung low.

There was a strange atmosphere throughout the whole

village that night, everything seemed eerily quiet. The Cross Inn enjoyed the usual Monday night revellers but tonight instead of the usual dirty jokes followed by bouts of laughter, everyone was just grimly holding on to their drinks. The novelty of the battle to come had worn off and all that was left was the reality of possible casualties, or even worse the end of the village if they lost the war.

However, it wasn't all doom and gloom in the pub. Over in the corner sat Penny and Ivor celebrating the success of their new protective headgear.

"Here I've had an idea!" smiled Penny. "Remember all of them large water pipe insulation sleeves we bought when we read about that arctic winter we were supposed to have a few years ago?"

"Yeah" said Ivor wiping the foam of his ale from his top lip. "They're taking up most of the room in my shed. Turned out to be the warmest winter on record!"

"Well" said Penny leaning forward so that no one could overhear. "What if I sewed leather gloves on the ends of em? We could sell them with the helmets as arm protectors."

"What a bloody good idea" beamed Ivor. "We could be 'arms' dealers."

Over at the blacksmiths, Griff was working late trying to keep up with the surge of spears, swords and knives that people had suddenly brought to him to sharpen.

Cribbins had persuaded a grumbling Wilf to work into the

night making coffins and also had Dug looking for spare shovels, 'just in case'.

Huw Puw was at his desk hunched over a crudely drawn map of Pant y Gussett. He was using different coloured boiled sweets to represent the warring factions as he experimented with different campaigns. Deep down he knew his efforts would be to no avail, but he felt better for doing, 'something'. While Dai the dwarf was busily filling a load of stirrup pumps, he had borrowed from a garden centre, with, well you know what'.

The Fat Wizard had taken a turn around the garden, and after checking that there was no one in earshot he had gone over to the petunias with a top secret, and very important 'mission' for Jed and his men.

Walking through the back door into his workshop, the Fat Wizard was impressed to find his good lady wife had commandeered his giant work table. She, and her friends, were frantically tearing up bed sheets into bandages, while others were busy sewing little canvas bags together, each sporting an embroidered red cross.

"I've emptied the shop of every treatment, remedy and medicine that we might need. My 'ladies' and I will be ready to help with any wounded; you can count on us."

The Fat Wizard was delighted to see that Goodwitch Evans was included amongst the 'my ladies'. She seemed to be having the time of her life.

"Right, what can I do?" said the Fat Wizard clapping his hands together.

"You, my love, can put the kettle on. About time you did something useful!" said Jean as the 'ladies' all burst out laughing.

"Fair enough," he smiled, but as he went to climb the stairs to the kitchen, he heard a knock at the front door.

He was amazed to find Kayls and Ellie standing there with a suitcase.

"Hya dad" said Kayls throwing her arms around him. "Rebe's told me what's going on and we're here to help."

"But I wanted to keep you out of it, it could get…. violent!"

"Oh dad, I know I'm your youngest but trust me, me and Ellie have played in some of the roughest punk rock dives between Carmarthen and Cardiff. We're more than capable of tackling some jumped up security guards!"

"You're probably right" smiled the Fat Wizard. Your mother's in the workshop, apparently I'm on tea duty."

About time you did something useful" laughed Kayls.

"Don't you start!" he laughed.

It had gone nine o'clock before Downwind walked into the pub. "Where have you been?" queried Double Dee. "Not like you to be this late. We haven't seen Dai or Dug yet either. Carry on like this and they'll make me redundant." she laughed.

"Uh…sorry I've been walking around thinking about

things."

"Blimey, you thinking, now I really do believe it could be the end of the village" smiled Double Dee as she poured his pint. "What am I getting your girlfriend?" she nodded, indicating the arrival of Miss Jones.

If the pub was quiet before, you could hear a pin drop now as Miss Jones slinked in, a vision of womanhood, her revealing new outfit having the desired effect. Even Gerhart the gnome seemed to be clutching his fishing rod a bit tighter than normal.

"Hello Downwind" she smiled sweetly. "Let me get that, and I'll have a glass of white wine please Miss Dee."

"Ta" muttered Downwind.

"You alright darling? You seem a bit...distracted."

"I'm fine" he replied unable to shake his earlier conversation with the Fat Wizard from his mind. "What have you been up to today?"

"Just a bit of shopping," said Miss Jones, stepping in front of him adopting a model like pose. "Do you approve?"

"Yeah, lovely" said Downwind in a very monotone voice. "You do anything else today?"

"No... nothing else, and I'm beginning to wish I hadn't bothered doing that!" she replied, sensing something was wrong.

"So your bosses haven't told you what happened at the

mines this morning?"

"No, what happened?" she asked with a horrible sinking feeling in the pit of her stomach.

"Charles was involved in an explosion that caused a cave in."

"What!" she exclaimed, horrified. "Is he okay?"

For some reason Downwind couldn't bring himself to actually lie to this woman but remembering FW's warning just said, "Nobody thinks anyone could survive such a terrible cave in."

"Oh my god, poor Charles. I didn't know him well but he seemed like such a nice man" she said as she took a big swig of her drink to help with the shock. This was followed by another big mouthful as it dawned on her that this might not be 'just a coincidence' after her morning 'report'.

"They wouldn't', would they?" she inadvertently said out loud.

"Who wouldn't what?" asked Downwind.

"Oh nothing" she replied, obviously upset. "Look I've got to go. I've got some urgent phone calls to make. I'll come and find you tomorrow." She pecked him quickly on the cheek and fled out of the door.

With more questions than answers, a bemused Downwind took refuge in another drink.

Sitting in her car in the Pant y Gussett village car park, a shaking Miss Jones took her mobile phone out of her handbag. She knew it was well out of office hours but being a trusted secretary at P.E.E.O.F.F. Ltd, she had her bosses' private numbers. For no other reason than 'B' coming before 'S' in her address book she rang Brimstone.

"Ah Miss Jones, have you some urgent news to report?"

"No not exactly" she replied, trying to control her temper. "Did you hear what happened at the mine this morning?"

"Oh yes, a terrible tragedy. We were going to ask you to arrange for some flowers to be sent to the widow."

"How did it happen?" she asked her voice trembling.

"Oh that's not something for you to worry your pretty little head about. There are much more urgent matters for you to deal with."

His smug unfeeling voice confirmed her worst fears. "Pretty little head...more urgent matters! You did it!" she yelled, "You and Sweetman had Charles killed, and it's my fault for telling you that he was helping the villagers." Crying, and shaking uncontrollably her final words were, "I quit! And you can whistle for your company car back," before violently throwing her phone out of the window.

Miss Jones sat rocking back and fore in the driver's seat, desperately trying to compose herself and plan her next course of action.

With a new resolve she jumped out of the car and headed back to the pub. Her face a picture of such fury that even

Eric decided against challenging her for her fare to cross the bridge.

Downwind almost dropped his pint when the pub door flew open and Miss jones shouted at him,

"You! get me a neat scotch, now! and then you can take me to the Fat Wizard's place."

It was unusual for the Fat Wizard to be up so late on a Monday night but Mrs FW's army of volunteers had not long gone, after preparing enough emergency first aid bags to put WW2 to shame. He was also enjoying the grilling that poor Jack was receiving from Kayls who, in the fashion of sisters everywhere, took it upon herself to see if this lad was good enough for her sister.

He seemed to be holding his own.

They had invited Jack to sleep on the sofa for the next few days. The Fat Wizard was concerned that P.E.E.O.F.F., might have been gunning for him too. He was delighted and offered to wire up some floodlights in the dragon pens, while he was there.

When someone started hammering on the front door, the Fat Wizard tensed and said,

"Right I'll go answer that, you lot better stay here."

"Not bloody likely" said Jean, "I coming with you."

"So are we!" said Rebe, Kayls and Jack.

"Me too" said poor Ellie, still a bit bemused by it all but

determined to pitch in anyway.

The Fat Wizard was relieved to find a confused looking Downwind and a very upset looking Miss Jones at the door.

"What's the matter? Said the Fat Wizard, "What happened?"

"Don't really know yet" said Downwind. "Ann said she had to talk to the two of us together, urgently!"

Miss Jones burst out crying again.

"Alright everyone" said Mrs FW putting her arm around the distraught young woman "Let's get her up to the living room, this looks like it's going to need a pot of tea!"

With a cup of tea battling for top position against the whisky in her stomach, Miss Jones came clean. She explained about her spying mission and she admitted to delivering her report to P.E.E.O.F.F. that morning.

"But I swear, I had no idea what they were going to do to poor Charles, I promise, I... I…"

The Fat Wizard took pity on her and explained that Charles was fine, and that actually, as he was currently staying with Melanie, he was probably more than fine.

"Charles… alive…thank God" she said, "Still I hope you can all forgive me, I thought I was just being a good employee. I hadn't realised how much danger this fracking was going to cause and now I've gotten to know some of you, especially you Downwind" she held his hand, "I couldn't bear the thought of hurting you."

"That's alright love, no real harm done eh," said Downwind suddenly picking up and smiling again.

"Oh, and that's not all, "said Miss Jones. "I don't know much, but I can tell you Sweetman and Brimstone have organised for the main equipment and more security guards to arrive here on Wednesday.

"Wednesday eh" said the Fat Wizard stroking his beard.

"They're also shipping in something from Europe, which will also arrive by Wednesday. I don't know what it is but they spent a fortune on it. Kept calling it a 'surprise' and then laughing. Knowing what I know now, I think it might be something awful, please be careful."

"Oh don't worry we will. Downwind do you think you could let Miss Jones stay with you for a few nights?"

"Of course she can" said Downwind with a huge grin.

"Good luck Miss Jones, you might be slightly safer with him." sighed the Fat Wizard.

"Ah, but will he be safe with me?" grinned Miss Jones.

The Fat Wizard cleared his throat and looked away, embarrassed.

Tuesday morning came all too soon. The Fat Wizard's shop was a hive of activity as it naturally evolved to become the centre of operations. A particularly chirpy Downwind accompanied by Dug and Dai, sallied back and forth with messages and instructions for the villagers. The basic plan was to ensure that everyone was ready at the car park at first light to ensure that the equipment couldn't be delivered to the mines and to try and destroy it before the security guards could get there.

The gnomes, who weren't generally good fighters had been instructed to gather, throwing size rocks and stack them into piles around the car park.

Dai the dwarf had come to see the Fat Wizard for some clay pots that he could fill with some unmentionable substances that could be used as stink bombs. The Fat Wizard supplied him with some thin glass bottles that would shatter more easily giving a more widespread coverage, though he did have some misgivings about sanctioning the use of these 'new clear' weapons.

Amidst all this chaos, Dorcas had called in asking if Jean had any cracked or misfired crockery she could have, explaining that her husband, Bill, had pointed out that she may not be very good with a club but by heck she was a markswoman with cups and plates.

Huw had been commissioned to gather all the elderly residents to form a home guard based at the pub. Their job was to ensure that none of the invading forces could sneak into the village to get food or supplies. He wasn't short of volunteers. Dobbs was ready with a catapult and half a dozen jars of boiled sweets, old man Cobbins had cut down all the rose plants from his cottage and wound them round an old cartwheel, ready to use as makeshift barbed wire and even old Arthur, the old man from the pub, had dug out his old bayonet, and being a fan of seventies sitcoms, was shouting excitedly something about, "they don't like it up em you know!"

The Fat Wizard was distracted by a loud whistle from the street outside, followed by a cry of; "FW come and have a look at this!"

He rushed outside to be confronted by a grinning Ed Dee.

"Whaddaya think?" asked Ed standing by his 'taxi' now adorned by thick leather panels covering the roof and sides. "It's our battle wagon" he exclaimed. "Me and Tom been up all night making this. Now we can move troops quickly and safely, no charge!" he grinned.

"Excellent!" said the Fat Wizard noticing Double Dee sitting up front with a determined expression.

"I've been chucking people out when they're not wanted for years" she said. "This aint so different".

"No... I suppose it's not" chuckled the Fat Wizard, but as he stood admiring this latest addition to their military might he heard his name being shouted frantically from further up the street.

"FW, FW please help!"

As he got closer he could see it was Melanie, and she was really distressed.

"What's happened, is Charles alright?" he asked concerned.

"It's not Charles, it's Pog" she cried desperately. "Pog left a note. Apparently he overheard the conversation with you and the Coblynau and he said he was going to avenge his father, he said he's going to kill Big Ron! Charles can hardly walk but he said he was going to the mine and save Pog. Oh please help!"

"Of course I will. Go inside, Jean will look after you. Ed, get me to the mine as quick as you can!" said a worried Fat Wizard.

"No problem!" said Ed determinedly. "Get in and buckle up. Oh yes we got seat belts now!"

The Fat Wizard wasn't the only one busy preparing for conflict. First thing that morning Big Ron had called his second in command, a weasley, sycophantic little man, called Davies to check on the 'arsenal' kept in a secure transit van on site. Big Ron had been delighted when Sweetman and Brimstone had told him they would pay for whatever 'equipment' he deemed necessary for the job. In Big Ron's mind that meant only one thing, guns, and plenty of them. He spent a small fortune, and called in every favour he could on amassing an armoury of all the unlicensed shotguns and ex-army small arms he could muster.

"Well there's no law here to worry about" he reasoned. "So let's make it easy!"

A few minutes later, and an ashen faced looking Davies stood in front of him. He was looking down at his feet and was fiddling with his hard hat, afraid to look up.

"Well, is everything alright?" growled Ron.

"Uh… not really no…" said a panic stricken looking Davies.

"What do you mean... not really no… are the guns okay or not?" said Big Ron menacingly.

"I dunno" said an increasingly fearful Davies. "They're not there."

"What do you mean not there? The van was locked wasn't it?" he snarled.

"Yuh yuh..Yeah but it's completely empty, not even a bullet left. There was a small hole in the floor of the van I could hear some laughing but there was no one there!"

"How the hell?" started Ron when he noticed a scruffy young boy wearing shorts with his socks around his ankles, walking up to him. "What do you want punk?" yelled Ron angrily. "I'm busy."

"You Big Ron?" asked the child coldly.

"Yeah what's it to you? Go away I'm busy" said Big Ron, dismissively.

"You killed my father!" said Pog.

"Possibly" smiled Big Ron. "Who was your father?"

"Evan, Evan Lewis" said the small boy, rage building inside him.

"The mine bloke, prove it!" demanded Ron.

"The Coblynau heard you bragging about it!" said Pog,

starting to lose control of himself.

"The who?" chuckled Big Ron. "Never heard of them. Besides what's a squirt like you going to do about it anyway.?

"You'll see" said Pog pulling a large stick out of his back pocket. With both his legs shoulder width apart, he pointed the stick at Big Ron and recited,

"YOU STANDING IN FRONT OF ME ON THE ROAD, NOW I'LL TURN YOU INTO A TOAD!"

Nothing happened.

"I don't know what you think you're up to" shouted Big Ron as he advanced on the child ready to give him a slap, when Pog trembling with fury, repeated,

"YOU STANDING IN FRONT OF ME ON THE ROAD, NOW I'LL TURN YOU INTO A TOAD!"

Now magic is an amazing thing, we all have a little magic in us, and we demonstrate it every day. Giving birth is magic; being good at sport is magic; writing a, hopefully funny book about magic is magic, but occasionally, extreme emotions can evoke deep magic. Like when a woman picks up a bus to save a trapped toddler or a soldier, though wounded, being able to carry a stricken comrade off the battlefield and when a small boy, confronted by the monster who killed his father, believes a stick to be a magic wand.

As Big Ron reached the small boy and raised his hand to give him a clout, he started to feel 'funny'. First he noticed a thin cloud of white smoke envelop his body, then his legs started to bow and he felt himself shrinking. This was followed by a loud 'pop' as he changed into a particularly ugly large toad, fighting an instant urge to eat bugs.

"What the hell…" exclaimed Davies who witnessed the whole thing and being the sort of cowardly little man that he was, quickly ran away.

With the path widened for P.E.E.O.F.F.'s vehicles, Ed had managed to drive his carriage right up to the mining area, picking up a badly limping Charles on the way. He had to stop suddenly when Pog appeared in the middle of the road in front of them. He was crying uncontrollably. He still had his stick in his right hand while in his left hand he was holding up a large, strangely marked toad by its back legs.

The Fat Wizard leaped off the cart and embraced the boy.

"Pog, are you hurt?" he asked concerned. The boy just stood there shaking but after a few seconds managed to mumble,

"No"

"So what happened?" continued the Fat Wizard noticing that the strange markings on the toad resembled tattoos.

Pog just held the toad up higher and asked in a pitiful voice. "Did I do wrong?"

It took the Fat Wizard a minute or two to work out what had happened. "No Pog" he said gently. "It's no more than he deserves, but let's leave the sticks alone for a bit eh, at least until you're a bit older anyway. What do you want to do with him?"

"I'm going to keep him in a cage in my back garden. That way he won't be able to bully the other toads."

"Sounds like a good idea" smiled the Fat Wizard noticing the toads eyes suddenly widening. " C'mon let's get you home" he said placing the boy carefully on Charles's lap. "I think I've got some explaining to do to your mother!"

It was a good few hours later before a trembling Davies could pull himself together enough to crawl out from whatever rock he had hidden under. He knew he had to phone Sweetman and Brimstone to explain what had happened to Big Ron.

"Pity" said Sweetman down the phone. "He was a good man, never mind Davies, that means a promotion for you. Now I want you to get the miners together…"

"Wh… what miners?" stuttered Davies. "They all scarpered after they heard about Ron."

"What!" snapped Sweetman. "I'll see to it they never get a job in the mining industry ever again! I take it the security gang is still there?"

"Yea…yes Mr Sweetman, they're all still here."

"Well that's something I suppose. Now listen carefully. I want you and your men armed and ready to meet the convoy in the car park first thing tomorrow morning…"

"B…B..But"

"But what?" shouted Sweetman. He could swear he could hear Davies sweating down the phone. "Spit it out man, what?"

"The..The..the guns"

"What about the guns?" shouted Sweetman in a tone that suggested he was about to shove his arm down the receiver and throttle Davies.

"They're all gone, stolen!" blurted out Davies, feeling a sudden urge to relieve himself.

"What? How? Never mind just arm yourselves with whatever you can find. It's imperative that you join the men arriving tomorrow, and make sure you guard the machinery. We've sunk a hell of a lot of money into this and we can't afford for anything to go wrong! Understand?"

"Yes Sir, understood Sir...I'll organise the men to find tools and meet in the car park tomorrow, consider it done." To his dismay, he found he had relieved himself already.

Sweetman slammed down the phone, "Wait until I tell Brimstone about this!" he growled.

25. CAR PARK CHARGES.

Dawn broke over the High Street in Pant y Gussett but there was not a soul in sight. The only sound was the snickering from a couple of horses tethered outside some houses, and the haunting strains of a child's music box, left open, drifting down from an upstairs window. A plastic bin bag, caught by the breeze tumbled across the empty street.

Of course, a bit further up the road, the Cross Inn was awash with pensioners, armed to the teeth with weapons ranging from simple broom handles to the deadly rolling pin. They had decided early on that it was best not to fight on an empty stomach so were cheerfully glugging away at a variety of shorts, for medicinal purposes only, you understand. If they could only stay awake then nothing was going to get past them.

On the bridge to the car park Jean, and her ladies had erected a giant gazebo to use as a first aid station. It was filled with hastily scrounged cots and tables and was manned by volunteers, many of whose only surgical experience was applying sticking plasters to skinned knees. They did, however boast a giant tea urn.

Eric stood in the centre of the bridge, a giant club in his hand. He had been assigned to guard the 'nurses'. He took this post very seriously.

All around the perimeter of the car park, villagers huddled in groups. Grimly silent, the men kept checking their makeshift weapons while the women gathered together around the rock piles prepared by the gnomes earlier, all with a rock in each hand ready to throw. The gnomes hid in the bushes ready to replenish the supplies should they become depleted. The Coblynau lay unseen, hiding in a network of tunnels they had just excavated that encompassed the entire area. Queen Megan and the Fat Wizard had formulated a plan to make best use of Jed and his men's special 'talents'.

Downwind, Dug, Dai and Wilf had hidden near to the main road entrance. They were surrounded by a mountain of pumps and glass jars. They knew that they were the best people suited for 'biological warfare'. Downwind was delighted when Miss Jones joined them.

"What" she said. "You didn't think I was going to miss out on the fun did you? Pass me one of those pumps."

Alongside them stood Griff and his son Ned. They both looked scary enough at the best of times, but with big hammers in each hand, they were terrifying.

Jack was standing in front of one of the vans parked near the bridge. He was armed with a simple cricket bat. "I've hit a few sixes with this in my time!" he explained to Kayls and Ellie who stood each side of him wielding some old electric guitars.

"Managed to escape some grotty clubs with these!" Kayls replied smiling.

"Not half" chorused Ellie, who if she was afraid, she didn't show it.

Rebe was standing on the roof of the van, her fingers already sparking in anticipation.

The Fat Wizard stood silently in the middle of the car park with his arms crossed.

Back at the mines Davies was checking that all his men were armed with all the hammers, pickaxes and spades left by the miners.

"Right men" commanded Davies, feeling brave with a small army behind him. "You know what we have to do, follow me!"

So off they marched, while Davies, in the true tradition of many military leaders, planned to be behind the men when the trouble started.

They hadn't got very far when they found the path blocked by the dwarf miners who were also carrying mining tools. At their head stood Brock.

"Well…. Well….Well, what have we here?" Brock said to

his men as he looked over his shoulder.

"They got the tools, but do they look like miners to you?"

"Not in the slightest!" someone shouted.

"Look little men" said Davies trying to keep the tremor out of his voice, "we've got urgent business to get on with, so clear off before you get hurt!"

"Little men is it?" sneered Brock. "Get hurt, will we?" he laughed. "Let me explain something to you laddie, you may be bigger than us but we've been using these tools since we were born. Half of your lot are holding them upside down. Now why don't you put your toys away and go home before YOU get hurt."

"I haven't got time for this!" said Davies walking carefully backwards through the ranks. "Get them men!"

Davies watched in terror as men in 'Strong Arm Security' hi vis jackets fell in heaps, groaning and bloodied to the floor before the onslaught of the dwarves, who weren't even breaking into a sweat.

True to form, Davies fled.

Back in the car park the convoy had arrived. A fleet of cars, vans and lorries rumbled in and started parking up.

"Okay everyone, stay calm and let me talk to them first" boomed the Fat Wizard.

"Oi! you seen Davies?" shouted the driver of an articulated lorry to the Fat Wizard, as he climbed down from his cab.

It took a while, the man was obviously more fond of beer than he was exercise. "He's supposed to be in charge."

Dozens of men in hardhats got out and stood around their vehicles. They didn't look like they were here to join the book club or play chess.

"I'm afraid I've never heard of this 'Davies' fellow" said the Fat Wizard, "and as for who is in charge…"

"Ah, you must be FW" said the driver grinning. "I've got something for you!" and as he went to unchain the lock on the back of his trailer, he called to the man by the large van parked next to him, "open yours up Fred, while I unchain this."

As Fred opened the back door of his van there was a really angry buzzing sound that could be heard all over the car park. Suddenly out of the van flew legions of scruffy unwashed fairies. These looked nothing like Queen Megan's clan. These looked primeval and savage, a far cry from the civilised and disciplined local fairies. They formed a dark cloud above the villagers and were obviously amassing together to attack.

"Leave them to us FW, we've got it!" came a shout from above the angry hoard.

The Fat Wizard was relieved to see Captain Riser leading a battalion of his 'men' in full formation, ready to repulse the invaders. Armed with clubs they swooped down to engage the enemy.

The other drivers started to unload the mining equipment

from the vans. Some were starting to drive a variety of tracked machines, bulldozers, dump trucks and hydraulic drills off low loaders all flanked by P.E.E.OF.F's men who were waving crowbars and hammers menacingly.

"Seems they don't want to talk" said the Fat Wizard as the unwelcome visitors started to march towards the villagers. Determined to keep the locals as safe as possible the Fat Wizard pulled his wand out from his sock and started firing a colourful mixture of red fire bolts and blue force waves at the feet of the first row of men.

"Bugger!" cried one of them as he hastily untied his now smouldering, and slightly molten, steel toe capped boots.

"Ouch!" cried another as a force wave knocked his legs out from under him forcing him to take a not too graceful swan dive face first into the soil of the car park.

"Leave some for me" shouted Rebe from the roof of the van. "I want to play too." she smiled as she directed her brand of fire bolts towards the now slightly more hesitant advancing army, unfortunately for them, Rebe had a slightly more vicious streak than her father and opted for the more comical crotch and posterior targets.

Horrified at seeing their comrades falling like ninepins, shoeless, prostrate or unlikely to be able to sit down for a few weeks, (And they were the lucky ones), the invaders started to spread out to the perimeter of the car park in the mistaken belief that the villagers would be an easier target. Housewives, with an endless supply of rocks, and honest hard-working men defending whatever they called home, soon shattered that illusion. For every villager that fell two more would take their place wielding frying pans, stale buns or pitchforks with a vigour that would daunt any special armed service in the world.

As the battle raged on the invaders were further dismayed to find themselves fighting villagers that they had already bested, many of whom, after two paracetamols and having been bandaged up with a beer towel held on with sticky tape (Courtesy of Jean and her makeshift hospital) had re-joined the fray.

Swelling with pride at how well the villagers were starting to repel the attack the Fat Wizard was about to turn his attention to the machinery the frackers had brought with them. He was about to point his wand at the first of the machines when he noticed that the overweight lorry driver had finally managed to unlock his trailer that was swaying violently back and fore. Suddenly both doors flew open knocking the unfortunate man to the ground.

The Fat Wizard watched with growing concern as a gargantuan block of ice seemed to unfurl as it exited the trailer.

"What the hell is that?" shouted Rebe from her vantage point on top of a van.

The creature stood up. It was massive, standing at over fifteen feet tall. It had legs like tree trunks with arms and shoulders to match. Its head looked like an evil cross between an ugly man and a seriously annoyed ape. It was also transparent and looked as hard as rock.

"It's a Scandinavian Ice Giant" shouted the Fat Wizard

trying to be heard over the creature's guttural growl that shook the ground. "I thought they were extinct."

The monster started to advance on the Fat Wizard and as it stepped forward its hand brushed against a parked car, screaming with rage it grabbed the vehicle and effortlessly tossed it at the Fat Wizard who instantly erected a transparent shield around himself. The car bounced off the shield and ended up in the river. The Fat Wizard returned the attack with beams of force emanating from his wand and his hand. He aimed at the creature's legs in an attempt to halt him in his tracks. The monster looked down at his feet confused by the twin beams of blue light that were hitting his legs and stopping him walking. He growled again in rage as firebolts thrown by Rebe stung his face.

Around the car park the villagers engaged in battle; men in hard hats swung their weapons at men who determinedly swung theirs back, all the while suffering under a barrage of rocks thrown by laughing women. Dorcas had already lain three men out, two with old water jugs and one with a cracked plate, a throw that, had it been a discus, would have qualified her for the Commonwealth Games.

The men at the back of the car park weren't faring very well either. At first they thought it was raining, then they thought it was hailing until, that is, they saw the broken glass all round them. Soon their eyes started watering, but when the realisation of what they were covered in sank in, then they ran for the bushes vomiting noisily.

Considering the seriousness of the situation, Downwind, Dug, Dai, Wilf and Miss Jones were altogether having way too much fun.

The few bad guys, presumably with stronger stomachs than their comrades, that tried to stop the aromatic onslaught, were quickly knocked out by Griff and Ned, who were trying to outdo each other with their quickly growing collection of cracked hard hats.

The Fat Wizard was starting to feel the strain of keeping the Ice Giant in check. Sweat was starting to roll down his face and his arms were beginning to ache. Noting how Rebe's firebolts were causing the creature pain he switched from force beams to flame. The creature roared in pain but despite a small amount of steam it started to advance again. Rebe, aware of the seriousness of this new threat, turned all her attention to bringing as much heat to her attack as she could muster but as a novice to such magic the effort was starting to take its toll.

The giant kept rumbling forward, closer to the Fat Wizard.

Suddenly a figure started running towards the ice giant, a figure that would normally be described as huge itself until dwarfed by this behemoth. It was Eric, he took a swing with his great club but could only reach the creatures knee. The creature looked down with a slightly puzzled look on its face, and with no more effort than you or I would deal with an annoying fly, swatted poor Eric leaving him tumble arse over tit down the length of the car park. Fearing he was dead the Fat Wizard breathed a sigh of relief when Eric sat up and shook himself.

"Thank you Eric," shouted the Fat Wizard, "but I need you to protect the nurses, We'll deal with this." he said, with a confidence that was waning fast.

Leaving Rebe to supply the heat, FW reverted back to blasting waves of force back at the monster, it seemed to slow him down and was obviously weakening him but who could last longer?

Some of P.E.E.O.F. F's men, too afraid of the force the Fat Wizard was directing at the creature, turned their attention on Rebe, reasoning that if they could stop the firebolts then the Ice Giant might be able beat the wizard. Unfortunately for them they hadn't taken into account the musical ability of her sister and her sister's girlfriend coupled with the sporting prowess of what might soon be Rebe's boyfriend.

"That sounded like a C major 7th chord" laughed Kayls after delivering a vicious blow to the head of an approaching thug with her cheap reproduction Gibson Les Paul.

"That's nothing" retorted Ellie. "I just managed, an A Flat miner, pardon the pun."

"Leave this one for me!" shouted Jack, as he spotted a man sneaking up on Rebe from behind the van. "I feel another six coming on. Cor if my old club could see me know I reckon they'd make me head batsman!"

High above, the aerial battle between the fairies raged on. Despite great heroics from the outnumbered Captain Riser's men, injured bodies from both sides started to trickle down to the ground. The gnomes had come prepared with fishing nets and darted out of the bushes to catch the stricken warriors before they could hit the hard ground. Riser's men were quickly taken to the first aid station, the others were locked in small cages. They would be treated, but later.

Jean and her emergency crew were out amongst the thick of it rendering aid to any stricken villagers. So far most of the injuries were superficial and were bandaged up on the spot. Any interference from the bad guys was quickly dealt with by well-aimed kicks to their most vulnerable places. Anyone with a serious injury was carried back to the emergency gazebo by Eric.

Funnily enough, no one tried to stop him.

Jean looked across to her husband. She knew him well enough to notice he was in trouble. She wasn't sure how long he could keep on holding that monster.

While the thugs from P.E.E.O.F.F were engaged in all the fighting, the other workers were trying to offload all the fracking equipment. Ignoring the melee all around them they were perplexed that most of the smaller vehicles were already empty. The bigger machines were also missing vital components, keys, steering wheels and in one instance a complete engine had vanished. With little to no direction from anyone in charge, and judging by the depleting number of hard hats around them, they came to the conclusion that they appeared to be on the losing side. They had a quick union meeting and decided to pile into one of the few intact vehicles left and seek employment elsewhere. They drove off just as one of Jed's men was about to unbolt the exhaust on the lead lorry.

They had timed it well. Fuelled by a modicum of Dutch courage, the elder villagers had tired of waiting in the pub and had demanded that Ed loaded them all up in his 'war wagon' to join in the battle. They may have been old but upon seeing the affray, Huw, now sporting a pith helmet he bought from a charity shop, led them into a fresh charge on the rapidly diminishing number of 'outsiders'. The thugs might have been reticent about fighting frail old pensioners but the pensioners had no such misgivings and laid into the thugs viciously.

Captain Riser had taken full control of the skies. As one, the primitive fairies had abandoned their fallen brothers and swarmed out to sea, presumably flying straight back to where they'd come from.

The Fat Wizard could see that the war around him was all but won but he also knew that he couldn't hold back the Ice giant much longer. If it got free then the battle was for nothing, Sweetman and Brimstone would have won. Sweat pouring down his brow and every muscle screaming in agony he feared that he was about to let everyone he cared about down but just as he thought that he couldn't go on any longer, he heard a voice behind him.

"I say, would you like a hand with that old boy"

"Surten?"

"Yes I'm certain" laughed the enigmatic mage. "What? Didn't Brian tell you I was going to visit?"

"He did but I wasn't expecting...Look help me with this and I'll buy you a pint" said the Fat Wizard exhausted.

"Hmm... he is a big bugger isn't he? Lets see..." Scarlet

red beams shot from Surten's hands into the centre of the outraged creature's chest. Rebe, herself as tired as her father, managed to increase the intensity of her firebolts aimed at its head.

The Fat Wizard redirected his power to join Surten's at the centre of the monster's body, somehow mustering enough reserve to increase the intensity of his own force beams. Under this combined power, the Ice Giant, finding his slow advance had been halted, looked down at his feet confused. Nothing had ever stopped him before and he wasn't enjoying this new sensation, he started bellowing, making guttural noises that were probably the ice giant equivalent of the sort of profanities we employ when standing barefoot on a plastic toy brick discarded by a bored child.

With so many of the invaders now running away, well those that were still able to anyway, the villagers turned their attention to helping the Fat Wizard, Rebe and the welcome stranger who had joined them.

The ice giant, weakened by the magical onslaught, now found itself under a barrage of well-aimed rocks, pots and bottles of something very smelly, almost immediately it started to tremble violently, it's clear body began to glow hues of blue and red, then lifting its head to the sky, let out one more defiant growl before exploding into a thousand pieces; pieces that Penny and Ivor would later collect to sell to the pub for their ice buckets.

Seeing the demise of their greatest ally and noticing how many of their men had fallen, the remainder of P.E.E.O.F.F.'s mercenaries decided to lick their wounds and retreat. They had been beaten, well and truly beaten. Ashamed that they had been bested by peasants in a village, in the middle of nowhere, they all thought they should go home and re-evaluate their career choices.

"Oi FW" said the red-faced driver of the Ice Giant's transport. "I've got a call for you!"

"Hello" said the Fat Wizard taking the mobile phone from him, so weak he could hardly stand.

"FW" said Sweetman, his voice dripping with venom. "So, I suppose you think you've won do you!"

"Well, we did alright" said the Fat Wizard facetiously.

"If you think you've got away with it, you've got another think coming."

"Ah" said the Fat Wizard recovering his breath. "But we did 'get away' with it. By all means feel free to try again. As you say there is no law to protect the village as indeed there is no law to protect your rights to the mines. So remember, we will be ready, and waiting. Oh…one more thing. If you do decide to interfere in any way with this village, or anyone in it ever again, be warned, next time I will bring the fight to you!"

The lorry driver just managed to catch the phone that the Fat Wizard had hurled at him. He wasted no time climbing back into his cab and starting his engine. "Damn where have my wipers gone?" he groaned as he drove out.

As the lorry passed them Downwind, Miss Jones, Dug, Wilf and Dai were joined by a grinning Griff and his son.

All were unhurt apart from an unfortunate incident when Downwind over pressurised one of the pumps and got himself covered, but this was Downwind, so no one really noticed.

"Bugger me!" he said looking at the carnage all around him. "If you expect me to clean this lot up, I'll be expecting some overtime pay."

The villagers started to congregate in the middle of the car park. They were congratulating each other and already swapping stories of their individual tales of personal heroics and comparing injuries, treating them as some kind of badge of honour. They all went silent when Queen Megan, with a bloodied and bruised Captain Riser at her side, hovered above them.

"Well done, all of you." she said. "A brave and glorious battle" and turning to the Fat Wizard, continued "I particularly want to thank you FW, and Rebe and of course you Mr…"

"Surten" said Surten.

"Oh quite certain…Surten" she laughed. Surten rolled his eyes good naturedly. "If you hadn't beaten the Ice Giant the war would have been lost, and so would Pant y Gussett.

I've sent some men to collect our injured. I wouldn't want them to miss the great feast we have planned for tonight. You are all welcome to join us of course."

Queen Megan looked around at the battle-scarred villagers

and added, "But I suspect you may have some celebrations of your own planned, down the pub I'll wager!"

"I should smile… your majesty" piped up Downwind, suddenly remembering who he was talking to.

Queen Megan laughed. "Well enjoy yourselves, you've earned it" and as she went to fly away, she stopped and turned to the Fat Wizard. "By the way FW, Brock and his men are on their way. I think they have a 'present' for you." Then smiling, she and Riser flew off.

Sure enough a few minutes later a band of dwarves with Brock at their head entered the car park.

"Look what we found hiding under a caravan" said Brock dragging with him by the ear, a bent over, dishevelled and thoroughly terrified looking Davies. "Where'd you want him?"

"Actually, I know just the place" said the Fat Wizard with a positively evil grin. "Would you mind following me? It's not far."

Melanie was taken aback upon answering a knock at her door to see the Fat Wizard, Rebe and Jack, a strange magical looking man and an army of dwarfs, one of which was manhandling a squirming, weeping and totally obnoxious looking man. Even more puzzling was the sight of all the curious villagers, some bleeding, some limping, most bandaged and yet all smiling, gathered in the road outside her front garden.

"Hello Melanie, is Pog at home?" he asked politely.

"Hi FW, I'm here" said Pog arriving at the door.

"Ah good, out of curiosity, do you still have your stick?"

Davies looked up and recognised the boy, he involuntarily relieved himself again.

☐

26. MY HERO.

The pub was so busy that night that Jack and Justin had had to roll up their sleeves and help Double Dee serve behind the bar. They were beginning to regret doing their 'bit' by offering beer at half price for the night. Their best customers had taken up their customary positions at the end of the bar. Dug and Wilf were swaying and talking, almost incoherently, to each other about nothing in particular. Dai was smiling happily with his arm around his new girlfriend's waist. He'd long given up trying to reach her shoulders, while Downwind, looking worried, was talking to Miss Jones.

"So what are you going to do now Ann?" he asked. "I suppose you'll be going back to London?"

"Well that is where my flat is." she replied. Then looking over her glasses at the increasingly despondent Downwind, "Of course I don't have a job anymore so I won't be able to keep it.... I'll certainly have to move."

"Where would you go?" asked Downwind seeing a little ray of hope.

"Actually, with my qualifications I could probably find work anywhere...maybe even around here," she smiled. "What do you think?"

"Oh most definitely around here!" he said and he kissed her passionately.

"Well that's settled then." she laughed, gasping for air. "Now let's talk about the bathing arrangements."

Over at another table, Huw, Cribbins and Dodds had all collapsed and were snoring. After all they had been drinking since first light. Alongside them Goodwitch Evans and Dorcas, were sitting with Jean's ladies, having the time of their lives, and were busy arranging to join their darts team, their book club and any other social activity they were in.

Dorcas even went so far as to fetch her husband Bill a pint from the bar. He was sitting with his leg up on a stool having had a blow from a thug wielding a pick axe handle.

"Am I going to die?" he asked Dorcas as she handed him his drink.

"Don't be silly it's just a bruise. Now call me when you're ready for another."

Bill felt his head for lumps, he was convinced he was hallucinating.

At the back of the pub Penny said to Ivor,

"Here what do you think the Coblynau are going to do with all the bits they've collected today?"

"Dunno, why?" asked Ivor.

"Cos maybe we could open up a vehicle parts stall?" grinned Penny.

"But there aren't any vehicles in Pant y Gussett. How much have you had to drink?"

Tonight was really special, even the dwarfs the gnomes and the elves were all socialising with the humans. One of the dwarfs noticed Peter, trying to sip his beer through a split lip. He also had a really nasty looking black eye.

"Cor, one of them buggers really laid into you!" said the Dwarf.

"Uh...no" said Peter, "Actually it was my girlfriend's father. He'd seen me with another girl last night!"

Everyone laughed, even Peter, eventually.

Seated around a large table near the fireplace were Charles and Melanie. Melanie had arranged for Ed to bring Charles to the pub. He still couldn't walk properly yet and was desperately upset that he couldn't do his part in the battle. Next to them Jack was explaining to Rebe, Kayls and Ellie that, as a self-employed electrician, it would be easy to relocate to somewhere near the village, and looking directly at Rebe said,

"Perhaps you would teach me more about dragons...if you didn't mind...and maybe you could help me with rescuing other reptiles, what do you think?" he asked hopefully.

"I think that sounds like an excellent idea" laughed Rebe. "Just you remember who's in charge, that's all."

"You poor man." said Kayls to a very happy Jack. "You should ask Ellie what it's like to get involved in this family."

"I'm saying nothing" smiled Ellie. "Apart from it's never boring."

Jean was sitting with her husband and Surten. They had been swapping tales of what magic they had used and how, to defeat a variety of entities over the years. Each trying to outdo each other in friendly rivalry. Jean, upon hearing of some of his exploits for the first time, was a bit miffed to find that her husband had obviously been keeping some secrets from her, even if it was just to stop her from worrying.

Charles spotting Brock in the pub called him over.

"Brock do you think we could have a chat sometime tomorrow?" Then noticing that Melanie had fetched him another pint, said "Actually you'd better make that the day after tomorrow. I think Evan may have been right. I think there could still be some seams of precious ore waiting to be found that could make conventional mining profitable and I would love to be your surveyor, if you'll have me?"

"What say you lads!" yelled Brock holding his tankard high in the air, well high for a dwarf anyway. "Fancy being miners again?"

"YAY" came a resounding chorus of gruff voices from all corners of the pub.

"See you Friday...boss" smiled Brock heading back to the bar for another beer.

"Does that mean you'll be staying?" smiled Melanie.

"Is that alright with you and Pog? I can help with the honey business as well, if you don't mind teaching me."

"Pog will be fine, he's taken quite a liking to you, you know."

"And you?" smiled Charles.

"Yes Charles, I've taken quite a liking to you too," and as if to prove it, she kissed him.

For the first time that he could remember, Charles was a happy man.

"So" said the Fat Wizard to Surten, "I'm grateful, but why did you decide to come here and help?"

Surten took a big drink of his ale, smiled and turned to the Fat Wizard. "I've already told you. I like you and I wanted to visit this wonderful village that I've been hearing so much about."

"And?" said the Fat Wizard.

"And… Brian said he wouldn't do my books for me anymore if I didn't help. Have you any idea how hard it is to find a good accountant these days?" laughed Surten.

"I see. Looks as if I owe my old friend a few drinks. All the same, thank you Surten. I couldn't have done it without you" smiled the Fat Wizard.

"To be honest" said Surten, "I think you and your daughter would have beaten that thing without me. I just speeded things up."

"You never struck me as the modest type" chuckled the Fat Wizard as Huw Puw, recovered from his little nap approached the table.

"Everyone, everyone listen to me" he shouted. "I'd like to propose a toast to the Fat Wizard for everything he has done for the village, so charge your glasses.

"TO THE FAT WIZARD!"

"THE FAT WIZARD" chorused the entire pub.

"The Fat Wizard" hiccupped Dug a second later, as he slid down the bar into an untidy heap on the floor.

The Fat Wizard, feeling a little embarrassed by all the attention, felt Jean's arms wrapped around his neck followed by a wet kiss on the cheek.

"My Hero" she said, sincerely.

EPILOGUE

Over the next few months, Pog's life had changed for the better. No-one could ever replace his father but Charles was proving to be a gentle and loving step-dad. It had been a long time since he'd seen his mother so happy and with Charles's income from the mines and the extra help with the honey business, money was no longer such a worry. He had friends now as well. The boys who used to bully him now wanted him to play with them. They were particularly fond of coming over to see the two big toads that Pog kept in a cage in his back garden,

"Cor... look at that big ugly brute with them blue marks all over him, I've never heard a toad growl before" remarked one of the boys the first time Pog had showed them.

"That's nothing!" laughed another lad, "Look at that scrawny one in the upside down flower pot, all he does is shake and pee."

THE END

ABOUT THE AUTHOR

Noel. P. Morgan was born in South Wales at an early age, and as a child enjoyed the natural delights of the beaches and countryside of the Gower Coast, which instilled a love of the magic of nature and animals.

He has enjoyed a varied career including car cleaner, love spoon maker, zookeeper, candle maker, and eventually college lecturer specializing in exotic animals and all things aquatic.

He has previously had a book published on lizard husbandry, but this is his debut novel based around his other passions of humour and fantasy.

A Tale of Wizards, Dragons and Fracking

Printed in Great Britain
by Amazon

28640712R00189